The House on
Riverdale Circle

A L   A U B R Y

Copyright © 2017 Al Aubry
All rights reserved
First Edition

PAGE PUBLISHING, INC.
New York, NY

First originally published by Page Publishing, Inc. 2017

ISBN 978-1-64027-493-8 (Paperback)
ISBN 978-1-64027-495-2 (Digital)

Printed in the United States of America

1

It all started just over two years ago. Tom and Irene had celebrated their granddaughter Geena's eighth birthday. It was March 1, 2014. Their son Trevor, his wife, Anne, and their daughter had been vacationing with them in Naples, Florida, for ten days.

The five of them had spent the entire day on the beach, building a huge sand castle. It was at least five feet tall with multiple towers. They had dug a tunnel that dipped through the center and had taken pictures of Geena as she crawled from one side of the castle to the other. By late afternoon, the tide came in and started to flood the tunnel. They went back to the condo where they enjoyed an elaborate dinner featuring pecan-crusted grouper in a lemon-butter sauce. Geena had no trouble blowing out the candles on her cake. She was a real sweetheart and the apple of Tom's eye. Her actual birthday wasn't for a couple more weeks, but the family had made it a tradition to celebrate it during their spring break vacation with Geena's grandparents.

Tom drove the three of them to the Southwest Florida International Airport the next day while Irene completed a major cleaning throughout the condo. The Gibsons had entertained guests for five straight weeks, and there was much to be done, not the least of which was to vacuum up all the sand that had accumulated all over the floors. First, there had been Tom's sister who had visited for the first two weeks in February, and then their daughter Christine, her husband, Alan, and their three boys were there for the second half of February. They had driven down and had left two days before Trevor and his family arrived. It was hectic, but Tom and Irene both loved it.

On the way home from the airport, Tom felt a little jittery. He wasn't sure what it was. He checked his blood pressure when he got back to the condo. He had been on blood pressure medicine for almost three years, and it seemed to be working just fine. His pressure reading was 125 over 79, so he knew there was no problem there, but his heart rate was 95 and he still felt some kind of anxiety for some inexplicable reason.

Tom and Irene had been married for thirty-eight years and were enjoying the kind of retirement everyone wants. Each year, they spent eight months in their rural waterfront home on Lake Erie and headed south to Naples for the winter. Tom retired in 2005 after a successful corporate career and continued to dapple with income property here and there. Irene was a child psychologist who had spent most of her career on consulting contracts with multiple school districts, helping them in the development and deployment of educational programs for kids with special needs. She too was retired, but she still accepted work on a project now and then. The two of them were avid tennis players and played organized matches at least three times a week, both at home and in Florida.

Tom found it difficult to get to sleep that night. He rolled over from side to side every half hour. He used his self-hypnosis tricks, staring at the ceiling fan, repeating the word "nothing" in his head, imagining himself pushing a kart down the aisles of a grocery store, but nothing seemed to work. He had never taken sleep medication and wasn't about to start. He got up at two o'clock in the morning and went out to the lanai to read a book. It was a fascinating account of Lord Chichester's solo sail around the world in 1966, at the age of sixty-five.

Tom went back to bed around four and finally fell asleep. He later wished he hadn't. He woke up in a cold sweat. He looked up at the ceiling as his eyes refocused and saw the time projected by the alarm clock. It was 5:31 a.m. He clearly remembered every detail of the eerie nightmare he had just woken from. He recalled being in the rear vestibule of a big old house that seemed somewhat familiar. It was a dreary day. There was a door on his left, leading into a screened porch. Another door, to his right, was wide open and led down the basement stairs. It was too dark to see the bottom of the stairs. He was about to open the outside door when he heard a voice. It was faint but clear and mournful. It was the voice of a child, a young girl in obvious distress.

"Help me ... Please help me," moaned the child. It seemed to be coming from the basement.

Tom remembered reaching for the light switch on the right-hand wall of the stairway. He felt the switch in his fingers, but, as so often happens in these dreams or nightmares where one seems unable to accomplish the simplest of tasks, he fumbled around the switch and couldn't turn it on. He decided to open the outside door to let more daylight into the vestibule. At that very moment, he heard the voice again:

"Oh, please help me. You're the only one who can help me ..."

He was torn. He didn't know if he should go down the stairs to investigate or just get the hell out of that place. He was frightened but didn't feel he was in imminent danger. It was more a matter of being fearful of what he might find.

A flash of light suddenly streaked over his head and down the stairs. For that fraction of a second, he was able to see down the stairs. They seemed to go on forever and he still wasn't able to see the bottom. That helped him make up his mind. He tried to run out to the porch but couldn't move his legs. It was as if his feet were glued to the floor. His heart began to race. That's when he woke up.

Tom was normally a sound sleeper and couldn't remember the last time he had had a nightmare. He was haunted by this one for a few days, but that was the end of it. He never saw any reason to share it with Irene. The two of them enjoyed their last three weeks in Naples and then packed up and headed home.

Tom and Irene always felt lucky to be able to spend their winters in the sunny south, but they equally relished coming home to the shores of Lake Erie, southwest of Buffalo, New York. Their waterfront home, on the western outskirts of Westfield, offered an idyllic lifestyle. The trees were budding, the crocuses were popping out all over the front garden, and a gentle spring breeze wafted through the house as Tom opened all the doors and windows. They had had the two-story Cape Cod–style house custom built in preparation for their retirement. The house sat at the end of a three-hundred-foot driveway, lined on both sides with tall sugar maples and ending in a circle in front of the house. The three-car garage was a separate two-story structure, about fifty feet from the house, sitting on the southwest side of the circle. A rock garden, one of Irene's favorite projects, filled the center of the circle.

They had been home just over a week when it happened again. Tom had another nightmare, even scarier than the first. Again, he remembered almost every detail. He was sitting in a tunnel of some sort, or perhaps a dugout with dirt walls. It was dimly lit by a candle in a tin can. There was a box of matches beside the candle. He looked around. There were a few pieces of wood and some candy wrappers strewn on the ground. The air was cool and damp. He picked up the tin can and moved it from side to side to try to find a way out. The space seemed to be about six feet wide and maybe eight feet long. The low ceiling looked and felt like concrete. Perhaps he was under a bridge abutment, he thought. He noticed a blanket bundled in one corner. It was light sea foam green with a silk border. It looked a bit familiar, but it was soiled and frayed. He crawled up to it, reached for one corner of the blanket, and pulled it toward him.

"Oh my God!" he shouted as he recoiled away from the blanket, blowing out the candle in the process. It was pitch-black. He wiped the sweat from his brow but couldn't see his hand. He started to hyperventilate as he tried to convince himself to remain calm. It was impossible. The sight of a young girl's face under the blanket was all he could think of. Her face was gray and gaunt. Her eyes were wide open and seemed to stare at him. He started to feel around the dirt floor, searching for the candle. He found the box of matches. He pulled open the box, but his hands were shaking so much he spilled the matches all over the ground. He felt around, found one, and began to strike it against the side of the box. The match didn't light. He turned it around and tried again. It lit briefly and went out. It had momentarily cast enough light to show him where most of the other matches were. He grabbed two of them and lit them together. He was able to find the tin can and the candle. The matches went out as he placed the stubby candle back in the can. He placed it on the ground in front of him, lit two more matches, and lit the candle. He raised the can and looked up at the corner. He hadn't imagined it; she was still there. Suddenly, her left arm flopped out from under the blanket.

Tom gasped and quickly scanned the area. He saw a piece of plywood propped up against the dirt wall to his left. He grabbed one edge and, as he pulled it away, saw a small crawl space about two feet wide and three feet high. It seemed to be the only way out. He crawled into it, holding the candle in front of him, but felt increasingly uneasy as the tunnel turned to the left and got narrower. He was finally able to see a faint light several feet ahead, but he was wedged and couldn't get any closer. He began digging around him with his bare hands, trying not to hyperventilate. That's when he woke out of his nightmare.

He was so agitated that Irene also woke up.

"Are you okay?" she asked.

It took Tom a few moments to respond. He was gasping for air and was unable to utter a word. Irene held his hand, and he began to calm down.

"I'm … I'm okay … It's okay … Just a nightmare," he finally answered.

"What could possibly get you so worked up?" she asked.

For some reason which he didn't quite understand, he wasn't ready to share the details of his nightmarish ordeal, even though it was all still so vivid in his mind.

"I don't know, I just can't remember."

Sleep became elusive for Tom over the next several nights. He remained very disturbed by the recent nightmares and feared what would happen the next time he slept. Inevitably, he fell asleep for an hour here and there, even catching an occasional afternoon nap. His nightmares, as brief as they were, adopted a consistent theme. He was usually among people he knew, sitting in a public place. It was often at a riverside park. The same young girl with the ashen and wrinkled face would ride by on her bicycle. Her pink shorts and light blue blouse were torn and smeared with dirt. Her bicycle was covered in rust. As she neared Tom, she turned to look at him. Her eyes were hollow. She then looked straight ahead and rode away. It wasn't as shocking as his previous nightmares, but equally eerie, as much for the horror in her eyes as for the frequency of these recurring images.

Tom thought there might be a pattern taking shape. Whenever he reflected on his nightmares during the day and tried to make sense of it all, he seemed to be able to get through the following night without another episode, although his sleep was light and sporadic. But whenever the images faded and he seemed to be moving on, he soon experienced another nightmare.

Irene and Tom had been back at their home in Westfield since mid-April. There was no change in his sleeping pattern. He began to fear he might have to live with this "curse" for the rest of his days.

2

One night in early May, Tom was lying in bed, flat on his back. After a while, he realized he couldn't hear Irene's usual rhythmic breathing.

"Are you awake, dear?" he whispered. There was no answer.

He began to worry, so he rolled to his right, reached up, and turned on the lamp on the bedside table. He rolled back to his left.

"Oh God!" he screamed.

It wasn't Irene in bed with him. It was the cadaver of the young girl with the same filthy blanket pulled up to her chest and her bony little arms stretched out over the blanket. Just as Tom tried to jump out of bed, she gripped his forearm.

"Wake up! Wake up! Please, wake up! You're having another nightmare!" Irene pleaded with him as she shook his arm.

"Oh, thank God, it's you," he uttered, still panting and trying to get his bearings. "I'm so glad you're okay."

"I'm fine, but I'm very concerned about you. Why are you sleeping so poorly and having all these nightmares? Maybe it would help if we talked about it. Can you tell me anything about them?"

Tom started to calm down and concluded the time had come to tell Irene what had been going on in his dreams. Perhaps she was right, he thought. Openly sharing his experiences could be helpful and could possibly shed some light on what might be driving these nightly episodes. After all, she was an experienced psychologist.

"Let's go downstairs and I'll make us some tea," Irene offered.

They sat across from each other, sipping their tea. Tom began describing each of his dreams, carefully keeping them in precise chronological order. He meticulously covered every detail. They were still vivid in his mind. Except for a few facial expressions, Irene didn't react. She said nothing and just kept listening until he was done. They were both quiet for a while as she reflected.

"I wonder … I'm wondering if you're experiencing some kind of anxiety about Geena. Perhaps you subconsciously feel that she's in some kind of danger and your anxiety is manifesting itself in the form of these nightmares," Irene postulated. "You did say that the first time it happened was just after Trevor, Anne, and Geena went home, right?"

"Yes, that was the first one," Tom acknowledged. "I'll have to think about that. It makes sense, although the young girl, with her blond hair, doesn't look anything like Geena, and some of the locations seem a little familiar, even though I don't recognize them."

"Dreams often have a way of warping reality, so it could still be triggered by your worries about our granddaughter for some reason," she explained.

"Thanks, this might be helpful. I'll have to reflect on it for a few days."

They went back to bed, and Tom was able to sleep reasonably soundly.

Several days later, Tom decided the lawn needed mowing. There were two acres of grass between the road and the house and only rock gardens and flagstone stairs between the house and the lake. He decided to tune up his riding mower before setting out on the two-hour job. He replaced the spark plugs, replaced the engine oil, and adjusted the drive belts on the blades. It was well worth the effort, he thought. The machine performed just as it had when it was new, as Tom wound his way around the trees and back and forth across the property. He parked it in the garage and decided to touch up a few scratches on the cowling with some matching enamel paint. Afterward, he poured some paint thinner into a tin can and dropped the small paintbrush into it. He placed the can on the steel shelf above his workbench.

He suddenly felt faint. He leaned forward and rested his hands on the workbench to steady himself. He took a few deep breaths, inhaling through his nose and exhaling through his mouth. He remained motionless for several minutes. His heart was pounding and his mind was racing. It was as if he had just seen a ghost, only worse. He slowly looked up, glanced at the tin can, and looked away. He had just understood, at that very moment, at least part of what had been haunting him.

A small detail from his second nightmare came back to him. He recalled that, as he was crawling through the tunnel to escape the dugout or whatever it was, holding the candle in front of him, the label was still on the tin can. It was a seven-ounce can of Green Giant corn niblets, the same type he had just used to clean his paintbrush. He thought about this singular detail over and over. He wanted to make sure he hadn't simply modified his recollection of his dream. The distinction was vitally important because, if the label was really part of his nightmare, it had a much more profound significance, taking him back to his childhood.

The more he thought about it, the more he was able to connect some of the dots. As an eleven-year-old boy, Tom lived in a big old three-story house with his parents, his older brother, Ronnie, and his younger sister, Sarah. Their father was one of the founding partners in a large accounting firm and was a regular lecturer at the nearby university, about a ten-minute walk from the house. Their mother was an at-home mom but was an active volunteer with a number of charitable organizations. Both parents were away much of the time, leaving the kids to fend for themselves. Marnie, their Jamaican housekeeper, was there five days a week. She kept the house clean and made the occasional meal when asked by Mrs. Gibson. Tom had very few pleasant memories from that time. In fact, he had blanked out that part of his life for many years, but many of the details were coming back to him.

Tom was a smart and well-behaved kid. He did well in school, and one of his passions was for electromechanical devices. From an early age, he tore apart household appliances and put them back together in order to understand how they worked. By the age of eleven, he could repair pretty well anything around the house, from the vacuum cleaner to the lawn mower. Almost all the devices in the house were from Sears. The phone number for the Sears parts center was permanently posted on the corkboard beside the wall phone in the kitchen. Initially, Tom's mom, Elizabeth, placed orders for him whenever he needed parts to repair an appliance, but after a while, the folks at the parts center got to know Tom and accepted his orders, even when these included some new tools or accessories. All orders were charged to the Gibson family account. Eventually, Tom's basement workshop became quite well equipped.

Another of Tom's passions, which he shared with his best friend, David, was building and "driving" soapbox gravity racing karts. Their neighborhood was ideally suited for soapbox derbies. The main thoroughfare, Ridge Road, wound its way from east to west along the edge of an escarpment, which overlooked the upscale enclave of River Heights Estates. Tom's street, Riverdale Circle, was actually shaped like a U, with both ends intersecting at Ridge Road and sloping down to the bottom of the U. Tom's house, 5 Riverdale Circle, was located at the top of the hill at the west end of the street, backing onto the inner circle. From their back porch, the Gibsons had a clear view of all fourteen backyards in the circle. Soapbox derbies were held every other Sunday afternoon throughout the summer. Although informal, the races were well organized and well attended. Volunteer parents at each end of the street controlled what little traffic there was, and the START line was mere steps from Tom's front door.

All of it should have been an ideal environment for a thriving young kid like Tom, and it would have been if it were not for his older brother. Ronnie was continually getting into trouble at school and after school. Mr. Gibson, like many parents, seemed to be toughest on the elder child. With every report of bad behavior came another beating. Their mother had tried to intervene on Ronnie's behalf on a couple of occasions, but it had only made their father even angrier and more violent. So she gave up trying, and just suffered quietly each time it happened. Late afternoon one Saturday, while Mr. Gibson was in the kitchen preparing his "prized" spaghetti sauce, Ronnie was brought home by the police after being caught shoplifting with some of his buddies. Mrs. Gibson was crying in disbelief. One of the officers explained that, because of the family's standing in the community, there would be no charges brought against Ronnie, as long as he stayed out of trouble. After the officers left, Mr. Gibson, his face boiling red with anger, unbuckled and removed his belt and chased Ronnie up the stairs to his room. Sarah was traumatized by Ronnie's pleas and cries and she covered her ears. Mrs. Gibson wept. Tom was worried because, after every beating, Ronnie took out his frustrations by bullying him. This one, he feared, was going to be the worst. Ronnie's abuse of his younger brother was physical, psychological, and relentless. The parents' frequent absence left Ronnie with plenty of opportunity to pick on Tom. He also treated Marnie like a slave and bossed her around. She never said anything to anyone for fear of losing her job.

Tom was unable to defend himself, so his only recourse was to stay out of Ronnie's way and spend as much time as possible next door at David's house. But that wasn't always an option. David attended a private school across town, and although he was a day student, his band practices and other activities kept him away from home much of the time. Tom resorted to finding hiding places at home. His relationship with his brother often came down to a sinister game of hide-and-seek. Ronnie relished the hunt as much as Tom feared it.

In the early stages of Tom's abuse at the hands of his brother, Tom innocently found refuge in places like his mother's closet, the second-floor linen closet, or the tight space behind the furnace in the basement. The house was old and larger than most. It offered numerous possibilities for anyone who wanted to hide. It was a three-story home with a full basement, half of which was nicely finished into a recreation room, a spare bedroom, and a washroom. The rest of the basement was a dark, damp, and cavernous area that housed the laundry room, the furnace room, Tom's workshop, and a long and narrow closet under the staircase where the family stored off-season clothing and Mrs. Gibson's furs. It was completely lined with aromatic cedar. On the main floor, there was the living room which was normally off-limits to the children, a formal dining room, a den which Mr. Gibson often used as a home office, and the kitchen. A wide staircase in the center hall led to the four bedrooms on the second floor, one for each of the children and a master bedroom for the parents. One washroom was part of the master suite, and another served the other bedrooms. A narrower staircase in the second-floor hallway led to the attic.

The attic was a vast and eerie place, stuffed with old furniture, wooden chests, old paintings, and stacks of boxes. Most of it had belonged to the grandparents and other relatives, all of whom were deceased. Tom feared the attic and only rarely used it as a hiding place. During the day, the four dormer windows offered enough light for any brave soul who wished to wander through the cobwebs to explore the attic's contents. At night, the two small lightbulbs didn't cast enough light to reach the four corners.

Regardless of where Tom chose to hide, he often got caught. The longer it took for Ronnie to find him, the harsher the beating. Ronnie was taller, stronger, and more athletic than Tom. It was never a fair fight.

One day, Tom had a brilliant idea for a hiding place, one that his brother could never find. He just had to wait for the right time to execute his plan. He didn't have to wait very long. After another beating by his father, Ronnie was assigned to two-hour tutoring sessions twice a week until he could improve his math grades. On those days, he didn't get home until just before dinner. Tom took advantage of Ronnie's absence to create his own secret room. He removed the cedar planks from the far end of the storage closet in the basement, right under the landing at the top of the stairs. He carefully cut and dismantled the studs and repositioned them four feet closer to the closet entrance, bunching the clothes on hangers closer together. He reinstalled the cedar planks, a section of which he hinged so as to create a secret door. He stocked his new secret room with a folding chair, pillows and blankets, a flashlight, food and water, reading material, and a transistor radio with an earphone. Whenever he chose to use his secret room, he stood on the landing at the rear of the house, opened and slammed shut the outside door, and then quietly tiptoed down to the basement and snuck into his room. It worked every time, and before long, Tom could sense his brother's frustration.

3

Tom was still standing in his garage, deeply troubled by his recollections of that passage in his life. But it wasn't the abuse at the hands of his brother that sent chills down his spine. It was something else, something more sinister.

In the early fall of 1963, just after school was back in session, Tom took up a newspaper delivery job. He had just turned twelve and wanted to earn some extra spending money. It was a local morning paper called the *Daily Record*, one of two newspapers that served the community. The other, called the *Journal*, was published and delivered late in the afternoon. On average, Tom had to deliver about fifty papers in his neighborhood every morning before six o'clock, six days a week. He usually got up at 4:45 a.m., got dressed, and walked to the corner of Ridge Road where the bundle of newspapers was always waiting for him. He transferred the papers into his carry bag which he strapped over his shoulder. He folded each paper as he delivered it. His delivery route took about forty-five minutes most of the time, a little longer in the winter. He worked in the dark for much of the year, so he carried a small flashlight. He visited each customer during his collection round every other Thursday at dinnertime. He always turned the money over to his mother, and she took care of settling with the newspaper's delivery supervisor. Tom never said anything to his mother, but he insisted on giving her the money for fear that Ronnie would steal it.

He saved his money to buy special wheels for a new kart he was building with David. These wheels were available in diameters that ranged from six to fourteen inches. They could be ordered in solid hub or spoked versions. Most importantly, they featured double sets of real ball bearings. This meant minimal resistance, which translated to higher speeds in a gravity racer.

David's father had recently built an entire wall of shelving in their garage. All of it was constructed from black metal tubing about one inch in diameter. He had brought it all home from the metal product distributing company he worked for. The idea for a new kart had come to David when his dad offered him the leftover pieces.

The two boys were excited about the prospect of building a racing kart with a metal frame and high-efficiency wheels. They spent some time on the design and then got to work on construction. Welding wasn't an option, so they used the drill press and pipe bender in David's garage. They used a hacksaw to cut the pieces of pipe. Each cut was arduous and took at least twenty minutes. As per David's father's instructions, they poured water on the blade during each cut and changed the blades frequently. They used bolts, nuts, and lock washers to assemble the frame. They designed the kart with a flat area behind the seat frame. They felt this feature would provide a footrest for pushing the kart back up the hill and, in their wildest dreams, could possibly house a gasoline engine one day. They realized that, as a motorized kart, it wouldn't qualify for the Sunday races, but they agreed it would be a lot more fun.

During those cold fall mornings when Tom delivered his papers, he kept himself motivated by thinking about their amazing new kart. He and David figured it would be ready by spring. He always finished his route one street away from Riverdale Circle and normally cut through two backyards to get home. One day, while cutting across, he happened to notice a rototiller behind the McPhersons' garage at the back of their yard. It hadn't been visible before because it was kept hidden by shrubs until all the leaves had fallen. It was semicovered by an old shredded tarp.

The idea of motorizing their new kart became a bit of an obsession for Tom. The next morning, he paused to examine the engine on the old rototiller. It was a single-cylinder four-stroke gasoline engine. He smiled all the way home. In the following days, although neither Tom nor David had ever done anything illegal in their entire lives, they plotted how they could steal the rototiller, bring it home, and remove the engine. They rationalized that it had become a piece of garbage for the owners and convinced themselves that the McPhersons would likely never notice. If they did, they would be relieved to have gotten rid of it. Their conviction wasn't quite strong enough to simply approach the owners and ask them if they were willing to give it up, so Tom and David knew they were about to cross a line.

That Thursday morning, David accompanied Tom on his route. He snuck out of the house, and the two of them left thirty minutes early and brought Tom's wagon. It was cold and dark. Tom had gone as far as lubricating the wheel hubs on the wagon the previous evening, wanting to make sure they didn't squeak. They walked stealthily along the route so as to make sure they didn't wake up anyone. Tom had wondered if the bundle of papers would be there so early in the morning. It was. They completed the route and pulled the wagon to the rear of the McPherson garage. They removed the old tarp and dragged the tiller about ten feet through various junk and into the open. Loading it onto the wagon was more difficult than they had anticipated. It was an awkward piece of machinery to handle.

"Let's both grab the rotor and rest it on the front of the wagon," Tom whispered. "Then we can both grab the handles, lift up, and swing the rest of the tiller onto the wagon."

They struggled but eventually loaded the tiller securely on the wagon. Just as they were about to pull it away, a light went on in the McPhersons' house. Light poured out of a second-floor window. Both boys were scared and froze on the spot. The window was small and frosted, so Tom figured it was a bathroom window.

"It's just someone going to the bathroom," he whispered.

"Goddamn it!" uttered David.

"It's okay … We're okay … Just stay calm! It's someone in the bathroom."

"That's not it … I … I wet myself …" David admitted.

Tom snickered nervously, knowing he had come very close to doing the same. They left the wagon where it was, beside the garage, and hid behind the structure. The light went out a minute later, but they remained hidden for what seemed like an eternity. Tom looked at the tarp and decided to move one of the old empty barrels to the spot where the tiller had been. They covered it with the tarp. The boys crept back to the wagon and slowly pulled it away. Tom did the heavy tugging while David held the machine steady. It took them ten minutes to reach David's garage. They unloaded the machine the same way they had loaded it and dragged it through the walk-in door at the rear of the garage. Opening one of the bay doors would have been too noisy. David's parents' bedroom was directly above the garage. They slowly eased the tiller into a temporary hiding space they had prepared and, for a few moments, felt good about their feat.

"We can't leave it here very long," David whispered, "or my dad will surely find it."

"I know … I know," Tom acknowledged.

Their hearts thumped as they simultaneously began to panic. Their planning had focused on stealing the machine and mounting its engine on the kart. Not much thought had gone into disposing of the carcass of the tiller, or explaining how they had acquired an engine for their new kart.

"What are we going to do with this thing? It's so much bigger than I thought."

"I think I've got it figured out," Tom answered, his voice still trembling. "After school today, we can remove the engine and get rid of the rest of this monster."

"But how and where?" David asked.

"Under the back porch of my house," Tom explained. "We're going to pull away some of the lattice, push the tiller under the porch and slip the lattice back into position. Nobody will ever see it."

"Brilliant," David commented.

The whole school day was a blur for Tom. He was fixated on what he and David needed to do after school and, in his daze, never paid attention to what was going on in class. He breathed a sigh of relief when the final bell rang.

The boys met after school. They ate some of the cookies that Marnie had baked and drank some milk.

"Where's your brother?" David asked.

"He's getting some extra tutoring at school. He won't be home until six."

"Good."

They got to work in David's garage and removed the four engine mounting bolts.

"We have to remove the throttle control from the handlebar," Tom explained. "The control and the steel cable stay with the engine. Everything else has to go."

They removed the two screws from the throttle control, and it slipped away from the handlebar. Tom wished he could have used the two wheels, shaft and differential, but the wheels were too close together and the gear ratio in the differential was so high that the top speed of the kart would have been less than five miles per hour.

"How are we going to explain where we got this engine?" David asked.

Tom paused for a few moments to think. He looked around the garage and spotted a shelf full of spray paint cans. He walked to the shelf, moved a few cans, and picked one up.

"This is perfect," he said. "We're going to use this bright yellow paint to spray the engine. We're going to do it right now. We can also spray some short sections of the frame on the kart so everything will match and look like they belong together!" Tom said with some excitement.

"Brilliant!" answered David. "But how are we going to explain it to our parents?"

"It's simple. You can tell your folks that I bought it from a friend. My parents never pay attention to this stuff and will never notice. But, if they do, I'll tell them that you bought it from a friend," Tom explained smugly.

"Got it! You're a genius," David exclaimed.

The boys cleaned up the engine with some old rags and then sprayed it. While it was drying, they grabbed a short pry bar, a hammer, and a few nails from the tool bench and walked over to the porch behind Tom's house. The floor of the large porch was over four feet above the ground. A wide set of stairs with a handrail sloped down to the patio from the south side of the porch. There was a gap of approximately eight feet between the stairs and the rear wall of the house. A cedar flower box filled most of the gap. The underside of the porch was hidden by lattice which hung down from the rim joists around the perimeter of the porch.

The boys looked around to make sure there was nobody around, then turned the flower box so it was parallel to the staircase. Tom carefully pried the nails out of the top of the lattice and pulled away a section of it. The boys went back to the garage and dragged the tiller to the patio. Tom got on his knees at the front of the tiller and pulled it toward the porch while David pushed on the handlebars. Once the tiller was fully under the porch, Tom crawled back out and repositioned the lattice. He hammered fresh nails into the top of the lattice, securing it firmly to the rim joist. They reset the flower box in its original spot. They sat on the porch stairs and instantly felt relief.

"Wow! I don't know if I would ever do this again," Tom admitted. "I've never done anything like this before, and I don't like how it feels." David simply nodded.

The next morning, Tom delivered his papers as usual. When he was done, he cut through the McPhersons' backyard. It was dark, but he was able to see enough to conclude that everything behind the garage looked pretty well the way he and David had left them. He got home, got ready for school, and had a hearty pancake breakfast. Just before leaving for school, he decided to go out to the back of the house and check out the scene around the back porch. The sun was just rising and shining through the poplars at the back of the yard.

"Holy shit!" he exclaimed.

Tom was horrified. The sun's rays angled straight under the porch and through the lattice. The tiller was totally visible. Tom's heart was pounding as he frantically thought about possible solutions. He was too upset to think clearly. There was nothing he could do immediately. It would have to wait until he got back from school.

He felt anxious and distracted all day, but eventually came up with a viable solution. After school, he patiently waited for David to get home. The school van dropped him off in front of his house just before five o'clock. Tom must have looked agitated when he greeted David.

"What's wrong, Tommy?" he asked.

"Follow me," Tom answered as he led David down the lane between their garages to the backyard. He stopped about ten feet directly behind the porch. He pointed under the porch.

"It's not very obvious right now," he said, "but early in the morning, the sun shines straight under the porch and you can see the tiller clear as day."

"Why don't we cover it up with something … something dark," David suggested.

"Sure, that'll work for now, but we need a more permanent solution."

"What do you have in mind?"

"We're going to bury it. We're going to bury it right there, under the porch. Nobody will see us digging, and nobody will ever find it. It will be gone once and for all."

"That's going to take days, maybe weeks. We can't leave the lattice open that long … Someone's bound to see it," David commented.

"You're absolutely right, and I've figured out a solution for that too. We're going to have to be able to get in and out of that space, quickly, easily, and often. Follow me."

They walked into David's garage. Tom looked around and pulled a few of pieces wood off one of the shelves. They were five-foot-long strips of one-by-three-inch pine.

"These will be perfect," Tom affirmed. "Do you think your dad will miss them?"

"I doubt it," David replied. "It's just scrap lumber."

The boys used David's dad's miter saw to cut the strips into a two-foot-wide and three-foot-high frame, complete with mitered corners. Then they cut the remaining strips into a slightly smaller frame that fit inside the first frame with a half-inch gap between the frames.

"We have to find some hinges," Tom declared.

There were tobacco cans full of various hardware. One was full of hinges of various sizes.

"These will do just fine," Tom said.

They grabbed a few pieces of burlap that David's mother had used to cover some shrubs in the winter, picked up the pry bar, the hinges, a handsaw, the frame pieces, a handful of screws, and a screwdriver. They walked back to the porch.

"What time does Ronnie get back from football?" David asked.

"They're playing an away game, so he won't be back until after six," said Tom.

The boys pulled away the flower box, and once again, Tom gently pried out the nails at the top of the lattice and pulled it away from the rim joist. Tom crawled under the porch with the pieces of wood, the hinges, and the saw. He shuffled to a spot directly under the stairs. He positioned one of the three-foot pieces of wood vertically against the inside of the lattice.

"Okay, you need to crawl under the stairs and drive four screws through the lattice into this piece of frame," Tom whispered from under the porch.

David did as he was asked. Piece by piece, they installed a rectangular frame inside the lattice. Using the shorter pieces, they affixed a slightly smaller frame inside the larger one, leaving a small gap between them. Tom used the handsaw to cut the lattice in the gap between the frames. David held on to the framed section of lattice while Tom completed the cut. With the final cut, the frame section of lattice came free and David was able to pull it out.

"Pass me the screws and the screwdriver," Tom ordered. "Now, just hold on to the door while I install the hinges."

At that very moment, they heard the creak of the door opening above them.

"Tommy! Where are you? I'm going to find you … You little runt!" Ronnie yelled.

The door slammed shut. Tom and David were shaking.

"I don't know why he's home so early," Tom whispered. "The game must have been cancelled, or something."

They heard some loud voices at the front of the house. They faded after a few moments.

"Okay, I think he's gone out with his buddies," Tom whispered. "Let's hurry up and finish this."

After a few minutes, they had a fully hinged and invisible lattice door in a discreet spot under the stairs. This, they felt, would allow them easy access to the area under the porch. They covered the tiller with burlap and repositioned the lattice and the flower box. They ran into David's garage and both breathed a sigh of relief.

"Thanks, buddy, I feel better now," Tom conceded. "This will buy us some time while we dig a nice hole for that tiller."

For the next three weeks, the two boys spent their after-school time on Tuesdays and Thursdays digging their hearts out. They dug a four-by-four-foot hole right up against the foundation of the house. They piled the loose dirt around the perimeter of the porch, up against the lattice, except where their hinged door was located. After a while, they ran out of places to stack the dirt so they used buckets to carry it out to the back of the garden and they spread it along the row of poplars. At a depth of about four and a half feet, they ran into a layer of tiles. They used a hammer to break up the tiles. It slowed them down for a while, but as soon as they got past the tiles, the digging got easier. They used scrap lumber from David's garage to build a small ladder to get up and down the hole. At six feet, they were amazed to see that they had dug past the foundation and could expand their dig westward under the house.

"Do you think there is any chance we're going to run into water soon?" David asked.

"If we were at the bottom of the street, maybe," Tom replied. "But we're almost at the top of the ridge, so we should be fine. We just have to be careful not provide any path for rainwater to get in here." David nodded in approval.

By the third week, they were ten feet down and four feet under the house. They sat down to rest.

"This is way more than we need," David commented as he caught his breath.

There was no immediate answer from Tom, who seemed to be deep in thought.

"Uh-oh … I don't like that look … What are you thinking?" asked David.

"Actually, I've been thinking about this for a week. You're right. This is way more space than we need to bury the tiller. But look around. Wouldn't this make the coolest fort ever?"

It was dark with only a bit of light slipping in from the top of the hole. But it was warmer in their "fort" than it was outside.

"Yes, but it's a bit snug in here. We need to dig some more if we're going to bury the tiller and still have space to move around."

"Of course … Let's do it."

A week later, they had excavated a six-by-eight-foot room, about four feet in height, plus a narrower channel where they jammed the tiller. It was getting late enough in the fall that the sun was setting around five thirty. They used candles to see their way around their new fort.

All these childhood memories came back to Tom as if they had happened yesterday. Every detail was vivid. He looked at his watch. He had been standing, leaning on his workbench, for more than thirty minutes. He started to breathe heavily again. He felt some tightness around his chest. He was horrified, not by the fact that he had committed some petty crime decades ago, but because he clearly remembered that he and David held their stubby candles in a tin can of Green Giant corn niblets.

4

Tom went back into the house, poured himself a glass of whiskey, and sat at his desk in the den. He started to write down everything he remembered from the images in his nightmares and memories of that period of his youth that he had just so clearly reconstructed. He understood the linkage between the images he saw in his dreams and his childhood house on Riverdale Circle. That cool dark place where he first saw the girl's body, in his second nightmare, was definitely the fort that he and his friend David had dug. But he couldn't see what a young girl could possibly have to do with it, especially a dead girl. As far as he knew, no one had ever been aware of their fort. However, he had a vague recollection about his mother trying to console Sarah over a period of several days. He wasn't sure what it was about, but it had left her quite distraught. It may have had something to do with one of her friends, he recalled.

Thoughts were flashing through Tom's mind. He started to speculate. What if a young girl, maybe one of Sarah's friends, had somehow seen the two boys crawling in and out from under the porch stairs and decided to investigate on her own? What if she panicked down in the hole and suffocated? But that didn't make any sense to him. He reasoned that he and David would have found her. Unless it happened after they stopped using the fort. That was a possibility. Or, what if he had actually found her and was so traumatized that he had completely blanked it from his memory? That too was a possibility.

At that moment, Tom's thoughts turned darker. What if a horrible crime had been committed? What if he or David, or both, had lured a young girl into their fort and committed unspeakable acts? He tried to concentrate on every detail of those years, searching for any moment when he might have felt some remorse. He recalled feeling some regret after he and David had successfully mounted the engine on the kart and got it running up and down their street. He recalled feeling more shame than pride as he received the accolades of his buddies. But he couldn't recall anything about a young girl. Perhaps, he pondered, if such an event had occurred, it was so horrific that it remained locked, deep in his subconscious. That was a possibility.

There was one way to find out, Tom concluded. He needed to search newspaper archives to find out if there were any missing person cases in his hometown during that period in his life. The first thing he had to do was to narrow the search down to a specific range of dates, starting with the date when the fort was completed. He was quite sure he and David had completed digging the fort sometime near the end of October 1963. It stuck in his mind because he recalled spending the following weekend working with Sarah on their Halloween costumes. Ronnie ridiculed him for going out as a pirate.

"What's that stupid thing on your shoulder?" he remembered Ronnie asking.

"That's my parrot," he had answered.

His brother laughed derisively.

"That looks more like a sick pigeon taking a dump on your shoulder," Ronnie had replied as he had reached over and snapped the parrot's neck.

Tom remembered running into the living room, crying, and complaining to his parents. Their father summoned Ronnie, made him kneel in front of Tom and apologize. Then he told Ronnie to go up to his room. He followed him up the stairs and another beating ensued. Tom knew he was going to pay a price, not just for his brother's beating, but for his humiliation.

Tom refocused his thoughts on the time line. Figuring out the completion date of the fort was easy. Determining the date when he last saw the inside of it was going to be much more difficult.

The very last time he could possibly have seen the fort was in November 1965. That's when his parents got divorced and sold the house. Tom's father moved into an apartment in a downtown highrise. He and his sister moved into a brand-new ranch-style house in a suburban residential development south of the river. Ronnie, he recalled, was away at a boarding school.

"That's right," Tom said out loud as he took another sip of whiskey. It was all slowly coming back to him. Ronnie was sent off to a boarding school in September 1964. He remembered that awful night when Ronnie cried and pleaded with his parents not to send him away. But he had failed his school year and Mr. Gibson had had enough.

"I'll try … I'll try my best!" Ronnie had cried.

"We're done. You're going and that's it. You're not going to fool us anymore. You had your chances and you blew it. Now, finish packing your stuff and make sure you pack everything on the list the school gave us," their father had asserted.

Tom concentrated on that time period before the family moved away from Riverdale Circle. He remembered that, at some time after his brother had left, he couldn't find his scout knife. It was one of those multipurpose survival knives with scissors, screwdrivers, corkscrew, bottle cap opener, nail file, and several folding blades of various lengths, all in a sleek leather case. He had looked everywhere for it to no avail. He remembered thinking that Ronnie might have taken it with him to boarding school. One day, he recalled, he went down to the fort to see if his knife might be there. He didn't remember using it in the fort, but he thought it might have fallen out of his pocket when he was crawling around. He remembered being stunned by what he found.

The walls of the hole, the entrance to the fort, had completely collapsed. There was no way to get into the fort. He thought about digging it all out again, but concluded that the stability of the walls had been compromised and may not be safe again, not without some shoring up with timbers. Besides, with Ronnie gone, he didn't really feel the need for any hiding places. There was nothing of value to retrieve from the fort, unless his knife was there. He recalled running over to David's house and informing him of what had happened. David showed no enthusiasm for redigging the access to the fort. So that was it, the fort was done, and Tom never did find his knife.

All these memories became clearer, although without any recollection of the approximate date of the collapse of the fort. Nevertheless, Tom felt he could narrow his media search to that period that ended in November 1965, when his family moved, and then, from that point, work his way back to October 1963, when the fort was completed.

Tom downed the rest of his whiskey, booted up his laptop, and got to work. He wanted to search online for the *Daily Record*, the morning paper he delivered as a lad, and the *Journal*. Those were the two local dailies that would have carried any missing person story, if indeed anything of the sort had occurred. Tom was determined to find the truth, no matter how benign or horrible. It was becoming an obsession.

5

It didn't take long for Tom to find multiple items under the *Daily Record*. It appeared the paper was still in business, touting its seventy-fifth anniversary. The *Journal*, on the other hand, had gone out of business in the late 1970s. Tom visited the *Daily Record* website and discovered how to retrieve digitally stored articles from past editions. However, there seemed to be no online access to any editions before January 1, 1990. Tom picked up the phone and called the paper. After waiting on hold for quite some time, and having his call rerouted multiple times, he finally landed at the desk of the paper's official archivist, a Mr. Donaldson. As it turned out, the archivist was away so Tom left a voicemail.

Tom was impatient and called Mr. Donaldson again the next day. He heard the same telephone greeting and didn't see the need to leave another voicemail. Several days later, when he returned home after a tennis match, Irene informed him that he had received a call from a newspaper.

"I wrote it all down on the telephone pad in your office," she said.

"Thanks, dear," he replied.

"What are you working on?" she asked. "What do you need a newspaper for?"

"Oh, I'm just looking for an article from when I was a kid," he replied.

Tom felt some trepidation as he dialed the telephone number.

"Archives, Donaldson here," a voice said softly at the other end.

Tom introduced himself and explained that he was interested in examining the newspaper's past editions from late 1963 to the end of 1965, without telling the man exactly what he was looking for.

"I was a young reporter then," he declared with a bit of laughter. "I'm retired now, but I seem to be the only one that can find anything around here, so I come back two days a week and help people, mostly our editorial staff, find what they're looking for."

The old man went on for some time, telling Tom all about his life. He had started working at the paper in the print room, right after his graduation from high school. He had never worked anywhere else. Tom wanted to be respectful and didn't want to interrupt. Eventually, there was a pause.

"I've been searching online, but I can't seem to find anything that was published before 1990," Tom explained.

"Yes, of course," the man answered. "Well, I have good news and bad news for you. The good news is that we have records of everything that was ever published by this newspaper. I'm surrounded by all this rich history."

"So, what's the bad news?" Tom dared to ask.

"Well, the paper has been slowly going back and converting all the old records to a new digital format. Don't ask me about that because I don't understand any of it. I have enough trouble trying to receive and send messages on this silly screen they gave me. Anyway, this conversion project has gone in fits and stops. It's taking a lot longer than they anticipated, and right now, it doesn't seem to be a high priority. So, the project stalled at December 31, 1989. All the editions before that date are stored on microfiche."

"Are these records accessible by the public?" Tom asked.

"Oh sure ... Yes, of course. People come in here and sit at the cubicle next to my office, load these microfiche slides into the viewer, and scan all kinds of old stuff. These are the only records in existence, so they can't take the slides with them, but they can spend all the time they want looking at them right here," the old man explained.

"Are the slides catalogued?" Tom continued.

"Of course, they're catalogued. That's my job. I've been doing this for almost forty years. But here's your problem. There are at least ten files per edition and, let's see, if you want to examine two years' worth, well …"

Tom heard some mumbling.

"Well, looks like you may need to look at more than five thousand slides to find what you're looking for. It's a slow, laborious process. It could take you months. What's more, that service is only available to the public two days a week, when I'm in the office. That's every Monday and Tuesday except on holidays."

Tom was somewhat discouraged, but no less determined. He tried to imagine the logistics of driving two hours to his hometown, spending one or two days there, perhaps staying at a hotel, and then driving back, every week, for weeks on end.

"Would I need to make an appointment to come in and view some slides?" Tom asked. "Would I have to tell you in advance which slides I want to view?"

"Yes and no," the man answered with a snicker. "Yes, you need to make an appointment, but no, you don't need to tell us in advance which records you want to see. There is one deck of slides per box, one box for every three months, all neatly stacked on our shelves. They're very easy to get at."

Almost as in a knee-jerk reaction, Tom went ahead and booked a tentative appointment for the following Monday at 10:00 a.m. After he hung up the phone, he began to think about what he was doing. A decision needed to be made. Tom felt he needed to pursue this line of inquiry, but wasn't ready to share his quest with his wife, Irene. He believed that, until or unless he could find more substantial evidence, there was nothing rational to discuss with her. Yet, he was about to consider making a significant commitment in terms of time, expenses, and perhaps more.

At dinner that evening, Tom and Irene sat on the patio and enjoyed a rack of lamb, which he had roasted on the grill. He thought about how he might approach the subject with her. He couldn't find an honest path, at least not at this point in time.

"Do you feel like taking a trip with me?" he asked.

"That depends. Are we talking about going to Europe, or South America, or to some exotic island? If so, yes, tell me more."

"No, it's nothing like that," he admitted. "I'm looking at going back to my hometown to look at some possible buys in income properties. It's one of the fastest growing communities in the country. We could spend a couple of days there, stay at a nice hotel, and try some new restaurants."

"And when were you thinking of going there?" she asked.

"On Monday," he answered.

"Oh, I'm sorry, honey. I have a tennis match on Monday. You can go ahead on your own."

Tom didn't sleep well for the next several nights. He didn't have any nightmares, primarily because he wasn't sleeping. He couldn't stop speculating about what his media search might turn up. Meanwhile, Irene felt a bit of trepidation about Tom's sudden interest in buying more property. Why now, and why in Rochester? She didn't question him because she felt he needed some distraction from his nightmares and concluded that his search for real estate likely wouldn't amount to anything.

Trevor and Christine, along with their spouses and children, all dropped by for brunch on Mothers' Day. Irene had prepared an elaborate hot and cold buffet. The highlight was her eggs Benedict served on Maryland crab cakes. Afterward, Tom and Irene took everyone out for a cruise on their boat. Irene served tea, coffee, and homemade apple pie on the boat. The water was still very cold, but it was a glorious sunny day, and sitting on the rear deck of the boat, it felt like midsummer. The kids and grandkids left by late afternoon. Tom and Irene always found it difficult to say goodbye, although the thought that they would all be back for extended stays during the summer made it easier.

6

The next day, Tom was on the road by 8:00 a.m., heading to Rochester. It was May 12, 2014. He wasn't in the mood for listening to news or talk radio. He spent the two-hour drive listening to classical music from his MP3 player. He stopped for a coffee and bagel en route and pulled into the parking lot at the *Daily Record* just before 10:00 a.m.

A nice young lady from the security desk escorted Tom to the Archives Department which was located on the lower level. She introduced him to Mr. Donaldson.

"Just call me Jerry," said the old man. "I have a feeling we're going to see a lot of each other if you're still looking at seeing two years' worth of newspapers."

"Thank you, Jerry, you can call me Tom."

The two men hit it off pretty well, talking about all the things that had changed in their town over the past four decades. The cubicle was an apt name for the small sterile room that housed the microfiche viewer. There were two small tables and one wooden chair. The viewer sat on one table, the other was clear. The old man pointed to it.

"That's where you can place the file boxes," he explained. "I can bring two boxes at a time. When you're done with them, just tell me. I'll take them away and bring you the next two boxes. That's how it works."

"That will be fine, thank you, Jerry. Can I start with the last two boxes for 1965?"

"Yes, of course. That will cover July to December 1965. I'll be right back."

Tom felt a mixture of emotions. On one hand, he felt right about following through on his instinctive desire to find the truth. He also felt nostalgic about visiting his hometown. On the other hand, he had no fond memories of the period of his life he had spent there, and in the unlikely event that he could find some piece of substantive information, he wasn't at all sure he would like it.

"There you go," said Jerry. "Here are the first two boxes. Good luck!"

The date, November 20, 1965, stuck in Tom's mind. That was the day he and his sister moved out of the old house with their mother. Tom fingered through the first file box until he found the slides for that day's edition of the *Daily Record*. He didn't expect to find anything interesting, but he wanted to use these slides to get familiar with the search process. It took him just over twenty minutes to examine the ten slides. He felt he could get much more efficient with experience.

By the end of the day, Tom was only halfway through the first box. He was very discouraged by the slow rate of progress. He thought about changing to a fast scanning process, but he was worried he could miss a small column, thereby defeating the whole purpose of the exercise. He checked into the Hilton hotel and ordered room service. He was determined to get a good night's sleep.

He was back at the newspaper by nine o'clock the next morning. He had decided overnight to speed up his search by scanning for only a few keys words in the headlines. These words included: *missing*, *child*, *girl*, *River Heights*, *kidnapping*, and *murder*. This quicker process worked well, and he got through the rest of 1965 by the end of the day. He felt good about his productivity, if not about the fact that he had come up with nothing. On the way home, he began to question his undertaking, if not his sanity. It didn't alter his determination.

A week later, he was back in the cubicle, scanning the files. He brought fresh coffee for himself and his new friend Jerry. He tackled the ongoing search with a new sense of energy. He started with December 1964. It didn't take long for him to find a photo of his mother with a feature article, even though none of his keywords were in the headline. It was from late November 1964, when his parents attended a gala where his mother was named Volunteer of the Year and received a lovely plaque. Tom remembered seeing the plaque on a wall in their dining room.

As he read various articles, Tom marveled at the rich history and the significant events that occurred in the fall of 1964. President Lyndon Johnson was reelected in a landslide victory, the Warren Report on the assassination of President Kennedy was released, the Boston strangler was captured, and the USSR's Khrushchev was given the boot.

That afternoon, Tom discovered among the October 1964 files a picture of him standing beside his science fair project. He had placed first in the annual Regional Science Fair and had won an eight-millimeter movie camera. The *Daily Record* carried the story and posted his picture for which he had posed wearing a new suit and tie. He remembered going to a fancy downtown tailor with his mother to get fitted for the suit. It was one of those rare pleasant memories from that period in his life. He recalled that, at that time, he was growing so fast he never got a chance to wear that suit again.

Tom left the newspaper at the end of the day. His search, although unproductive, had been stimulating and, more importantly, was progressing rapidly. He felt he was developing a strong consciousness about his past. He was eager to come back. That night, he dined at an old Italian family-owned restaurant where his parents occasionally took the family for dinner.

The next morning, Tom realized that his search was approaching a crucial time period. His patience and determination paid off. He was stunned, almost in disbelief, when he spotted a tiny column on page 5 of the August 27 edition of the paper. The headline read: **Hope Fades for Missing Girl**.

Tom took a deep breath, leaned forward until his face was only inches from the screen, and read the piece. A young girl, eight years old, by the name of Jennifer "Jenny" Dawbrowski, had been missing for a week. She had disappeared without a trace. She lived with her mother and older sister in the Westgate district. Tom was familiar with that community. It was a modest neighborhood just west of River Heights, near the bridge that linked the north and south banks of the river. It was where the huge Westgate Mall was located.

The article went on to say that the police had very few clues to go on. Jenny had ridden her bike after school, heading to River Heights to visit a friend. She never arrived. There were some eyewitness reports that an unfamiliar old and rusty Chevy sedan had been seen on the streets of River Heights that day. The lead detective was quoted as following two possible theories of what had happened. Someone in that sedan could have kidnapped her and taken her somewhere. But there had been no demands for a ransom, which led the detective to the possibility that they were dealing with a parental abduction. Mrs. Dawbrowski's estranged husband had returned to his native Poland. He or his surrogates could have carried out the abduction and taken Jenny to Poland.

Tom requested a printed copy of the article and quickly advanced to the August 21st edition, the day after the abduction. There was nothing on the front page, but there was a piece, three columns by two hundred lines, on page 3, complete with a photograph of a sweet-looking young blond and blue-eyed girl. It was Jenny. The headline read: **Abducted in Broad Daylight**. Tom had no recollection of ever meeting Jenny, and she didn't really look like the young girl in his nightmares, although the comparison between a vibrant young girl and a cadaver was a complex matter. More importantly, he tried to understand why he had no recollection of this compelling story, one which occurred in his very own neighborhood. He reasoned that, during that summer, he had been so bullied by Ronnie that he had spent most of the summer in hiding. His brother had failed his school year, setting the stage for continual abuse from their father and leading to an increasingly intolerable degree of bullying at Tom's expense. Tom lived in fear the entire summer and was oblivious to anything else that occurred around him. His wasn't a happy home. Either or both parents were out most of the time. When they were home, they fought constantly. That span in Tom's life was characterized by long periods of anguish separated by brief moments of elation.

Tom continued to read the article. There were more questions than answers at press time. Among them was the question of what happened to her bicycle. Police found no trace of her bike. However, some facts emerged: the girl had disappeared sometime between four and six o'clock in the afternoon of November 20; her mother and older sister had searched frantically for her and called the police just before 7:00 p.m. After interviewing some of the witnesses that had come forward, the police launched an APB for an old light gray Chevy sedan. Mrs. Dawbrowski was a single mother who worked as a waitress at a restaurant in Westgate Mall. Tom got a printed copy of the article and revisited the files dated after November 20th, thinking he might have missed something. The only thing he found was a tiny piece in the September 4th edition which indicated the old Chevy, the one that had been the subject of an APB, had been located and turned out to be a false lead. It belonged to a woman who occasionally worked as a house cleaner in River Heights. The rest of his search came up with nothing. Tom chatted with Jerry for a while and explained that he had completed his search.

"That's too bad," the old man lamented. "I was really starting to enjoy the company and I was sure you would be here for quite some time. Did you find what you were looking for?"

"Yes, I did, and I want to thank you. You have been very helpful and you have helped make a tedious task more pleasant."

"It was my pleasure, sir. Have a safe drive home."

Before getting on the highway, Tom drove to the old house on Riverdale Circle and parked across the street. He stayed there for a while and took pictures with his phone. The gray stone house was exactly as he remembered it. The neighborhood had matured. The street was now completely shaded by the oak trees that lined each side. During the drive home, Tom was so captivated by his thoughts that he was home before he knew it, with little recollection of the actual trip. Irene was putting the finishing touches on dinner, poached salmon and risotto.

"Well, did you find anything interesting?" she asked.

"Yes, yes, I did," he replied, realizing they weren't talking about the same thing.

"Tell me, what did you find?" she persisted.

"I'll show you after dinner," he assured her.

Tom was pensive throughout the meal. He felt the time had come to tell Irene the whole story and he was trying to figure out where to start. They sat on the patio after dinner and sipped the rest of their wine.

"Do you remember those nightmares I was having a little while back?" he asked.

"Yes, of course I remember. I have never seen you so worked up."

"Well, as you know, there was a consistent theme to those nightmares. I don't think they were the result of any worry I might have about Geena's safety. I believe very strongly they were triggered by something that happened when I was a young boy."

"And why do you suppose some event from your childhood would suddenly come back to mind, so many years later?"

"I'm not sure. It's a good question. I have speculated, it might be possible that, watching Geena crawl in the sand under that castle we built on the beach in Naples could have evoked some memories."

"I'm sorry, I can't follow you on that one."

"Of course. I have to explain."

Tom continued by revisiting each of his dreams in detail.

"Yes, I remember," she said. "It's all very disturbing but I don't see a connection to you."

"Just wait, I'm just getting started," he continued.

Tom went on to describe the atmosphere around his family home in the early sixties.

"Yes, I remember some of the things you shared with me when you and I went to your brother's funeral, just after Trevor was born. It was the strangest service I had ever attended. It was somber, but there was no crying or any signs of grief. You felt obligated to explain to me why that was. Your mom was the only one who showed any emotion."

"Yes, it was tragic but I never shed a tear. My brother, Ronnie, had a difficult life. He dropped out of college and got odd jobs here and there, never able to hold on to them. He lived in a rooming house and got mixed up with some hooligans. When he was thirty years old, he was arrested for his involvement in a series of burglaries. He was convicted and sentenced to five years in jail. A year later, he got into a fight in the prison's exercise yard. Before the guards could step in, Ronnie had suffered severe head trauma. He was in the ICU when he died from his injuries a day later. I never spoke with him after he was shipped off to boarding school."

"I remember being shocked by what you told me at the funeral, and wondering why you had never shared those childhood details with me before. But as I looked at you and admired how you had emerged so well from such a toxic environment, I reasoned that you had locked it all away to preserve your sanity. I was curious, but I didn't want to roil up your past."

Tom further described how he had had to build hiding places to get away from Ronnie. Then, with his voice trembling, he described the circumstances that led to digging an underground fort under the porch of the old house.

Irene's facial expression suddenly changed, not just because of the tone of Tom's voice, but also because she was beginning to sense some linkage to the nightmares he had described. Her jaw dropped when Tom zeroed in on the tin can of Green Giant corn niblets. She gasped and covered her mouth with her hands.

"Did something happen with Sarah when she was little?" she asked with fear in her eyes. "Your sister and I are close. We share everything, and she has never mentioned …"

"No, no, it has nothing to do with Sarah," he assured her.

Tom continued and explained that, as far as he knew, his younger sister was never aware of the underground fort.

"Then, one day when I was searching for my survival knife, I went down to the fort and found the walls had collapsed. It had served its purpose, we thought, and we chose not to redig it."

"Okay, honey, I get all that. But if nothing happened and nobody got hurt, what's the big deal? Are your nightmares driven by worry over what could have happened, like if it had collapsed while you and your friend were in there?"

"No, I don't think so. This is the point where I have to share with you what I found during my trip this week."

"You mean you've been traveling back to your hometown these past couple of weeks because of this?" she asked incredulously. "This is way out of character for you. These were nightmares. They're not real!" she asserted with emphasis.

Tom went into the house and came back out to the patio with a file folder. He showed Irene the article from August 21st, 1964.

"Oh my God!" she gasped.

"Here's the second article, a week later," he whispered as if he was worried that someone might be listening.

Irene sat back in her chair, deep in thought.

"Did you have any idea, back then, that this had happened?" she asked.

"Not a clue ... I had no idea. I went there last week strictly on a hunch and searched the media files for a time period that corresponded with the beginning and the end of that underground fort."

"Did you know this young girl?" she continued.

"No, I had never even heard of her, although I remember Sarah being upset over something that happened to one of her friends, or a schoolmate ... I don't know."

"Does the girl in the article look anything like the one in your nightmares?"

"No, not really, but it's hard to compare a picture of a pretty and vibrant young girl with the image of a cadaver." In my dreams, she sometimes has blue eyes that stare at me. At other times, her eye sockets are hollow."

"So, now what ... What are you going to do?" she asked.

"I'm thinking of going to the local police and sharing what I know."

"Are you out of your mind? Think about it!" she exclaimed as she raised her voice. "They're either going to think you're crazy or they're going to follow through and find enough circumstantial evidence to pin you for the crime."

She paused to take a breath.

"You and I have worked very hard to have the wonderful life we have," she continued in a softer voice. "Do you really think this story is worth putting all of it at risk? Do I get a say in this?"

"You're right … What purpose would it serve now?"

The next day, Tom felt he could clear his conscience by sending an anonymous tip. He typed up a brief note indicating he had had a vision that something related to the Jennifer Dawbrowski case from August 1964 could possibly be buried under the back porch at 5 Riverdale Circle. He was careful not to leave any fingerprints. He addressed it to the chief of police and mailed it. He didn't tell Irene.

7

The Gibson family all gathered at Tom and Irene's home for the Independence Day holiday weekend. Trevor and Christine and their families arrived on Thursday evening, July 3rd, 2014. All four grandchildren loved the lake house. They had hardly been there an hour when they pleaded with their parents to let them stay the entire summer. They settled on letting them stay for the rest of the month, as long as it was okay with Grandma and Grandpa. That was a given, so everyone cheered.

After consulting with the kids, Irene called the tennis club and registered all four children into tennis instruction. Friday, July 4th, was a beautiful warm day. After breakfast, the family climbed aboard Tom's cruising boat. Irene brought a cooler full of chicken wrap sandwiches and drinking boxes. They spent most of the day touring Lake Erie. Irene served a big brunch on Sunday, and then the parents gave their kids the usual lecture on good behavior before they got on the road. Tom chuckled as the kids enthusiastically waved goodbye to their parents. He always marveled at the fact that the kids always behaved better when their parents weren't there and, in his opinion, it had nothing to do with the lectures from their parents.

It seemed the kids spent half their days in the water. They all improved their swimming and diving skills and couldn't wait to show off for their parents. They developed their own traditions together. There were Monday Movie Nights, the only time they were allowed to eat dinner in front of the TV. There were Taco Tuesdays and Spaghetti Saturdays. They normally went out for dinner at the marina restaurant at least once a week. The kids did so well in their tennis lessons that Tom and Irene talked about getting a court built on their own property.

"Besides, it would cut down on the amount of lawn I have to maintain," Tom commented.

"But summer is half over," Irene countered, "so let's get some quotes and line up a contractor, but let's not build it until next spring."

"You're right. I'll find out which contractor the club used and I'll start there."

It seemed to Tom as though the summer was over in a flash. He and Irene hosted Trevor and Christine, their spouses, and their kids, as well as their in-laws for the Labor Day long weekend, as had become their practice. People who had lived their entire lives in urban areas, as in the case of the in-laws, always seemed to have particular appreciation for an opportunity to spend a weekend at a lake house. It was a little crowded but everyone got along. The five pairs of adults had their own bedrooms while the kids set up camp in the downstairs family room. After the weekend, it was time to clean up the water toys and put them away. It was a quiet period that Tom usually found a little depressing. Although the fall was wonderfully picturesque, that was when he started to look forward to going south to Naples where he and Irene had a busier social life.

Tom hadn't had any nightmares for months and felt comfortable that the anonymous tip he had sent had been sufficient to clear his conscience. He was sleeping reasonably well, or as well as someone his age normally sleeps.

One morning in mid-November, Tom heard the doorbell. Irene was at the supermarket in nearby Erie getting an early start on preparations for Thanksgiving. Tom was startled to see two police officers standing on his doorstep. They introduced themselves and asked for Mr. Tom Gibson.

"I'm Tom Gibson," he replied. "What is this about?"

They were very polite and simply indicated they had been asked to hand deliver a letter to him.

"Here it is. Have a wonderful day," one of them said as they tipped their caps and walked away.

Tom felt his heart was going to pound through his chest. He quickly scooted to the den where he opened the envelope. The letter was from a detective named Phillip Carter, the officer in charge of cold cases at the police department back in his hometown of Rochester, New York.

Detective Carter began his letter by describing how his research had found that there were only two people still alive who had lived at 5 Riverdale Circle during the time of the disappearance of Jennifer Dawbrowski: Tom and his younger sister. So he had assumed that the anonymous tip had come from Tom.

The letter went on to thank Tom for his tip and invited him to call the main station to book an appointment for an interview. Tom was dumbfounded.

"How could I have been so stupid?" he said to himself.

He suddenly felt that his efforts to do the right thing were turning into a horror story. How was he going to face Irene with this new development? He didn't have much time to think about it. Irene came home thirty minutes later, shouting for help to carry in her purchases. At dinner that night, Tom let Irene in on the police visit that had occurred earlier in the day. Tom was forced to admit he had sent an anonymous tip.

"How could we have been so stupid!" she exclaimed. "It wouldn't take a genius to follow a straight and narrow path right back to you. How could you be so naive? Why didn't you talk with me first?" she continued as she shook her head in disbelief.

"What did you say? Did you admit anything?"

"No, of course not. They were just delivering a message. They know nothing about the case."

"I think we need to get a lawyer," she asserted.

"Yes, I think you're right. I feel I have done nothing wrong ... Actually, I'm convinced I have done nothing wrong, which is why I have no qualms about pursuing the truth. In fact, I want to find the truth."

"Before we retain a lawyer, maybe we should ask Dr. Mansfield to meet with us. Edward is the psychiatrist I have worked with on some school programs. You met him last year at the fund-raiser for special-needs schooling. Perhaps he could use hypnosis to find out if you have any deeply guarded secrets about what happened in that dugout."

"Again, I think you're right. It may give us a point of reference, going forward. If nothing else, it might tell us what we're dealing with and whether or not we need to be defensive. I won't book an appointment with Detective Carter until we've had a chance to meet with Dr. Mansfield."

A week later, Tom and Irene sat down with Dr. Mansfield at his clinic and explained the situation. Tom described his nightmares and the history of his childhood during the period relevant to the disappearance of the young girl.

"Are both of you ready for the truth, no matter what it is?" asked the doctor.

"Yes, absolutely, we need to know," Tom answered. Irene didn't seem to be as confident.

"All right then, here's how we're going to proceed. I'm going to use a technique called eye fixation to induce a state of hypnosis. Then I will mention certain things to try to invoke something we call an abreaction. An abreaction is a kind of emotional outburst or reliving of an experience and can release suppressed emotional material. The patient stays in control throughout the session and cannot be compelled to do anything he or she doesn't want to do. Are you ready?"

"Yes, let's go for it," Tom replied.

"Very well," the doctor continued as he pulled his chair over and sat down facing Tom. "I want you to relax your arms down each side and look at the picture on the wall over my right shoulder. As you stare at the picture, I want you to clear your thoughts. Think of nothing but the picture as you stare at it. Let your jaw drop slightly so there is no tension in your mouth. Keep staring at the picture. You can blink if you have to, but just keep staring at the picture on the wall. It may seem like it's moving or distorting at some point. That's perfectly okay. As you keep staring, your eyelids are going to start to feel heavy."

Tom started to blink and then his eyes were half closed. When his eyes finally closed and his shoulders sagged, the doctor knew he had successfully induced a state of hypnosis.

"Tom, I'd like you to go back in time, to the day you and Irene got married."

A few moments later, Tom smiled.

"Oh, there she is," Tom exclaimed. "She's so beautiful. And look, guys, look at my Mom and Dad. I haven't seen them together since I was thirteen."

Irene shed a tear as she listened. Tom's words evoked her emotions from that wonderful day.

"Now, Tom," the doctor continued, "I want you to think back even further, when you were a young boy, and you and your friend David dug that fort under your back porch."

There was silence for a while. Then Tom's smile turned to a frown. The doctor was about to say something when Tom erupted.

"Ouch, that hurts, leave me alone. You know I'm going to tell Dad."

There were a few quiet moments.

"I know, I know, Dave, we have to get rid of this thing. We have to do it before the McPhersons realize it's gone and call the police. I know just the place.

"You know, Dave, even though it's cool, damp, and dark in here, I feel safe and secure. And Ronnie will never find us."

Another period of silence followed.

"Look, see, when I hold up the candle, you can still see part of the handlebar. We need to pack some more dirt over it," Tom whispered as if he was sharing a secret.

"Oh no, what the hell? What happened?" cried out Tom

"What is it, Tom, what's happening?" asked the doctor.

"The whole thing has caved in! There's no way to get into our fort! All that work … And it's gone. I have to go tell David."

"Tom, tell me, did you ever see a young girl in the fort. Was there ever a girl in the fort?" the doctor pressed as Tom became more agitated.

There was no answer.

"He's getting quite worked up," commented the doctor. "I'm going to have to bring him back."

"Okay, Tom, you're going to wake up soon. I'm going to count to three and snap my fingers and you're going to wake up and open your eyes. One … Two … Three …"

Tom immediately awoke upon the snap of the doctor's fingers.

"Well, did we learn anything?" Tom asked immediately.

"Yes and no," replied the doctor. "Things seem to have unfolded pretty well as you have described them, bullying by your brother, stealing the machine, burying it, but no indication of any girl. But, at one point, while in the fort and holding up the candle, you mentioned something intriguing. You said that a portion of the handlebar was still visible and needed to be covered up. I immediately thought of the newspaper article you showed me and wondered if you were possibly referring to the handlebars from the bicycle that disappeared with the young girl."

"No," Tom answered. "Well, I can't be sure, but I think I was talking about the part of the tiller frame where the handle grips are … I don't ever remember seeing a bike in there."

"Very well. In my opinion, there is definitely some trauma associated with that underground fort. It has to do with hiding from your brother, and it has to do with the fact that you did something wrong and felt remorse for stealing that piece of equipment, but I don't see any link to any girl. Now, that doesn't mean that there was no girl. It can simply mean that, either you weren't aware of it, or it could possibly be that, whatever happened, it was so horrific that you can't overcome your suppression of it, even under hypnosis. Remember, as I told you, hypnosis can't make you do anything you don't want to do. So, I don't know what else I can tell you."

"Thanks, Edward, I think this was helpful," Irene responded. "It gives me a little more confidence that, whatever happened, if anything at all happened, Tom was probably not directly involved. But it doesn't explain his nightmares. If he wasn't aware of the girl's disappearance, or of any connection between her and the dugout, what could possibly be generating these images?"

"That's a good question, Irene," replied the doctor. "All I can tell you is that there have been well-documented cases of unexplainable sensory perceptions that have been helpful in solving crimes. So this, if it turns out to be something like that, is rare but not unprecedented."

Tom and Irene didn't say a word on the way home. That evening, during dinner, Tom finally broke the silence.

"I'm sorry to drag you through all of this, dear, all because of some silly nightmares."

"I don't think there is anything silly about any of it. And there is certainly nothing silly about the disappearance of that young girl. It's tragic; I can't imagine how her mother has suffered all these years without knowing what happened to her daughter. And you, you have been emotionally touched by whatever you experienced. There's a reason you've been taking them seriously. You're not a flippant kind of person. And whatever it is, you find it compelling enough that you feel the need to follow through. I don't like the fact that we find ourselves in this mess, but we're a team, you and me, so we'll see this through to the end, together."

"Thanks, I can't tell you how much I appreciate your support."

The next day, Tom called Detective Carter. Tom felt awkward at first but was soon comforted by the detective's calm and conciliatory tone.

"I want to thank you, sir, for coming forward and helping us with this case," said the detective. "We may not be able to solve this case, but every little bit of information gets us a little closer."

"Did you get a chance to research the file?" Tom asked.

"Yes, of course I did. To be honest, the case had been filed away on the assumption that it was a parental abduction. It was assumed that the father took her back to his home country, and since we have no extradition treaty with Poland, the case was filed as requiring no further action."

Tom heard the shuffling of some papers at the other end.

"So, based on your tip, I did some digging," the detective continued. "I'm afraid I have to admit the detective work that was done on this case at the time was rather shoddy."

"How do you mean?" Tom asked.

"Well, at the time, Poland was still a member of the Warsaw Pact and was still under significant Soviet influence. So the borders were very tightly controlled. Perhaps they weren't willing to share border information with western police forces back then, I don't know. But it only took me two days to find out that Michael Dawbrowski returned to Poland in 1963, alone. There was no record of a Jennifer Dawbrowski entering Poland in 1964, or at any time since. Our own government records show that Jenny's name never appeared on any passport application. All of this suggests two possibilities: One, she was abducted and the perpetrators took her over the border by car either to repatriate her to Poland or to realize some kind of financial gain. None of it was likely because she never entered Poland, there was no apparent motive, and there was no ransom demand. Possibility number two, the one I believe is most likely, is that she never left the country, and is likely dead. All of this is based on the facts I have examined so far and doesn't even take into consideration your tip or any new information that may come from it."

After a brief pause, the detective continued.

"Just for absolute certainty, I did some more digging. Mr. Dawbrowski remarried in 1966. He died in 1998 and his second wife died two years ago. They raised two sons who are both still living. One still lives in Poland and the other now lives in England. I was able to reach both of them, one by phone and the other by e-mail. Neither was aware of the existence of a half sister from North America. So, as far as I'm concerned, that's the end of that line of inquiry."

"I see ... That's very fascinating. You are certainly very thorough," Tom commented. "So what do you want me to do?"

"I'd like you to come in for a chat. I'd like to know all the details you can recall about what was going on at your house at that time. I'd like to know why you think there might be some evidence under the back porch of your childhood home. I'd like to reconstruct who was where and when, who had access and opportunity. With all that as a base, we can start down an investigative path."

The two men agreed to meet at the detective's office on Tuesday, December 2nd, 2014, at eleven o'clock.

"Normally, Irene and I would be on our way to Naples at this time," Tom explained. "That's where we spend our winters. We'll delay our departure for a few days so I can meet with you."

"Thank you, sir, that's very generous."

"Do I need to bring a lawyer with me?" Tom asked.

"It's up to you, sir, but at this time, I'm just suggesting that we have a chat. If we get to a point where we need a deposition, then yes, by all means, you should be represented by counsel. You'll know if we ever reach that point because I'll have to read you your Miranda rights. Anything you tell me before that would be inadmissible anyway."

"Very well, I will see you at eleven on Tuesday."

8

Tom and Irene shared a steak for dinner on Sunday. Tom cooked it on the grill while Irene prepared dirty-garlic-mashed potatoes and asparagus.

"Do you want me to go with you on Tuesday?" she asked.

"No, I don't think so. It's all very informal at this point. But thank you for offering. I may take you up on your offer if things get more formal or if we ever get to a point where they consider me a possible suspect."

"Okay, but I think you're being a little naïve, again. If they ever find something in that dugout, you can be sure you'll be a prime suspect."

"Perhaps, but I can't believe they'll ever find any evidence that links me directly to the case."

Both of them had difficulty sleeping for the next couple of nights. On Tuesday morning, Irene walked to the SUV with Tom. They kissed and hugged.

"Drive carefully. You haven't had much sleep and they're calling for a bit of snow later in the day."

"I'll be fine. I'll be back in time for dinner."

Tom felt considerable trepidation en route to Rochester. He wondered if he was starting to lose his mind. He weighed the possible consequences of his actions and tried to reason whether his search for the truth was really an act of good conscience or the result some kind of early dementia. He felt quite sane, but knew he probably wasn't the best judge of his sanity. He also believed he had nothing to hide, but couldn't be absolutely sure; there was a tiny bit of lingering doubt that gnawed at him.

A few snow flurries had started when Tom pulled into the underground garage of the police station. It was 10:45 a.m. when he walked up to the reception desk on the main floor. He was greeted by a tall redheaded staff sergeant.

"How can we help you, sir?" his voice echoed through the main hall.

"I have an appointment with Detective Carter."

The staff sergeant summoned one of the other officers and handed a clipboard to Tom.

"Could you please print your name and sign the register, sir. Please wear this guest badge at all times and return it to this desk before you leave the building."

He picked up the phone and pressed a few buttons.

"Yes, sir, this is MacBrian at the front desk. There is a gentleman by the name of"—he looked at the clipboard—"Gibson here to see you … Very well."

He turned to the other officer.

"Please escort this gentleman to Detective Carter's office on the fourth floor."

Detective Carter didn't look anything like what Tom had expected. He was a jolly fellow that looked more like Colonel Sanders than a seasoned police officer.

"Mr. Gibson, welcome, and thank you so much for coming in!"

"No problem."

Tom looked around. Detective Carter's office looked like a scrapbook. Three of the walls were almost completely covered with newspaper clippings. The fourth wall, the one beside the doorway, only had a dozen or so articles pinned on it, including one about Jenny's disappearance.

"Those are the unsolved cases," the detective commented. "I just added the piece about our missing young girl."

"And all these other ones have been solved," Tom asked.

"Yes, sir, some by virtue of good police work and some by sheer good fortune."

The detective invited Tom to follow him into the conference room next to his office. He walked up to a large whiteboard and picked up a marker.

"Let's get started, shall we? Let's go back to the summer of 1964 and name all the people you knew at that time."

Tom started with his family, then his neighbors. Detective Carter wrote the names on the whiteboard as Tom spoke.

"Good, and now I'd like you to think about everyone who stepped into your house that summer."

"That's easy, because there weren't many. There was my best friend, David, and both of his parents. They were the most frequent visitors. Two of Ronnie's friends came over a few times, Billy Shmale and Tim … I don't remember his last name. And the only others were the officers who brought Ronnie home that day when Ronnie got caught shoplifting. Oh, and there was one more. My father's secretary was there a couple of times to drop some files off. That's it."

The two men spent the next several hours going over every detail of what happened from the time Tom and David stole the tiller to the point when Tom discovered the fort had caved in. Then they meticulously covered each of Tom's nightmares.

Tom looked at his watch. It was almost four o'clock, and the two of them hadn't even paused for lunch.

"I think that's pretty well it," Tom sighed. "Now you know everything I know. So where do we go from here?"

"Well, I'm going to have to digest all of this and determine our next steps, if there are any next steps."

"What do you mean? Aren't you going to dig up under that porch and see if there is any evidence there?"

"It's not that simple. You can't just dig up somebody's property. You have to get the district attorney to request a warrant. Then a judge has to issue a warrant. I'm not sure we have enough here to convince the DA to seek a warrant."

Tom seemed perplexed.

"Let me ask you this," the detective said. "How strongly do you feel about the possibility that there is evidence under that porch that relates to the disappearance of that young girl?"

Tom paused to think.

"I'm not sure how to describe how I feel. But the very fact that I reached out to the police, and the fact that I'm here with you right now, should say a lot about how I feel."

"Yes, of course."

Tom stood up and picked up his jacket.

"I'd better get going," he said.

The men shook hands.

"Thanks again for coming in. Have a safe trip home and have a good winter in Florida. Here's my card. Please send me a brief e-mail when you get home and give me your contact information in Florida. I'll keep you posted on our progress and I'll call you if I come up with more questions."

"I'll send you an e-mail, but here is my card. It has my contact information."

As Tom pulled out of the underground garage, he decided to take a side trip and drove to his childhood neighborhood. He parked across the street from his old house, again.

Tom just sat in his SUV and stared at the front door. Many unpleasant memories came back to him. He was about to drive away when a black Range Rover pulled into the driveway. A man wearing a beige trench coat stepped out. He had a short white beard and looked a bit like Ernest Hemingway, Tom thought. He walked up the four steps, opened the door, and went into the house.

Driven by impulse more than anything else, Tom turned off the engine, stepped out of his vehicle, and walked up to the front door. He stood there for a moment and then rang the doorbell.

The man he had just seen entering the house was the one who answered.

"Yes, whatever it is you're selling, we probably don't need it," he said as he looked at Tom.

"Oh no, I'm not selling anything and I'm sorry to disturb you. My name is Tom Gibson. I was in the neighborhood and I thought I would drop by. You see, this was our home when I was a young lad."

"The Gibsons, of course. Your family sold this house to the Collins family, and they sold it to us. We've been here since 1982. Would you like to come in?"

"Oh, I don't want to impose," Tom replied.

"Who is it, Jim?" asked a voice in the background.

"We have a visitor. This is Mr. Gibson. He and his family used to live here!"

He gestured at Tom to enter.

"Come in … Come in," he said. "I'm Jim Alford and this is my wife, Connie."

"Tom, I'm Tom Gibson. I lived here until the age of thirteen. We moved out at the end of 1965."

"Give me your coat and Jim can show you around so you can reminisce," she said.

Tom wasn't sure he wanted to rekindle anything from that period in his life, but his curiosity was not to be denied. Besides, a live tour could possibly evoke fresh memories or new information. The house was essentially as he remembered it, with the exception of some renovations in the kitchen and bathrooms. The rear wall of the living room had been punched out and sliding doors had been installed, leading down some steps to the patio. Tom felt a chill when he stepped into the rear vestibule. It was just like the one in his nightmare. He chose not to go down to the basement.

The three of them sat down in the kitchen and shared a pot of tea.

"When we bought this house in 1982," Jim Alford explained, "Connie and I were recently married and were both teaching at the university. We had carpenters come in and build three bedrooms and a bathroom in the attic. We rented those three rooms, as well as the bedroom in the basement, to students at the university; mostly foreign postgraduate students. It helped us carry the mortgage payments for the first few years. Then we raised our two girls. It has been a wonderful home for us. Our girls are now married and we have five grandchildren."

"Congratulations!" Tom exclaimed. "Isn't grandparenthood great?"

"Absolutely!" Connie answered. "If I had known grandchildren were going to be so much fun, we would have had them first!" she replied in jest.

"Connie retired last year and I plan to retire next May," Jim explained. "We plan to travel for about a year before starting our next book project."

"Good for you," Tom answered. "I think you'll find retirement almost as enjoyable as having grandkids. And it will give you the opportunity to enjoy your grandchildren even more."

A thought crossed Tom's mind. He wondered if he should share with them the reason he was in town. He concluded it might be too abrupt and he didn't want to cast a shadow on their happy feelings regarding the house. Instead, he took a different approach.

"This is a mighty big house for the two of you. Do you think you'll continue to live here after retirement?"

"You're right. It is way more house than we need, and as a matter of fact, we're contemplating moving into one of the new condo buildings on the riverfront."

"Sounds like a good plan," Tom commented. "I'll tell you what … I'm retired but I still dabble in real estate, particularly income properties. I'll give you my contact information. If or when you decide to sell, I would be interested in making an offer on this house. Who knows, if we can agree on a price, you may be able to save the cost of a realtor's commission."

"Very good!" said Jim. "When the time comes, we'll be sure to get in touch with you."

"I should get going," Tom declared as he stood up. "Thank you so much for inviting me in and allowing me a retrospective look at my childhood home, and thank you for the tea. Here is a card with my contact information."

On the way home, Tom reflected on what had just transpired and was amazed by his audacity. Once again, he wondered if his curiosity had become an obsession. The idea of buying an expensive property, just to excavate the area under the back porch, seemed like lunacy. He decided, at that very moment, to apply some rationality to any future decision. That meant that, before making any important decision such as buying a property, he needed to complete a full business analysis, just as he would for any other investment. No decision was going to be skewed by his curiosity about a missing girl, regardless of any disturbing dreams or nightmares.

Tom was home by seven o'clock and sat down to dinner with Irene. He recapped the highlights of his day, including his visit to his childhood home. He omitted the discussion he had with the Alfords about the possibility of buying the house. He fully realized that the mere idea would cause Irene to come unglued.

Two days later, Tom and Irene were on their way to Naples. They spent one night on the road and stayed at one of their favorite hotels in Atlanta. They soon settled into their winter routine and played tennis three or four times a week. They flew home to spend Christmas with the kids and grandkids and were back in Florida ten days later.

They hosted a Super Bowl party on February 1st, 2015, with eight other couples from the tennis club. The next morning, the phone rang just after ten. Tom answered.

"Oh, hello, Detective, how are you?" Tom listened for several minutes, nodding at times and shaking his head at others. Irene stood patiently beside him.

"I understand, Detective," Tom finally answered. "I have to concede that I'm disappointed. I guess I'll just have to let it go. I want to thank you for trying and doing the best you could … Yes, we will … We always enjoy our winters down here. Thank you for getting back to me … And a happy new year to you also … Goodbye."

"Well, what was all that about?" Irene asked anxiously.

"He said he and the DA looked at all the facts and were unable to justify a request for a warrant to excavate private property. He said it would have been different if had I stated that I remembered actually seeing some evidence under that porch. He said that would make me a witness and could constitute a basis for a search. But a dream or vision are not sufficient grounds. So that's the end of it. They're not pursuing the case any further unless some new evidence surfaces."

"Well, it doesn't solve the case but it means we don't have anything to worry about." Irene observed.

"Yes, that's right. We can just get on with our lives knowing we did what we could."

All was well until the end of February. That's when Tom began feeling the same kind of anxiety he had felt just before his first nightmare, almost a year earlier. He expected the nightmares to start again at any time.

One night, just after two in the morning, Tom sat up abruptly out of his sleep, choking and coughing.

"What's wrong, Tom! Are you okay?" Irene cried out.

It took awhile for Tom to catch his breath. He finally began to breathe somewhat normally.

"My God, what an awful experience," he finally uttered.

"What? What?"

"I dreamt I was buried alive … I couldn't open my eyes … My mouth was filled with dirt. Some of it got sucked down my throat as I gasped for air … It was so real!"

"Oh, honey, I don't know what to say. I don't know how I can help you …"

"It's okay, I'll get through it over time."

From that point on, Tom feared going to bed at night. He also began to experience brief daytime hallucinations. He would open the pantry door and, for a fraction of a second, would see the young girl's cadaver lying across one of the shelves. Occasionally, he would see her in the trunk of his car. Tom was startled each time, but eventually convinced himself that it was just his mind playing tricks on him, or more specifically, his conscience prodding him, and he needed to just get used to it. He felt he needed to even go as far as anticipating the visions. He succeeded so well that he was almost disappointed when he expected a sighting and it didn't happen.

All of it, the lack of sleep, the hallucinations, and the mind control games left Tom physically and mentally exhausted. He couldn't imagine spending the rest of his life this way. He felt some temporary relief during Christine and Alan's visit with the boys, and again when Trevor, Anne, and Geena followed for a two-week visit which started on March 7th. Their visits couldn't have come at a better time. Tom was relaxed and slept better than he had in months. Unfortunately, it was over all too soon. It was Saturday, March 21st, when Tom and Irene drove them to the airport. Tom was already feeling some anxiety.

The following Monday, Tom and Irene got back from their matches at the tennis club and sat by the pool to relax and read. She was into a novel and he was scanning the *Naples Daily News*.

"Do you think I should make an appointment to see Dr. Bennett?" Tom asked.

The Gibsons had a family physician at home and another in Naples. They had met Dr. Bennett through the tennis club.

"Sure, perhaps he can at least give you something to help you sleep."

Tom picked up his cell phone, found the doctor in his directory, and called to make an appointment. He was able to see him that afternoon. Tom explained that he was feeling anxious and losing sleep. His hallucinations were likely the result of being exhausted. He didn't see the need to get into the details of his nightmares or the whole story about the young girl.

"I don't think I'm the right person to explore the underlying reasons for your anxiety," the doctor explained, "but I can give you something to help you relax. I'm going to write up a prescription for valium," he continued as he typed away on his laptop.

"Which pharmacy do you normally use?" he asked.

"Irene and I tend to use the CVS near the tennis club."

The doctor keyed in a few more strokes and turned to Tom.

"Okay, you're all set. They'll have it ready for you in the next half hour."

Tom truly disliked taking any medication. He was already taking meds for his blood pressure, reluctantly, and was less than enthusiastic about adding another daily medication. However, he was becoming desperate and realized he couldn't let things go on the way they were.

"Do I need to worry about any interaction between valium and valsartan?" Tom asked.

"As far as I know, there are no known interactions between valium and your blood pressure medication," the doctor assured Tom. "But let me check the database, just to make sure."

Dr. Bennett punched away on his keyboard and read something on his screen.

"Looks like we're good to go. I don't see any issues. However, different people react differently to valium. If you feel any adverse physical or emotional reactions, stop taking the medication and call me right away."

Tom filled the prescription and took his first capsule just before dinner that evening. He slept reasonably well that night. After a few days, he found he was feeling light-headed when he got out of bed or got off the couch. He also experienced muscle control issues to the point where he couldn't play tennis at his usual level. He seemed to be unable to concentrate enough to complete his crossword or sudoku puzzles. Finally, after two weeks, he stopped taking the valium.

"I just can't continue taking this stuff," he explained to Irene. "It's destroying me."

"Yes, I've seen some changes in you," she confirmed, "but I was hoping you would come to this conclusion on your own. I've noticed that you're jittery and your eyes are glassy. It can't be good for you."

Tom called the doctor and explained what was happening. He got a referral to see a psychiatrist, hoping there might be a different way to help him deal with his issues. Thanks to a recent cancellation, he was able to see Dr. Christy Gormley the following week, on April 14th.

Tom found her to be warm, pleasant, and understanding. He had no difficulty opening up to her and describing the whole pattern of recurring themes in his nightmares and daytime hallucinations. She listened attentively and did not interrupt.

"So, Doctor, what do you think? Am I going crazy?"

"I don't think so, but let me ask you a few questions. Are you able to go about your daily routines, are you functioning normally, aside from these visions?"

"Yes, other than that short period when I was on valium, I'm doing everything just the way I always have."

"Are you depressed?"

"No, not at all. I'm a little worried about having to experience these nightmares and visions for the rest of my life, but other than that, I feel great about my life."

"In retirement, are you finding enough to keep you busy?"

"Yes, in some ways, I'm busier than ever. Between our tennis, our grandkids, our travels, and the real estate investments I manage, I'm never short of things to do."

Dr. Gormley was busy writing notes as Tom spoke.

"Very well, here's what I think is going on. No, I don't think you're going crazy. You seem sane and rational. But, you are suffering from an obsession that was triggered by dreams that somehow connected with an episode in your childhood. Obsessions, by their very nature, take up a disproportionate amount of a person's thoughts. When obsessions are based on imaginary conceptions, they can lead to forms of psychosis like schizophrenia and other delusional behavior. However, in your case, there was a young girl who disappeared in your neighborhood; you have concluded that there might be a connection to your underground hideout; you were experiencing psychological trauma at that time in your childhood. All these things follow a logical pattern and do not reflect any kind of psychosis."

She paused for a moment as her face took on a more somber look.

"However, even though I don't know you very well, from what I have learned, it seems that you have guided yourself with rational thought rather than emotion. Your decisions are based on facts. Therefore, I'm afraid you will likely continue to be dumbfounded by this until you're satisfied that the facts have been fully exposed. Sure, I could prescribe some medications that might help mask the problem, but nothing will solve this until you feel that you have followed your conscience and exposed the truth, even if the truth is that there's absolutely no evidence in that dugout."

Tom took a deep breath. He was relieved, in a way, firstly because she had confirmed that he wasn't suffering from a mental disorder, and secondly because he had known, in the back of his mind, that the only solution was to follow his instincts and uncover the truth.

When he got back to the condo, Irene had already returned from her tennis match and seemed quite irritable.

"What's wrong? Did something happen at the club?" Tom asked.

"No, that's not it. There was a message on the recorder when I got home, a message from a Jim Alford. He mentioned that the two of you had discussed the possibility that you might want to buy his house. You never said anything to me about that. What are you up to? You and I always discuss these things. We don't keep secrets from each other, do we?"

"I'm so sorry. We had a very brief conversation during my visit. He mentioned they might be ready to downsize and I just wanted to plant the seed. I felt it was way too early to discuss it with you. It was a mistake. I should have mentioned it. In any case, I won't consider any such investment unless it makes perfect business sense, and of course, I won't do anything without first discussing it with you."

Tom called Jim Alford and found out the house was going to be listed for sale in May. The Alfords were moving to the newest riverfront condo tower. Their closing date for the condo was set for early August.

"Thank you for giving us a heads-up. Yes, we are interested, but I need to build the business case. My wife and I will be back home on Sunday. Would it be all right if I made an appointment to meet a real estate agent at your house sometime next week?"

"I thought you said you wanted to do a direct sale and forgo an agent and save the fees?"

"Yes, of course, Mr. Alford, but we would be looking at this as an income property and I need to assess the income potential with the help of a local expert."

"Oh, okay, I see. Sure, just let us know when you want to be here."

"In that regard, you mentioned you had rented out the rooms on the third floor at some point. Did you keep any of the documents that were issued by the municipality, allowing you to operate a rooming house?"

"Yes, of course, we had to convert the window at the south end of the hallway into a door and install a fire escape down to the flat roof over the garage and then over the parapet and down to the ground level. I kept all the paperwork."

"Great, I'll call you early next week and make an appointment."

Tom felt a sense of excitement. He got on the Internet right away and started to research the most active real estate agents in the area. It seemed that the undisputed king of real estate in River Heights Estates and the entire university district was a woman by the name of Marcia Tilley. Tom took note of her contact information and called her. He got her voicemail and left a message. She called back in less than ten minutes, which in itself gave Tom a favorable impression.

After their hellos and introductions, Tom explained what he needed.

"My childhood home in River Heights Estates is coming up for sale and I'm seriously considering buying it as an income property. Specifically, I want to turn it into a rooming house. Given the close proximity to the university and the attributes of the property, I think it would be a good investment. However, I need to work with real numbers to see if it makes sense."

"What address are we talking about?" Marcia asked.

"Number 5 Riverdale Circle," Tom answered.

"Oh yes, I know the property quite well. I sold the house across the street last year."

"Very good, but here's the thing," Tom continued.

"If I buy this property from the Alfords, it will be a direct sale. So there won't be any commission in it for you. However, if you are interested, you could act as the property manager and I would be happy to pay you a generous monthly fee."

"That sounds fine to me. What do you need from me to go forward?"

"Glad you asked. Here's what I need: I need an analysis of the comparable sales in the area so we can establish a fair purchase price for the house. I need to know the annual property taxes. I need to know how much revenue each room will likely generate."

"Do the current owners have municipal approval to run a rooming house?" she asked. "Because I know there has been a major clampdown on illegal rooming houses in the past couple of years."

"Yes, the Alfords have the documents in hand, although it has been many years since they have rented any rooms."

"That's fine. That means their approval has been grandfathered and remains valid. I'll need to tour the house and see each bedroom you plan to rent out."

"Right, so would you be available to meet me at the house next Wednesday?"

"Let me check my calendar … Yes, yes, I could meet you there at two o'clock."

"Great. I have your e-mail address from your website. I'll send you a brief note with my contact information."

"Very well, see you next week."

9

Tom and Irene headed home on Friday, April 27th. They were on the road by eight o'clock, and they knew they had about a ten-hour ride to get to their overnight stop in Atlanta.

"I expect most of the traffic to be southbound today," Tom commented after they had been on I-75 for about twenty minutes.

"You were snoring like a trooper last night," Irene said. "You must have had a decent sleep for a change."

"That was the best sleep I've had in a very long time," Tom replied.

Irene had prepared some sandwiches the night before. They stopped once to gas up and had their lunch on the road. They pulled into the St. Regis Hotel just after six and checked into their suite. After freshening up, they had cocktails at the bar and then walked over to the Atlas where they looked forward to a gourmet dinner. They looked at it as their reward for a long day's drive. Tom's main course was a rack of lamb while Irene's was a bison rib eye. They had been there many times and always seemed to order the same dishes. Everything was as good as ever.

Tom started to yawn before they had even finished their bottle of wine.

"Let's get back to the room and go to bed," Irene suggested.

Tom nodded, signed the bill to their room, and got up to stretch his legs. The two of them were asleep before ten, and Tom enjoyed his third consecutive uninterrupted sleep.

The next morning, they skipped the lavish breakfast offered by the St. Regis, picked up coffee and muffins at Starbucks, and were on the road before seven. They pulled into their driveway just after six o'clock that evening. It took Tom about an hour to get the house up and running. They ordered pizza and then started to unpack. They were happy to be home.

On Monday morning, Tom called Jim Alford to make sure it was okay for Marcia to meet him at their house on Wednesday at two o'clock. Jim confirmed there was no problem and he looked forward to seeing them.

On Tuesday, the contractor came over to meet with the Gibsons to go over the final details and options for the construction of their tennis court. The best choice was an omni-court surface, which consists of a synthetic grass carpet-like material stretched out over a paved surface. Several tons of silica sand are then spread into the fibers of the carpet. The contractor explained that the advantage of this type of court is that it is much gentler on the legs and body than a hard court, and requires much less maintenance than a clay court. It provides about the same playing conditions as a grass court.

"It will be an extra $8,000 for the omni-court," the contractor informed them. "The rest will be the same as I quoted you … So we're looking at a total of $46,000. Assuming you're okay with that, I'll get my team started here on Monday of next week."

Tom caught a glimpse of Irene's expression. He could tell she was having second thoughts. This was no time to add more stress to their relationship.

"I think my wife and I need to give this a bit more thought. I'll be in touch," Tom answered.

After the contractor left, it only took five minutes for Tom and Irene to conclude they didn't need a tennis court after all. They smiled and kissed.

On Wednesday morning, Tom got on the road around eleven o'clock. He picked up a cheeseburger along the way and parked in front of his childhood home ten minutes before two. A woman got out of an Audi which was parked in the Alfords' driveway. Tom got out of his SUV and met her on the front steps.

"I assume you're Marcia," Tom said as he extended his hand.

"Yes, pleased to meet you, Tom. Can I call you Tom?"

"Yes, of course," he replied as they shook hands.

The door opened just as Tom was about to ring the doorbell. Jim stood in the doorway.

"Hello, Jim, I'd like to introduce you to Marcia Tilley. Marcia, this is Jim Alford."

Jim shook Marcia's hand and then Tom's. Marcia handed her business cards to both men.

"Please come in," Jim offered as he stepped aside. "Unfortunately, my wife couldn't be here; she's attending a faculty meeting at the university. But I'll be happy to take you on a tour of the house."

Marcia pretty well took over from there. She was very professional in her looks and demeanor. Tom guessed she was likely in her midforties. She had shoulder-length blond hair and deep blue eyes. She was very attractive, well-spoken, and friendly. There were some very specific things she wanted to see, starting with the bedrooms and bathrooms. They started in the third-floor attic which, as Jim had explained to Tom, had been converted to three bedrooms and a bathroom. In each room, Marcia scribbled notes and drew pictures on her clipboard. She also took pictures with her digital camera.

"That's a lovely camera," Tom commented. "What model is it?"

"This is a Sony Alpha a7S II with a wide-angle lens," she replied as she handed the camera to Tom.

"Wow, I'm a bit of a photography buff and this is an amazing piece of equipment," he went on as he looked through the viewfinder and took a couple of pictures. They stepped down to the second floor and visited the four bedrooms, starting with the master. Tom, once again, felt more anguish than nostalgia as he progressed from room to room in his old home. He overcame his emotions by trying to focus on Marcia's reactions, observations, and questions.

"So, you have seven bedrooms and three bathrooms on the upper floors and a powder room on the main floor," Marcia commented. Tom was about to correct her, but Jim Alford beat him to it.

"Actually, Ms. Tilley, there is another suite in the basement," he said. "It has a bedroom, a full bathroom, a sitting area, and its own separate stairwell and entrance on the north side of the house."

"Good, I'd like to see it," she replied.

Tom felt an eerie sense of déjà vu as they stepped through the rear vestibule and started down the stairs to the basement.

"This is very spacious and the ceiling is nice and high," she commented. "When was the basement finished this way?"

This time it was Tom who answered.

"It was done when my family lived here," Tom replied. "My guess is sometime around the early sixties."

"Could I see the furnace and the electrical panel?" she asked.

Jim obliged and led Marcia and Tom to the unfinished part of the basement. While Jim was busy showing her around the new furnace, Tom walked to the storage closet and flipped on the light switch. He tugged a few hangers aside and was able to observe that the small hinged door to his secret room was still intact. He felt a chill up his spine. He suddenly relived all those times he spent in that room, hiding from Ronnie. He acknowledged that there was something comforting about that room. He felt it represented a small victory at a time when there wasn't much to be happy about. But it also felt strange, and perhaps ominous, that this secret room had gone undiscovered all these years. He saw no reason to tell Jim or Marcia about it.

Tom heard Jim explain that the new electrical panel had been installed in 2010 and the new furnace and electronic air filter in 2012.

The three of them went back up to the kitchen.

"I just need to ask you a couple more things, Mr. Alford," she stated. "Could I see the document from the municipality which confirmed their approval for you to rent out rooms?"

"Of course, I retrieved it from my files and I have it on my desk in the den."

Jim stepped out and came back into the kitchen holding a manila folder. He pulled out a letter and handed it to Marcia. She examined the letter and then placed it on the kitchen table. She took a close-up picture of it and handed it back to Jim.

"And when was the current roof installed?" she asked.

"It was installed in 1999," Jim answered. "We chose premium shingles and they should normally be good for forty years."

"Well, I have everything I need," she stated. "I want to thank you, Mr. Alford. This has been very helpful."

The three of them ambled quietly toward the front vestibule.

"I just wanted to let you know, Tom," Jim spoke out. "I have an appraiser coming in tomorrow. He will present us with a formal appraisal. I thought this might be helpful in establishing a price that would be fair for everyone."

"That's excellent, Jim. So here's what I'm thinking. I have to do some number crunching with Marcia, and then decide whether or not to make an offer. If the decision is to go ahead, it will of course be contingent on agreeing to a price that falls within our expectations. I will do my best to get back to you by this weekend, if that's all right with you."

"That will be fine. I look forward to hearing from you."

Tom and Marcia walked down the front steps and heard the door close behind them.

"There's a Starbucks at the Westgate Mall, just a few minutes from here. Let's go there so we can talk about this," she suggested.

"Sounds good, I'll follow you."

Marcia and Tom sat down in a quiet corner with their coffees. She wasted no time getting down to business. She pulled a file and her clipboard out of her leather briefcase.

"I pulled out the comps for this house," she began. "There have been six sales in River Heights Estates in the past two years. Even though the overall real estate market is pretty hot right now, these big old homes have been difficult to move. All six comparable homes were on the market for more than six months. Mature families and seniors want to downsize and young families don't want anything that big. Add to that the fact that most of these homes are money pits, that is, they require a ton of work, and that explains why there are very few buyers."

"But the Alfords have done a lot to this house: a new roof, electrical panel—"

Marcia cut him off.

"Yes, but much remains to be done. The kitchen and bathrooms are outdated, and all the windows are more than fifty years old. They all need to be replaced with new casement windows. You're looking at more than $150,000. That's if a buyer wants to move into it. But, in your case, given that you want to use it as a rooming house, you could forgo these changes for now. But when you decide to sell it, you're going to face the same issues."

She pulled out her comp report.

"Bottom line is this," she continued. "This house should fetch between $700,000 and $750,000, no more."

"That's lower than I expected," Tom commented. "But, given the work that needs to be done, that price range seems about right to me. How about the income potential?"

"That part is pretty easy because room prices have been fairly consistent and have been well established for some time. Your three rooms on the third floor will each generate $600 a month. On the second floor, the master will get you $900 and the other three rooms on that floor will get you the same as the rooms on the upper floor: $600 a month. The basement suite, because it has its own bathroom and sitting area, and its own entrance, it will get you at least $1,200 a month. That adds up to $5,700 a month. You'll have no trouble renting these rooms, given the close proximity to the university and the city's recent clampdown on illegal rooming houses."

She paused to sip her coffee.

"Now, what kind of down payment and financing did you have in mind?" she asked.

"I'm ready to invest $250,000 in cash and finance the rest."

"Good, so you have two options, as I see it. You can amortize the mortgage over thirty years and generate some pretty decent net monthly income. Or, you can pay it off aggressively, say over fifteen years, and generate much less income on a monthly basis but add about $30,000 in real equity each year. Either way, the rental income more than covers the cost of carrying the house."

"That sounds great. So let's look at the numbers for the fifteen-year plan."

"Okay, so you have income of $5,700 a month. We'll factor that down by 10 percent to account for brief vacancies when you replace tenants. So let's say that leaves you with $5,100 a month. How much did you want to pay for a management fee?"

"I was thinking of paying you $1,000 a month. Would that be acceptable to you?"

"Yes, I would accept that. So your monthly expenses will be $3,000, for mortgage interest and capital, $1,000 for the management fee, and the remaining $1,100 will cover taxes, insurance, and minor maintenance items. That will leave you with a breakeven situation before taxes. You'll most certainly be generating a net after-tax profit, but you'll have to consult with your accountant to determine exactly what that is."

"I'll do that, but it won't materially affect the decision. We don't need the income. As long as the place carries itself, and I don't have to deal with the tenants, I'm okay with it."

"So, as I said, with this aggressive pay-down schedule, you'll be adding about $30,000 in real equity each year, plus a bit of net after-tax income. On an initial investment of $250,000, that's better than a 10 percent annual return. If the property appreciates over time, then the return goes up from there."

"In these days of low interest rates, it's hard to find that kind of return anywhere, especially where there is virtually no risk at all. Okay, that's good enough for me. I'm going to review this with my wife, and then I'll call you."

The two of them said their goodbyes and left. Tom caught some of the rush hour traffic on the way out of the city and didn't pull into his driveway until just before seven o'clock.

Irene greeted him warmly and served a delicious prime rib dinner.

"So, how did it go?" she asked as they sipped their wine.

"I think there's a good investment opportunity there," he replied.

Tom went on and described in infinite detail all the income and cost elements. He went into his office, grabbed a couple of blank sheets of paper from his printer and came back to the dining room where he sat beside Irene. He drew a plan of each floor and showed the rental income potential for each bedroom. He supported his assumptions with Marcia's expert opinions and research. He itemized all the cost elements and concluded with the bottom line. He compared the net gains with the yields that were being generated by their other investments.

Irene thought about it for a few moments.

"You're going to dig it up, aren't you?" she asked.

They both simultaneously burst out in laughter. It helped relieve the slight tension that was in the air when Tom was making his case to Irene.

"Yes, if we agree to make this investment, and if we can make the purchase at a reasonable price, there are some changes I would like to make, and these include potentially tearing out the screened porch and replacing it with a sunroom that would span across the rear vestibule and the rear of the living room. So, what do you think? Should we go ahead?"

"I know you feel you need to do this, and if the numbers look okay, then sure, you have my blessing," Irene whispered affectionately as she leaned toward Tom and kissed him.

"Thank you … I'm going to call Marcia right away."

Tom picked up his cell phone and called Marcia. He got her voicemail greeting, as usual, but knew she would call him back in a matter of minutes. She did, and Tom explained he was ready to make an offer at $710,000.

"Do you think that's too low?" he asked.

"No, I think that may be a good place to start," she answered. "You'll need to go over the items that need to be updated and how those affect the price, just as you and I discussed."

"I will, thanks. And, if possible, I'll need referrals from you for a good local lawyer who can handle the private sale, and a contractor who can build a new sunroom at the rear of the house."

"No problem, I'll send you an e-mail with my recommendations. And, if I were you, I wouldn't make the offer right away. You committed to Mr. Alford that you would call him on the weekend, and he was okay with that. So, I would call him on Sunday. This will do two things: it will let him wonder if you're going to make an offer, and it may allow sufficient time for him to receive the formal appraisal. I'm sure the appraisal will come in at a lower value than they are expecting, and this will soften them up a bit before you make your offer."

"That's very good advice, Marcia, and I appreciate it. I'll let you know what happens."

Tom called his bank and had no problem lining up the necessary financing, subject to an appraisal of the home.

"Can't you use the appraisal that was commissioned by the current owner?" Tom asked.

"No, unfortunately, we have to order our own. But, given the scope of your relationship with us, I'm pretty sure I can get the bank to eat the cost of the appraisal," the branch manager explained.

"That would be nice," Tom commented.

On Sunday, just after five o'clock in the afternoon, Tom called Jim Alford. After a bit of small talk, Tom got down to business.

"I discussed it with my wife and I have decided to proceed with an offer," Tom explained.

"That's great!"

"So, if we can agree on a price and on a closing date and whatever other provisions might be appropriate, I'll submit a written offer through my lawyer, along with a deposit check which the lawyer will hold in escrow."

"That will be fine," agreed Jim.

"So, I'm willing to offer $710,000 accompanied by a deposit check in the amount of $100,000. In total, we would pay $210,000 in cash and finance the rest. I already have approval for the financing."

There was nothing but silence at the other end. Tom had enough experience to understand that the next person to speak would likely give up the most. He waited for Jim to speak. Finally, Jim broke the silence.

"That's quite a disappointing offer," Jim commented.

"Jim, I should explain. Normally, your house would be worth over $800,000 but, there are some things, costly things that need to be done. You have done a lot of great work on the house over the years, the furnace, the roof, etc. ... But the kitchen and bathrooms need to be updated and all the windows are well past their useful lifetime and need to be replaced. In total, we're looking at more than $150,000 worth of work. It was almost enough to discourage me from making an offer. But I decided to go ahead because I can get this work done over a period of time."

"The appraiser mentioned those same things to me," Jim answered meekly.

"So, you have received the appraisal?" Tom asked.

"We haven't received the full document yet, but the appraiser gave us the bottom line number. We were in shock, so he went on to explain what would need to be done to bring the value up. The appraisal came in at $720,000."

Tom chose not to comment.

"So, as I think out loud," Jim continued, "I would be tempted to just forget it. We had banked on getting much more for this place. But, we're already committed to the purchase of the condo, and we can't turn back now. So, I'm thinking that if you raise your offer to meet the appraisal value, we can throw in most of the furniture. All we want to take from this house is my oak desk and bookcases in the den, the marble tables in the living room, and the artwork on the walls."

Tom paused to think about what Jim had just put forth.

"And when did you want to close the deal?" Tom asked.

"I was hoping we could wrap it up before the end of August."

"Okay, Jim, I think we have a deal."

Tom heard a sigh of relief at the other end.

"I'll have a written offer delivered to you in the next week or so. My bank will need to send another appraiser, so we'll have to inconvenience you one more time."

"I understand and it won't be a problem for us. Just get them to call us ahead of time."

After the call, Tom felt some empathy for the Alfords, but he rationalized that they might have been much worse off if he hadn't come along and made an offer. And, after all, they were saving the realtor fees, so the net proceeds from the sale should turn out to be quite respectable, he thought. He was pleased to have settled on a price that would leave him close to $30,000 for the sunroom project and allow him to stay on budget.

Tom continued to have nagging doubts about this undertaking. He wondered if the positive business case for this investment was simply a way to rationalize actions that were driven by an obsession. He had to repeat to himself, over and over again, the words of the psychiatrist who had said that he was perfectly sane but troubled by a sincere belief that would not fade away until he discovered the truth.

10

The kids and grandkids arrived on Saturday, May 9th, for Mother's Day weekend. Tom, Alan, and Trevor took the kids fishing. They took the boat to a spot that had been recommended to Tom by one of the neighbors. They weren't disappointed. The fish were biting. Every time one of the kids caught one, it was bedlam in the boat. All the kids screamed each time, as if it was the first time they had ever caught a fish. Tom filmed the excitement, and even stuck his camera below the surface to catch the underwater action as Trevor scooped up the fish into the net. The whole family enjoyed watching the fishing adventure on the big flat-screen TV after dinner. It was another memorable weekend, and just what Irene and Tom needed.

The grandkids were back by late June and stayed for most of the summer while their parents commuted on weekends. Between the tennis lessons at the club, water sports, boating, and fishing, there was hardly a dull moment. The weather was magnificent, allowing the Gibson family to enjoy most of their meals out on the patio or in the gazebo. The grandkids, in accordance with the rules that had been set by their parents, were allowed one hour on their tablets in the morning, and one hour after dinner. They had the opportunity to earn more time by completing various chores around the house.

As usual, the presence of the grandkids was the kind of distraction Tom and Irene needed to relieve the ambient stress they had felt for months.

The Gibsons took possession of the house on Riverdale Circle on August 27, 2015. The grandkids had just gone home, so the timing was perfect. Irene had never been there, so after signing all the documents at the lawyer's office, Tom took her there and toured her through each floor. He even showed her his old hiding place at the far end of the storage closet in the basement.

"Very spooky," she commented as Tom briefly relived some of the painful episodes from those years.

The two of them drew up a list of the furniture and furnishings they needed, then drove to a consignment store on the other side of the Westgate Mall and found everything they needed. They managed to get it all back to the house in two trips in Tom's SUV. Tom's cell phone rang just as they were hanging the last picture.

"Hi, Tom, it's Marcia," said the voice on the other end. "I just wanted to bring you up-to-date with a few things. I got a copy of the lease agreement your lawyer recommended. I posted notices on the university bulletin boards a week ago and I have had several responses already. I also posted a notice on the school's room-finder app. The question I have for you is this: do you want to personally screen the renters or do you just want to leave it in my hands?"

"I'd prefer to just leave everything up to you. The only thing I want to insist on is that their rent payments be made by e-mail transfer to me. I'm going to ask the lawyer to add the appropriate words in the lease document and I'll ask him to forward the file to you. I have already signed a limited power of attorney which will allow you to sign the leases on my behalf. Oh yes, and one more thing. I'm meeting with the contractor tomorrow morning, before Irene and I head back home. I hope to get the work started on the new sunroom early next month. So you should advise the prospective renters about the nature of the renovations and possible slight inconvenience."

"Got it! No problem, I will do that."

Tom and Irene stayed at the Del Monte Lodge and celebrated their new purchase with an elegant meal.

"How much are you going to tell the contractor?" Irene asked.

It seemed she always had a way of getting right to the crux of the matter.

"I was just thinking about that myself," Tom whispered back as if to indicate he was about to reveal a secret. "I think I will give him specific instructions on handling the digging in the sensitive area, but I won't give him any of the background. I don't want to start rumors, or attract undue attention. I don't want, most of all, to draw curious freelance diggers."

Tom parked in the driveway of 5 Riverdale Circle the next morning. The contractor arrived at nine o'clock, right on schedule. Tom was suitably impressed. The Larson brothers had come highly recommended by Marcia.

Tom introduced himself and led Mike and Art Larson around the garage to the back of the house.

"So, here is what I would like to do," Tom started. "I want to tear down this screened porch and I want to replace it with a sunroom that will cover the current footprint of the porch and extend over here to the back of the living room. I want to remove these sliding doors so people can just walk into the sunroom from the living room. There's a door from the rear vestibule to the porch. I want to leave that door intact."

"Do you want a simple footing and crawl space under the new sunroom, or do you want a full basement?" asked Mike Larson.

"I want a full basement which I plan to use as a storage room," Tom replied.

"Very well, so we're talking here of a full excavation," Mike commented. "I can get a backhoe in between your garage and your neighbor's. We'll use that to excavate, and use a Bobcat to get the dirt out to the driveway where we'll load it into a dump truck."

"Okay, that sounds fine with me, but there's one really important thing I need to cover with you regarding the excavation. After you have removed the porch, I need you to dig very carefully in the area of the porch footprint. The rest of the excavation doesn't matter, but in this area, I want you to drag the bucket on the backhoe so as to dig down about two inches at a time. If you find anything other than dirt, I want you to call me right away."

Tom realized he had to give them some kind of explanation.

"This is my childhood home. I have reason to believe there may be something buried under there that could offer clues to something that happened fifty years ago, or there could be nothing. But, we need to proceed delicately, and most of all, we need full and absolute discretion. If any evidence is there, we don't want to destroy or contaminate it, but we don't want a public circus here. Are you okay with that?"

"We can handle it as you wish, no problem. But it will add a few hours of backhoe time. I'll include that in our quote."

"I understand," Tom agreed as he pulled out a piece of paper. "Here is everything else you'll need to know in order to come up with a quote. Here is the layout, the location of the windows and exit doorway, the brand and dimensions of the door and casement windows I want to use, the siding material, and the roofing. You can use drywall on the inside and dark oak flooring. My e-mail ID and cell phone number are at the bottom."

"Very good … Very thorough … I like that. I'll look up these materials and I'll try to have a quote out to you by the end of day on Monday."

"Excellent, and if we decide to proceed, how soon can you start and how long will it take to complete?"

"We can start by the end of next week. It will take four to six weeks."

Tom and Irene had lunch on the riverfront patio of one of the new restaurants where all those condo buildings had popped up at the south end of River Heights Estates. It was difficult for Tom to conceive how this natural riverfront, where he had romped as a child, could have been turned into a sea of concrete. It was also unimaginable that these busy streets were once used for their Sunday kart races.

The two of them got on the road after lunch. Tom's mind wasn't focused on driving. He thought about everything he had done in such a short time. He felt a sense of accomplishment, but he also felt some anxiety. This wasn't about dreams and visions and hallucinations anymore; it was all becoming very real very quickly. He realized he was taking giant steps and that the truth, whatever it was, could soon be revealed. He pondered about whether or not these efforts would finally bring an end to his torments or raise more questions than answers. More importantly, he wondered if their decisions would irrevocably change their lives.

"I have to admit I'm a little scared," Irene blurted out, breaking a long silence.

"Are you worried about the investment, or the excavation? Tom asked.

"Oh, I'm not one bit concerned about the investment ... It's solid and pretty well risk free. It's a lovely old house. No, I'm somewhat worried about what we're going to find. The uncertainty is driving me crazy," she admitted.

"I feel the same way. I fear my instincts may be leading us astray, or even worse, into the abyss. In fact, I'm not even sure if I should trust my instincts anymore. I admire you for sticking with me on this. I want you to know how much I appreciate your support. I love you."

"I'm not going to abandon you now," she replied. "You have given us so much. We've been a great team, and we'll stay that way, no matter what happens. I just wish this whole chapter in our lives could be over tomorrow."

The two of them stopped at a restaurant for dinner and got home around ten o'clock. Tom fell asleep watching TV in the family room. He was sleeping so soundly that Irene decided not to wake him, concluding he needed his sleep. She went to bed, read for a while, and fell asleep. Tom came into the room just before five and started snoring almost right away.

11

Tom got home from the tennis club just before eleven o'clock on Monday morning. It was a beautiful late summer day, the last day of August. He checked his e-mail account. There was a note from Mike Larson with two attachments: one was the written quote, and the other was the proposed contract. At $32,000, the quote was a little higher than Tom had expected. He pondered the idea of getting other quotes and then bartering with Mike Larson. He concluded it might be best to accept the proposal and thereby build some goodwill with the Larsons. He realized that, if they were to dig up any kind of evidence, the project would be delayed and he would have to rely on their patience.

After reviewing the proposed contract, Tom printed two copies and signed them both. He sent them by courier, along with a deposit check as stipulated in the contract. Another payment was due upon completion of the exterior walls and a final payment was due upon completion of the project. He sent a reply to Mike Larson's e-mail, informed him that he wanted to proceed and that the paperwork and deposit were on their way.

By Labor Day, Marcia had signed up tenants for the basement suite and five of the seven bedrooms. All the renters were postgraduate students. She had solid prospects for the remaining two rooms and expected to have leases signed within two weeks.

The Larson brothers arrived at the Riverdale Circle house on the morning of September 8th. Before starting any work, they installed a security fence around the perimeter of the backyard with a gate between the garage and the neighbor's garage. They placed sheets of plywood on the grass between the garages to avoid tearing up the lawn with the Bobcat. They sealed off the door into the rear vestibule with a sheet of plywood. And, to Tom's surprise, they installed a webcam with its own router and called Tom on his cell phone to give him the URL he would need to access the webcam.

"We've got it aimed at the back of the house. That way you will be able to log on and watch our progress in real time," Mike told him proudly.

"That's very cool and totally unexpected. Thank you," Tom replied.

It took all morning for the brothers to set up the site. After lunch, they got to work on the demolition of the screened porch. It wasn't just a simple matter of tearing it down with the bucket on the backhoe. The floor joist which was closest to the house was bolted into the brick siding of the house. The same was true for the roof truss closest to the house. These had to be unbolted in order to avoid damage to the brick wall. It took all afternoon to remove the bolts and the flashing which was tarred to the siding.

The next day, they were able to pull the structure away and break it up into small pieces which they loaded into the bucket of the Bobcat and loaded the debris into one of the two Dumpsters that were sitting in the driveway. Tom watched all the action on his laptop. He couldn't get away from it. It was as if he was in a trance. Irene was equally curious, but she found it too tortuous and couldn't bear to watch. She went to their son's place for the week to look after Geena while Trevor and Anne travelled to Las Vegas. Trevor was attending a conference and Anne decided to accompany him. It was Geena's first week back in school; she was just starting grade 4. Tom and Irene had opted, after considerable discussion, not to tell the family about what was going on with Tom's childhood home, at least not until there was something more definitive to tell them.

The excavation started in earnest on the morning of September 10th. Mike's brother, Art, operated the backhoe and did it with such precision that Tom was mesmerized. Art started in the area behind the living room, swinging the bucket back and forth within a half inch of the foundation of the house without ever touching it. He gently lifted the patio stones one by one and stacked them on a skid. Tom felt that Art's skill was exactly what they were going to need when they started to dig in the sensitive area. Once the stones were gone, Art dug deeper and started to pile the dirt on a tarp. Mike used the Bobcat to transfer the dirt into the second Dumpster. Tom figured they would likely have to dig down at least eight feet in order to pour a footing and floor. After two full days of digging, Art and Mike were ready to start working on the area where the screened porch had stood. But they didn't work on weekends, so that next phase would have to wait until Monday.

Irene was home by dinnertime on Friday. Tom felt he needed to get out of the house. They took the aluminum fishing boat to the marina and, after a couple of cocktails, enjoyed a healthy serving of local perch for which Lake Erie is so famous.

"So, did you stay glued to your computer all week?" she asked as she sipped her wine.

"I'm afraid so."

"Well, are you going to tell me what's happening? I've been trying to get it out of my mind all week, and I haven't had much luck."

Tom gave her a detailed account of everything that had transpired. She wasn't very interested in Art's prowess at the controls of the backhoe and was impatient and frustrated that Tom didn't have anything meaty to report.

"What about the tenants?" she asked. "Are they in the house yet? Are they okay with all this?"

"Most of them have moved in. Marcia informed them ahead of time that this kind of work was going to occur for four to six weeks. It didn't seem to be an issue. I saw some of them watching from the sliding doors in the living room."

Tom paused.

"Anyway," he continued, "the interesting part starts on Monday. That's when they start digging where my childhood fort was. I was thinking the other day, maybe they'll find my survival knife. I never found it and I was thinking I might have left it in the fort."

"Really, you were thinking about finding your knife? How will you feel if you go through all this and all they find is your stupid knife?"

"Well, actually, when you think about it, that might be the best of all possible outcomes," Tom answered, sensing that Irene's frustration was likely the product of months of uncertainty and worry.

Neither of them had much to say for the rest of the evening. They did some reading and retired early.

"Good night," Irene whispered as she turned off her bedside lamp. "I hope you didn't forget we're hosting Trina and Jay and the others for dinner here tomorrow."

"I had forgotten all about it but I saw your entry on the calendar. I took some steaks out of the freezer. I assume they're bringing munchies, salad, and dessert. Good night. I love you."

The Gibsons' dinner was a success. Tom and Irene were gracious hosts even though they both had difficulty focusing. Their minds were elsewhere. They never said a word to each other about it, but they were increasingly nagged, if not haunted, by the thought of what was going to happen on Monday.

On Sunday, they took a long cruise in their powerboat and stopped at the marina for a late lunch. They ran into some friends and shared a table with them. Neither Tom nor Irene had any appetite for dinner that night, and they were emotionally drained. They went to bed early and watched a bit of TV until they fell asleep.

12

Tom took his coffee and bagel into the den on Monday morning and booted up his computer. He wasted no time logging on to the Larsons' webcam site. It was 8:45 a.m. and there was no visible activity.

A short while later, he saw Art walk up to the edge of the excavation, coffee cup in hand. Mike soon walked up and stood beside him. There was no sound to go along with the live video stream, so Tom was unable to discern what they were talking about. Both disappeared from view for a few moments, and then Art walked by and climbed up into the backhoe. A puff of black smoke blew out of the exhaust and work was under way.

The webcam was mounted on a tripod about twenty-five feet behind the edge of the excavation, so Tom couldn't see into the hole. He estimated the depth of each pass by the portion of the two-foot-tall bucket he could see. It appeared Art was being very careful, as per Tom's request. He scraped a few inches of dirt at a time, piled it up in one corner, then occasionally scooped up the dirt pile and dropped it on the tarp. It was slow and methodical. It took all morning to get down where the top of the bucket was no longer visible. The work wrapped up for the day around five o'clock, without incident. Tom didn't know if he was relieved or annoyed. He figured they had dug down about three feet.

A thunderstorm blew in overnight and carried on into Tuesday morning. As far as Tom could tell, there was nothing going on at the site. At 10:30 a.m., Mike walked into view lugging a piece of equipment with the help of someone Tom didn't recognize. He saw

Mike stand up and pull out his cell phone. Moments later, Tom's cell phone rang. It was Mike.

"Hi, Mr. Gibson, Mike Larson here."

"Yes, I saw you from the webcam as you placed the call," Tom answered.

"Right, well, we got a lot of rain overnight and it's still coming down pretty hard here. We couldn't come out here until the lightning stopped. We have about two feet of water in the deeper part of the excavation, behind the living room. We just rented a pump and we're going to start pumping the water out to the front of the house and into a storm drain."

"I understand. Just go ahead and do whatever you need to do."

"The forecast doesn't look much better until around midday tomorrow, and we're going to need the site to dry up before we can carry on."

"I see. Well, just keep me posted."

The work didn't resume until Friday morning, September 18th. After a couple of hours of digging, Art climbed down from the backhoe and jumped into the hole. He stooped down for a few moments and disappeared from view. Then, when he stood up, he was visible from the chest up. Mike soon joined him in the hole, then pulled out his cell phone and called Tom.

"Hi, Mr. Gibson, Mike Larson here."

"Yes. Yes, what's going on?

"Well, we're not sure. There's something poking out of the ground that looks like it could be a handle grip."

"I see …" he said, thinking it might be one of the handle grips from the frame of the old rototiller that was buried there. "How deep are you right now?"

"We're down just about four feet."

From what Tom remembered, he would have expected the tiller to be deeper than that.

"How close is it to the house?" Tom asked.

"It's about two and a half feet away from the foundation."

Tom realized something wasn't right. The tiller should have been underneath the foundation of the house.

"So, what do you want us to do?" Mike asked.

"I'd like you to continue digging very carefully, with a shovel, until we can expose enough to see what we've got. I realize it's going to add some labor cost, but I don't have a problem with that."

"You got it. I'll move the tripod to the edge of the hole and point the webcam down a bit so you can see what we're doing."

"That's great, I really appreciate it."

Both men disappeared from view. Suddenly, the webcam shook, then pointed up to the sky, then down to the ground where Tom could see Mike's work boots walking. Finally the camera settled, and Tom could see into the hole. The detail wasn't sufficiently fine for him to see the handle grip sticking out of the ground.

A few minutes later, Mike and Art both jumped into the hole with shovels in hand. They gently pulled dirt away from the tiller, scooped it up, and flung it toward the edge of the excavation away from the house. They seemed to be very careful not to come into contact with the tiller as they progressed. After five minutes of digging, the handlebar was visible on Tom's screen. About an hour went by. Then, Tom was able to see enough of it to determine that, as he had suspected, it wasn't the tiller, or at least not the way he remembered it. After another forty-five minutes, Mike pulled out his cell phone and called Tom.

"Hi, Mr. Gibson, Mike Larson here."

"Yes! Yes! What have you found?"

"It's a small bicycle. It's very corroded and rusty, but it's definitely a bike."

There was a short pause. Tom could see from the webcam that Mike was peering into the hole.

"It's got a lower slanted and curved crossbar. It's a small girl's bike."

Tom took a deep breath. His heart was pounding. He realized he had found the answer to the mystery that had dogged him, or at least part of the answer. He suddenly feared the truth like he never had before. But he had crossed a line and there was no going back. He tried to compose himself.

"Okay. I need you to listen very carefully," he said with a slight tremor in his voice. "We're going to have to suspend the work for a little while. This bike could be a piece of evidence in a criminal case. Did either of you touch the bike at any time?"

"No, we were careful not to disturb it as we dug around it. And almost half of it is still buried."

"Good. Now, I'd like you to lay a tarp over it and secure the perimeter of the site. I'm on my way. It will take me about two hours to get there. I'm going to call Detective Carter. Please don't leave the site until he gets there."

Tom gathered a few items of clothing and threw them into a duffel bag along with his shaving kit and laptop. He brought Irene up-to-date.

"I think it's time to retain a lawyer," Irene suggested. "I really mean it. I'll call my brother's office and see who he can recommend from his firm or from among his colleagues."

"You're right. Give them my cell number. I'll book a room at the Hilton on the way there."

"Do you want me to go with you?"

"No, I'll be fine, but if I feel I need moral support, I'll call you. In fact, I'll call you anyway and keep you up-to-date. I love you."

"I love you too. Please drive carefully."

Tom got on the road and called Detective Carter from his SUV. He explained how he had come to buy his childhood home and turned it into a rooming house. He described the nature of the renovations that were under way. And finally, he described what the workers had just unearthed.

"I have to tell you I'm quite amazed at the trouble you've gone through," Detective Carter admitted. "I'm not sure what's driving you, but I respect your determination. Now, please call the contractor and instruct him to avoid touching anything. We don't yet know if this is a crime scene, but we have to preserve its integrity."

"Yes, I've already asked them to cover it with a tarp, secure the perimeter, and stay there until you arrive."

"Very good. I'm on my way. I won't call in the forensics team yet. I need to have a good look at that bicycle."

Tom called the Hilton reservations line and booked a room with an open checkout date. A short while later, he received a call from Denis, Irene's brother.

"Hi, Tom, this is Denis. Irene gave me a brief rundown on your situation. She's absolutely right in recommending that you retain legal representation. As you know, I only deal with real estate and estate law. But our firm has two excellent litigators who can assist you. One of them, Graham Stoddart, has agreed to represent you. He doesn't come cheap … His rate is $500 per hour. But he is the best."

"Thanks, Denis. I really appreciate your help, and of course I would be delighted if Graham could represent me in this case. I'm on my way to meet the detective right now. If it turns out that we have uncovered some key evidence in a criminal case, I'm sure I'll be considered a prime suspect."

"I'll send you an e-mail with Graham's contact information. Please let him know as soon as the detective makes a determination on that bicycle. And please, don't make any statements to the police without first consulting Graham."

"I understand."

By the time Tom arrived at the house, a police forensics trailer was already parked in front of the house. Police tape had been strung around the backyard, and two uniformed police officers were standing between the garages, guarding the site. Tom introduced himself to the officers. This was all becoming too real for him He was in a daze.

"Yes, sir, Detective Carter told us you were on your way," one of the officers said.

"He wants to see you. Please follow me."

Tom stooped under the police tape and followed the officer around to the backyard. He immediately saw a white tent that had been erected over the dig area. Detective Carter was standing in front of the entrance to the tent. He shook Tom's hand firmly.

"Hello, Mr. Gibson. Thank you for coming. I'm not at liberty to tell you very much. But you're the owner of this property and I can confirm that, by virtue of identifying this bicycle as one that exactly matches the description of the one that disappeared along with Jennifer Dawbrowski in 1964, we have declared this area a crime scene. Our forensic team is here and we will not release the site until we are sure we have determined that we have collected all the relevant evidence. That's all I can tell you at this time. Separately, as a person of interest in the case, you will be asked to come to the station and make a formal statement. I can't tell you exactly when that wi' be. It will depend, to a large degree, on the evidence we find here

The detective's demeanor and tone were completely different from what Tom had observed in their previous meeting. He wasn't the same folksy guy. He was very formal and terse.

"I understand."

"Now, can you tell me who is living here?" asked the detective.

"Oh, God, I forgot all about them. These are our tenants. We rent rooms out to them. Should I tell them to leave, or will they be able to continue to stay in the house while your team works on the site?"

"They can stay as long as they keep away from the area that is cordoned off. The door into the vestibule has already been sealed. We have strung police tape across the sliding door but we haven't sealed it because there has to be some kind of emergency exit at the rear of the house in case of a fire."

"Very well … I'll make sure they understand. You have my cell phone number. Please call me if you need anything or if you want me to come in to make a statement. I'm staying at the Hilton."

The Larson brothers were standing in the driveway, scratching their heads in disbelief. Tom walked over to them to explain a bit of the background.

"I'm very sorry about this," he said. "I have no idea how long it will be before they release the site back to us. As soon as they do, we can resume work on the project. I'll keep you posted."

A man approached them as Tom was speaking. He was wearing press credentials.

"Hello, my name is Brent Aldridge. I'm with the *Daily Record*. We received a tip about the forensics team being posted here. Are you the officer in charge?" he asked as he looked at Tom.

"No, I'm the owner of the house," Tom answered, regretting it almost instantly.

The last thing he wanted was to attract media attention.

"Detective Carter is the one in charge. He's back there somewhere in the area that is cordoned off. These officers can direct you to him," he said as he pointed to the two officers.

Tom left and drove to the Hilton to check in. He called Irene and gave her a brief update. Then he called Marcia and explained what was going on. He felt an obligation to let her in on some of the background.

"Wow, you pursued this purchase knowing this was probably going to happen?" she asked.

"Pretty much … It was just something I had to do."

"Are you worried?"

"I feel some anxiety, but if a serious crime was committed, I don't think I had anything to do with it. The problem is, there is a definite shortage of other possible suspects here."

Tom reflected for a few moments.

"In any case, I wanted you to know what's going on, and I wanted you to reach out to each of the tenants. They don't need to know the details, but they should know that the forensic team will be there for a few days and they should understand that they are to stay out of the cordoned area until the team releases the site. The sliding doors at the back of the living room are to be used only in the event of a fire emergency."

"I understand and I will get in touch with them today."

Tom spent the rest of the day searching the Internet to find his old friend David. He reasoned that, if he could locate him, he might be able to add a few pieces to the puzzle. He hadn't spoken with him since he, his sister and mother moved to the suburbs in November 1965. It wasn't because of any falling out between the two boys, but it had more to do with the fact that David was sent to a prep school near Boston that fall and the boys just lost contact.

Tom's searches on Google for David Strohman turned up ninety-six matches. There was a police detective in Long Island, a couple of lawyers in Texas. Tom examined each one, but none of them turned out to be his old friend. Tom had another idea. David's mother, as Tom recalled, was a freelance reporter and writer who had gained a bit of notoriety. He had no trouble finding her on Google. There were ample articles about her and her writings. He discovered she had died in 1992 and he read her obituary, but none of it offered any clues about where he might find David.

Tom spent most of the weekend watching sports on TV and taking long walks. He picked up a copy of the *Daily Record* and scanned it during breakfast on Monday morning. It was September 21st, 2015. There was a small piece on page 3 about a forensic investigation taking place in River Heights Estates related to a cold case. It offered no details, and Tom concluded that Detective Carter was loath to give the reporter any information at this time.

Tom spent a half hour on one of the stationary bikes in the gym and then went up to his room to have a shower. His cell phone was ringing when he came out of the shower. It was Detective Carter.

"We have recovered skeletal remains in the dugout under the foundation of the house. We haven't formally made an identification yet; that will take several days, perhaps even weeks. But the clothing matches the description of what Jennifer Dawbrowski was wearing the day of her disappearance. So we're pretty sure it's her."

Tom was silent for a few moments. Some of the images from his nightmares flashed through his mind. He didn't know how to react or what to say.

"My god, my instincts were right!" Tom exclaimed. "Perhaps the poor young girl will finally get a chance to rest in peace."

"On that note, I would like you to come in to the station and make a formal statement. Can you drop by this afternoon?"

"I would like to meet with my attorney first and fill him in on the whole story, then the two of us could meet with you at the station."

Tom and the detective tentatively agreed to meet at 1:00 p.m. the next day, subject to Tom's attorney's availability.

Tom ended the call and immediately called Graham Stoddart. He gave his barrister an update on the situation at the crime scene and explained that he had been asked to come into the station to make a formal statement.

"I can be there shortly, Tom. Where are you staying?"

"I'm at the Hilton."

"Very well, I just have to clean up a couple of things here. I can be there by dinnertime. I'll get a copy of the original police report before I leave the office. How about we meet for dinner at seven o'clock in the main dining room?"

"I'll be there at seven."

Tom spent the rest of the day preparing notes that he planned to use to give Graham the full background. The two men met at the restaurant at seven as planned. They asked for a table in a remote corner so as to have some privacy. They ordered their drinks and got to work.

"What I would like to do first is to tell you about the circumstances at that time in my childhood and how it came to be that my best friend and I dug an underground fort under the screened porch of the house."

Tom described the house and spoke about each member of the family. He went on to explain how his father was very tough on Ronnie and the relentless abuse he suffered at the hands of his older brother as a result. He described his hiding places, including the secret room at the end of the storage closet.

"I can't imagine how you suffered during that time. It must have been unbearable," Graham commented.

"Well, they weren't happy times for sure, but I was a survivor. It turned out there was some room between happiness and despair. I found it, and that's where I lived."

Tom went on to tell the story about stealing the rototiller to salvage the motor and then digging a hole under his porch to hide the remaining frame.

"It occurred to me that this dugout could be the best hiding place of all time. So we kept digging and disposed of the dirt along the row of poplars at the back of the property. We eventually got under the foundation of the house and created a cavity that was about eight by six feet and about four feet in height. We extended one end of the dugout to bury the rototiller frame. We made a hinged door in the lattice, under the stairs. It was all very covert and cool. Best of all, Ronnie never found me."

"So, you and your friend David, as far as you know, were the only ones that were aware of the existence of this hiding place."

"That's correct, as far as I know, but I can't be sure."

"Unfortunately, that doesn't leave us with a long list of suspects. So I have to ask you this, only once, as I do with all my clients: did you have anything to do with the disappearance and death of that young girl?"

"No, I don't think so. I mean, I'm sure I didn't have anything to do with it. I even went as far as subjecting myself to hypnosis to see if I was harboring any guilt, deep down in my subconscious. The psychiatrist said that it didn't appear I was suppressing any inner feelings about it, but he couldn't be 100 percent sure. He explained that some events can be so horrific that they can't easily be recalled because of the pain associated with them. So, the short answer is no, I didn't do it."

"Did you know this young girl?"

"No, I had never seen her or heard her name? But, in my nightmares …"

"Nightmares?"

Tom went through the whole chronology of his nightmares, visions, and hallucinations. Then he shared the results of the research he had conducted in the archives of the *Daily Record*. He also recounted his clumsy effort to send an anonymous tip to the police, and his subsequent conversations with Detective Carter.

"When I discovered those two articles about her disappearance, it was the first time I had ever heard of Jennifer Dawbrowski."

"You and your friend David were the only ones who knew about this dugout? Do you think it might have been possible that someone else could have discovered its existence? Perhaps your brother, or someone else?"

"I'm pretty sure he would have caught me in there and beat the crap out of me. I don't think he was smart enough to just hold on to that knowledge and play possum. Although, I think he was certainly evil enough to carry out that kind of crime."

"Right, and we know the girl didn't wander in there by accident because we now know that her bicycle was also buried there. So, logically, it was you or David. And if it wasn't you, it had to be David. Were you both the same age?"

"No, David was a year older. But he was such a gentle soul, I can't imagine him hurting anyone. He once nurtured a black squirrel back to health after it had been partly run over by a neighbor's car across the street."

"Do you know his whereabouts?"

"No, I don't. We lost touch after my parents split up and we moved out of the house. I've just tried using the Internet to locate him, with no success. I can't find any sign of him. I don't even know if he's still alive."

Graham sat back, took a sip of his single malt, and paused to think.

"This is going to be tough. You're in quite a pickle, my friend. There were likely only two of you who had access to the crime scene, or at least the scene where the police discovered the body. And you are the one who had all these nightmares, as far as we know. They, the police, are going to assume your feelings of guilt have finally got the better of you. So, here's what you have to remember tomorrow: firstly, look at me before you answer any question; if I nod, go ahead and answer the question succinctly without adding any more information than necessary; yes or no are good answers. And secondly, always tell the truth. The good thing about truth is that there can only be one version of it. You can't get your stories crossed when you tell the truth."

The two men ordered their meals and steered clear of any discussion about the case while they dined. They talked about the business climate, politics, and family. Tom picked up the tab knowing he would ultimately pay for it anyway.

"I'm going to get my staff started on some background stuff in the morning," Graham stated, "and we can drive to the station together. We should leave around twelve thirty."

Graham and Tom arrived at the police station ten minutes before one o'clock. Detective Carter led them into one of the interrogation rooms. It was a small room with a table and six chairs. There were two cameras mounted on the ceiling in opposite corners. The detective was stern but polite.

"Before we start," the detective announced, "I'd like to introduce Barbara ... She is our stenographer and will be capturing every word spoken here today. We are also recording this session. Everything you say can be entered as evidence. However, any prior conversations you and I had cannot be used as evidence. Is this clear?"

"Yes," Tom answered.

"Very well. Let me tell you a little bit about where we are in our investigation. We know that this young girl, Jennifer Dawbrowski, was murdered. She was likely murdered in that cavity behind the house at 5 Riverdale Circle, under the area where a screened porch once stood. Are you the one that dug out that hiding place?"

"Hiding place is a prejudicial term," Graham intervened. "Let's call it the dugout."

"Very well. Are you the one who dug this hole in the ground?"

"Yes, my friend David and I dug it," Tom answered after getting the nod from Graham, as he did for every question.

"What is David's last name?"

"Strohman ... His last name is Strohman."

"And, can he corroborate that he was involved in the digging?"

"I'm sure he can, but I have no idea where he is. We haven't talked in fifty years."

"Did you know Jennifer Dawbrowski?"

"No."

"Did you know of her? Had you ever heard about her?"

"No."

"Well, let me tell you a few other things we know: the slits in her T-shirt suggest she was stabbed multiple times in the chest and stomach ... We found a knife, one of those scout knives with all kinds of tools and blades. I think they called them survival knives. Did you own such a knife?"

"Yes."

"When was the last time you saw your knife?"

"It was sometime during that summer in 1964. I lost track of it and I suspected my brother might have taken it to boarding school with him in September of that year."

"Well, he didn't. We found your knife in the dugout. It has fingerprints on it. I have a warrant here to obtain your fingerprints and a DNA sample."

The detective picked up his cell phone and entered a number while Graham examined the document. He concluded the warrant was valid.

A few moments later, an officer entered the room carrying a box that looked like a large first aid kit. He took Tom's fingerprints and then used a cotton swab to retrieve a sample of saliva from Tom's mouth.

"Very good, I'm done," said the technician as he closed up his kit and left.

"Let me tell you some more," the detective continued. "There was blood on one of the knife blades. We're sure it will match the blood stains on her T-shirt and will match her DNA. There are also stains on the front of her shorts. We think these are semen stains. Our tests will confirm this and will give us a DNA sample of the perpetrator. So this is all likely to be pretty straightforward."

The detective paused and stared at Tom.

"Why don't you admit that you are the one that did this? Maybe you didn't mean to kill her ... Maybe things just got out of hand and you reacted without thinking. We're going to have all the evidence we need within a few days. Obviously, your conscience is telling you that it's all over, that you need to bring this story to an end. Did you kill her?"

"That's enough, Detective," exclaimed Graham. "My client is here to assist you in this investigation. He is not here to make a confession."

Detective Carter summed up the evidence again.

"Let me add to that the fact that, by your own admission, you are the only one who knew about this dugout ..." the detective continued.

"No, David also knew about it!" Tom intervened.

"According to you, but there is nothing to corroborate that he knew. You may be inventing this whole story about an accomplice," the detective suggested.

"And, it's entirely possible that others might have seen us going in or out of the doorway under the porch and discovered our fort," Tom added.

The detective tried two more times to get a confession out of Tom, who was beginning to show signs of weariness. Tom's lawyer protested each time.

"Okay, I think we're done here," Graham intervened as he stood up.

Detective Carter sighed. He was visibly frustrated.

"Very well, you can go back home. I'll call you and ask you to come back in after we get all the test results from the lab. You can call me anytime if you have a change of heart."

Graham and Tom didn't say another word. Once they were outside the police station, they agreed to touch base once they had heard from Detective Carter about the lab results.

"I know this was quite upsetting for you," Graham observed. "Are you okay to drive?"

"Yes, it's been a tough day, but I'll be fine."

During the drive home, Tom relived the interrogation over and over. He concluded that, without David's testimony, he was in a trap. Even with David's account, there didn't seem to be a lot of wiggle room. Tom felt the whole situation was turning into a living nightmare. He regretted trying to find the truth. He rued the day he sent the anonymous tip to the police. But, there was no going back. He imagined being wrongly convicted and spending the rest of his life in jail in spite of his innocence. He recalled that morning when he and David stole the rototiller. Little did he know at that time that this petty crime would eventually bring about his undoing.

When he got home, Tom gave Irene a detailed description of what happened during the interrogation. He also gave her a brutally honest assessment of where he stood. Irene was in tears and didn't know what to say.

"Now, we're waiting for the test results, and I have no idea what they're going to show. Of course, my fingerprints will be all over the knife. I don't know what else they're going to find."

The following two weeks were quiet and agonizing. Tom fell into deep depression. He entertained suicidal thoughts. He felt he would rather take his own life than suffer the indignity of life in jail. He wasn't interested in conversing with anyone. Even the incessant misery he had experienced as a young boy, at the hands of his brother, wasn't as painful as the mental torture he was feeling. He had changed so much that Irene contemplated leaving him. But she genuinely feared he would take his own life, so she decided to stay.

On the morning of October 7th, the phone rang and Irene answered. She had cancelled her tennis matches for the week because she didn't want to leave Tom alone. He was still in bed.

"He's in the shower at the moment, sir," Irene told the caller. "He'll call you back shortly."

Irene got Tom out of bed and informed him that Detective Carter had just called and wanted to speak to him about the case. Tom's heart was pounding. He had a brief shower, and Irene poured him a cup of coffee. He took a deep breath and then called the detective.

"Thank you for returning my call, sir," said the detective. "I wanted to let you know that we have received some reports from the lab. I'm not going to ask you to come to the station at this time because some of the tests are inconclusive."

There was a pause that seemed unbearably long to Tom, but he remained quiet.

"At this point in our investigation, we have positively identified the remains as being those of Jennifer Dawbrowski. We have also confirmed that the stains on her shorts are human semen. The DNA of the semen matches your DNA."

Tom's jaw dropped. He felt he was about to faint.

"But," the detective continued, "it is not a perfect match. What I mean is that the lab has found a partial match, which, as I understand it, means that there are two possibilities here. Either we have an issue with the sample taken from the scene, or the perpetrator is not you but is related to you. In any case, the lab is going to take another sample and repeat the entire DNA test protocol. It will take another week."

Tom felt more confused than relieved. What if that second test somehow came back positive? At the same time, he felt there was a glimmer of light at the end of the tunnel, a small ray of hope. Tom's thoughts were interrupted by the detective.

"In the matter of fingerprints, we found your prints on the knife. But, since you have already confirmed that you owned and lost track of a similar knife, we would expect to find your fingerprints on it. However, there are other prints on the knife which, at this time, remain unidentified. So, I have to ask you, who else might have had access to the knife?"

"I suppose anyone in the family could have held the knife at some time or other. And there was also our housekeeper, and my friend David. But to me, this is all starting to point toward my brother. Who else could it be? We have a partial DNA match to me, we have someone else's fingerprints on the knife ... Add to that the fact that he was the only person I knew who was evil enough to do something like this ... What do you think?"

"I've been in this business a long time and I've learned to follow the evidence and not jump to conclusions too early. We have other information on the cause of death, but I'm not at liberty to share that with you."

"I understand, Detective."

"I'll call you as soon as I get the new lab report. Oh, and by the way, our forensics team is done with the crime scene. You can inform your contractor that we're releasing the site today. Also, we're getting a lot of pressure from the media. They want to know what's going on. Now that we have located Jennifer's older sister, her only living relative besides her half brothers in Europe, and we have brought her up-to-date, we have scheduled a press conference for four o'clock today. We are not planning to share any more information than what I gave you, at least at this time, and we're not mentioning any identities other than the victim's."

"Thank you, I appreciate that. I look forward to hearing about the results of the new test."

Tom ended the call and looked at Irene. She had been watching the whole time. He tried to smile. She tried too. He briefed her on the lab reports.

"So, it doesn't sound like you're out of the woods yet. I'm still worried sick. But, from what I heard you say, we'll have to hang on to the possibility it was your brother ... That poor young girl ..."

"Yes, I'm more and more certain it was him. He must have seen us go in or come out of the fort. I was always careful, so I don't think he ever saw me, but he might have seen David go in or come out. Then, instead of trapping me in there and beating on me, he did something incredibly more heinous. He dragged the young girl in there, assaulted her, and killed her with my knife, undoubtedly hoping to pin the blame on me. What a demon."

Irene walked up to Tom and hugged him. They were both teary-eyed. They finally admitted openly just how much stress they were feeling. As they hugged, they could feel their tension easing a bit. Their affection gave them strength. They stood there for quite some time.

"For the first time in quite awhile, I have hope," Tom whispered. Irene simply nodded.

"Let's go to the marina for dinner tonight. I don't feel like cooking," she admitted.

"Good idea ... I need to get out of the house."

The phone rang just as they were about to leave. It was a reporter from the *Daily Record*.

"Good evening ... Yes, this is Tom Gibson ..."

Tom listened as the reporter explained that he had just attended a press conference where the police described their progress in the investigation of the 1964 kidnapping and murder of a young girl from the Westgate neighborhood. The reporter informed Tom that he was writing an article for the morning paper. He asked a series of questions. Tom tried his best to divert them back to the police department.

"Are you the present owner of the house at 5 Riverdale Circle in River Heights Estates, where the body of a young girl missing since 1964 was discovered?" the reporter asked.

"Yes, I am the owner of the house ..."

"Are you the current occupant?" the reporter continued.

"No, it is an income property ... I rent out the rooms to university students."

"How did you come to discover the body of Jennifer Dawbrowski?"

"Well, first of all, let me say that we were all horrified by the news. I didn't discover the body. A contractor, hired to build a new sunroom, came upon a small bicycle buried under the old porch. It looked a little suspicious, so we called the police. They matched it to the description of the bike that went missing at the same time as the young girl, way back in 1964. They took over the site and found the body. That's all I know."

"What else have the police told you about the case?"

"Nothing ... I've told you everything I know."

"Given these developments, do you plan to keep the house?"

"I don't know. We're still in shock."

The reporter confirmed the spelling of Tom's full name and thanked him for answering his questions.

As they ended the call, Tom was haunted by a sense of guilt for omitting to say anything about the fact that he lived in that house as a boy when the crime took place. He steered clear of that fact because he worried the public would jump to conclusions. He certainly didn't want himself and his family to be dogged by reporters. It was better to let the investigation draw to an end, he believed, although there was a possibility some of these facts could somehow come to light.

Tom and Irene went out for dinner, their mood sullied by new worries about the media.

13

The next day, Tom remained troubled by the uncertainty of the outcome of the DNA retest. He was hoping the evidence would ultimately point to his brother. He wondered if the prison records contained any DNA samples from Ronnie. This was such an important point, he thought, that he called Detective Carter to ask him. He didn't get to speak directly with the detective, so he left him a voicemail which simply said he had a question. The detective returned his call just after lunch and Tom posed the question.

"We requisitioned the prison records and have just received them, so your question is very timely," said the detective. "Unfortunately, we didn't have DNA testing technology back then, so no, these records won't tell us anything about DNA. But, they will contain detailed fingerprint information which will be helpful."

"That's very disappointing," Tom commented.

"Well, just hold on, it's not hopeless."

"What do you mean?"

"Well, if you could find, somewhere in your family possessions, any items that related to your brother … It could be a lock of hair, a tooth, a whistle, or harmonica or anything that might have been in contact with his mouth, there could be a trace of DNA that we could test and match against the samples from the crime scene."

"Fascinating … I'm going to start searching right away."

Tom ended the call, grabbed a flashlight from his desk drawer, and walked out to the garage. All the old family photographs, records, and souvenirs were in the loft. He hadn't been up there since the day he and Irene moved into their house. The only possessions that remained from his parents were in two old steamer wardrobe trunks that his mother had left him when she died. Tom had never had the curiosity to examine their contents. They both measured about four by two feet and about three feet high. One was dark blue and the other was black. Tom opened the black one first. It was full of family pictures, some framed, some not, and some in photo albums. There were stacks of boxes which contained 35 mm slides. There was nothing in there that might provide the kind of DNA sample Tom was looking for. He opened the second trunk. It had all kinds of items wrapped in newspaper: some figurines, china, silverware, and fine crystal. Tom removed them carefully and placed them on the floor of the loft. There was a shoe box that contained letters addressed to Tom's mother, Elizabeth. They appeared to be letters from admirers and, apparently, lovers. They were stacked in chronological order, which was not surprising to Tom because he recalled that his mother was always meticulously organized. He scanned a couple of letters. He didn't recognize the authors but was stunned by the contents. They were full of admiration and passion. They were somewhat explicit. Tom suddenly felt he was invading his mother's privacy. He placed the letters back in the box, vowing that he would never again be so disrespectful as to look at them again. He took the box back into the house and was about to throw it into the fireplace. He held a lighter to the corner of the box, and then changed his mind. He took the box into the den and placed it in the bottom right-hand drawer of his desk. He headed back to the loft and resumed his examination of the blue trunk.

There were manila folders in two file boxes. There were school report cards for Sarah, Tom, and Ronnie. There were newspaper clippings. There was another shoe box full of matchboxes from all over the world. There were three pairs of baby shoes. There were souvenirs from trips to Europe and South America. Then, at the very bottom, there was a slender leather case. It was about two feet long, five inches wide, and four inches high. There were two brass initials in one corner of the hinged top. The initials were R and G. Tom was excited.

THE HOUSE ON RIVERDALE CIRCLE

"That's got to be Ronald Gibson," he muttered out loud.

Tom opened the case. It contained a soprano saxophone wrapped in a felt sleeve. He put everything back in the trunk, grabbed the leather case, and went back into the house. He called Detective Carter again. This time, the detective answered.

"I'm sorry to bother you again, Detective Carter, but I've been going through our family souvenirs, as you suggested. I found a musical instrument, a soprano sax, in a leather case that has the initials RG, as in Ronald Gibson, my brother."

"That's great news. How fast can you get it here?"

"I can send it by courier and I'm pretty sure we can have it there by end of day tomorrow."

"Perfect, I'll let the lab know it's coming."

Tom drove to the UPS store in town, about ten minutes away, and shipped the sax. He felt things were finally starting to roll his way, except for one thing that was gnawing at him. He had no recollection of his brother ever playing a musical instrument. In his judgment, his brother didn't have the patience or mind-set to learn to play a musical instrument, particularly something as refined as a soprano saxophone. However, Tom considered the possibility that his brother had perhaps learned to play when he went to boarding school. Maybe Ronnie had been driven to learn new skills by the austere and structured environment, he thought.

On October 15th, Tom received a call from Detective Carter. Irene was at the hairdresser's.

"Just got the latest lab report," the detective announced. "It confirms the findings of the earlier report. That is, to be specific, the DNA from the semen at the crime scene is a 25 percent match with your DNA. So you are clear, my friend, and I want to apologize for being so tough on you during the interrogation. I hope you understand that we have a process to follow. I was doing my job, as I always do."

Tom slumped in his chair, unable to speak. His eyes welled up.

He needed to digest the news. After a few moments he regained his composure.

"It was indeed quite unsettling, and I haven't really been able to sleep or relax since then, but I understand. So, I guess you're agreeing with me that it had to be my brother."

"Well, it's not going to be that simple."

"I don't understand …"

"Are you sitting down?"

"Yes, I'm at my desk in the den."

"That's good. We've been examining Ronnie's prison records. We've learned a lot. The first thing is that he wasn't your brother."

"What? That's impossible!"

"The prison records show that his parents were Robert and Mary Goodman. His mother's maiden name was Mary Atkins."

"Atkins? That was my mother's maiden name. Grandma and Grandpa Atkins had five kids: my mother, her three brothers, and a sister who died before I was born. I think her name was Mary. My grandparents died when I was quite young, and we didn't see much of my uncles because they lived on the east coast."

"Your mother's sister, your aunt Mary, and her husband, were killed in a horrific car crash on their way to Boston in 1949. Ronnie was with them. He was two years old. He was seriously injured but he survived."

"So, how did he end up in our family?"

"Your aunt and uncle did not have wills. So the Massachusetts Probate and Family Court made all the decisions with regard to their estate and Ronnie's fate. The court awarded his custody to his aunt and uncle, your parents, Elizabeth and Fredrick Gibson. They officially adopted him. It all happened before you were born."

"My God, I'm stunned. But, in retrospect, it explains a lot. Like, why my parents seemed to favor me and my sister … Especially my father; he was always so tough on Ronnie. I'm sure he was psychologically traumatized and he took it out on everyone, but particularly on me. My mother showed some affection for him, but I guess it wasn't enough."

"So, back to what I was saying about the DNA. Ronnie was in fact your cousin. As such, he wouldn't have a 25 percent match to your DNA. It would be about half that, around twelve and a half percent, according to the lab. So that pretty well rules him out."

"That's shocking and very disappointing."

"In addition to that, we didn't find his fingerprints anywhere at the crime scene, although, if we had positive DNA evidence, we could have assumed he was wearing gloves. But it's all academic now."

Tom sighed in frustration and disbelief.

"So, where does that leave us?" Tom asked.

"I'm afraid we're back to square one. It wasn't you, and it wasn't your brother, or rather, it wasn't your cousin, but it was someone related to you. Obviously, we're missing a key piece of information."

"I hate to bring it up, but could it have been my father?"

"No, we considered that, but the lab says your father would have had a 50 percent DNA match with you. Our sample from the crime scene has a 25 percent DNA match. So no, it could not have been your father."

"Well, that's a relief. Is there anything I can do to help you?"

"Actually, yes, there is. I would like you to make a list of all your relatives who were alive in 1964. On that list, indicate if any of them had ever visited your house, to the best of your recollection, and approximately when you last saw them. Don't worry if you can't remember exactly. I would appreciate it if you could send me the list as an e-mail attachment as soon as you can."

"I'll get on it right away."

"Oh, and one more thing before I let you go," the detective continued. "Now that you have been cleared, I can tell you that we have other forensic evidence from the crime scene, but I'm not at liberty to disclose it to you at this time. We hope it will help us when we close in on the right suspect. None of these details will be released to the public or to the press at this time."

"I wish you hadn't told me that. It's going to drive me crazy trying to figure out what that evidence might be."

Tom felt an uneasy sense of relief about being cleared of any involvement in Jennifer Dawbrowski's murder. But he was frustrated that the evidence failed to pin the culpability on Ronnie. He pulled out a pad of paper and started to make a list of his relatives. It was fairly straightforward. Tom's father, Fredrick, had one sister. She was a nun and never had any kids. His parents, Grandma and Grandpa Gibson, were long dead in 1964. So Tom's only relatives at the time were on his mother's side. He wasn't sure if any of his cousins were born by 1964, so he decided to go into the garage loft to look at some of the pictures in the black trunk. Some of them had names and dates handwritten on the back.

Irene pulled into the driveway just as Tom approached the garage. He greeted her and hugged her.

"I just spoke with Detective Carter. The new test results are in. I'm officially off the hook. They confirm I had nothing to do with the crime."

"Oh my God! What a relief!"

He went on to explain about the remaining mystery. She was only slightly interested and didn't really care, and was actually rather pleased to hear that Ronnie wasn't his brother.

"It was a horrible crime and I feel so sorry for that young girl and her family but that's for somebody else to worry about now," she stated in a serene tone. "You've done your duty and your conscience should be clear. I'm proud of you."

Tom told her about the list of relatives the detective had requested.

"That should be pretty easy for you," she commented. "It's a good thing he didn't ask for a list of my relatives …"

Irene was the middle child of seven. She had twenty-six nieces and nephews, most of whom had their own families. Their occasional family reunions were big affairs. Almost seventy had attended the one hosted by Irene and Tom in 2012 at their home. There were tents and campers and RVs all over the property.

Tom went up to the loft and started taking photographs out of the black trunk and placing them in stacks on the floor. He began with the framed pictures. Most were very old, probably from a time well before he was born. He didn't recognize anyone in those pictures. He spent the rest of the day sorting through this rich collection of history. He recalled the last time he had seen any of these photographs. It was when his mother was dying from cancer and he sat by her side. They looked through the photo albums together as she told family stories. He hadn't been able to summon the courage to look at them since that time. His thoughts were interrupted as he heard Irene calling him for dinner.

Tom got back to work in the loft immediately following breakfast the next day. He brought a large mug of coffee with him. He soon discovered an album at the bottom of the trunk that piqued his curiosity. The inscription written on the spine of the album cover read: ATKINS FAMILY. Tom grabbed the album and took it into the house. He grabbed his reading glasses in the den and sat down at the kitchen table where he laid down the album. The first few pages featured pictures of Grandma and Grandpa Atkins. There were photos of their wedding. Some showed Grandpa in uniform. He had been an officer in the US Navy. He was very handsome, Tom thought. The middle of the album was dominated, it seemed, by pictures of Tom's mother, Elizabeth. They showed her from a very young age to about the time she married his father, Fredrick. Then, he found the shocker. It was a family picture of Grandma and Grandpa and their five kids. It was the first time Tom had ever seen a picture of his aunt Mary, so he thought. She and his mother, Elizabeth looked identical. Tom went back and examined the photos from the middle of the album. He removed some of them to look at the backs. As he suspected, his mother didn't figure in all those pictures in the middle section of the album, some of them were of her sister, Mary.

"They had to be twins!" he shouted. "They had to be identical twins."

It appeared that Elizabeth and Mary were the eldest, followed by their three younger brothers. Tom remembered his parents had taken him, Ronnie, and Sarah to the east coast to attend the weddings of two of his uncles: once, when Tom was about seven years old, and again two years later. On the second trip, he had heard his parents say that the third brother was unlikely to ever get married. It wasn't clear why. So, Tom deduced, it was unlikely that any of his cousins, other than Ronnie, could have been more than seven years old by 1964. And, for some reason, Tom's parents never seemed to talk about his aunt Mary and uncle Robert, at least not when the kids were present. Perhaps they were concerned that the kids would be curious and ask questions which they preferred not to answer.

Tom shared all of this new information with Irene. She wasn't very excited, but she was happy to see he had regained his energy.

"I don't know much about DNA tests," he admitted, "but I'm sure this changes things. Maybe it puts Ronnie back in the picture."

Tom picked up his phone and called Detective Carter. He got his voicemail. The greeting indicated he was away for the day. Tom was disappointed but remained resolute in following through with this new information. He didn't leave a message.

"It will have to wait until Monday," he conceded.

He went back to the album; there were only a few pages left to see. There were graduation and wedding pictures of his parents and of Aunt Mary and her husband. Then, on the next page, he saw a picture of the couple with young Ronnie. He wished he had had the sense to look at these pictures many years ago. Then came the next shocker. There was a photo of what seemed to be a small chamber orchestra. In the middle of the picture was a man playing what looked like a soprano sax. Tom went back to the den with the album in hand and pulled a magnifying glass out of the middle drawer of his desk. He pulled out the picture. The man in the middle was Aunt Mary's husband.

"Damn it!" Tom exclaimed. "The initials RG on the saxophone case don't stand for Ronnie Gibson, they stand for Robert Goodman, my uncle, Aunt Mary's husband. Shit!"

"We've got a lot to do this weekend," Irene shouted from the family room. "Why don't you give that up for a little while?"

"You're right. I'll just get on my laptop and prepare that list for the detective, and then I'll be done."

Tom spent the weekend getting the boats out of the water, except for the cruiser. They didn't have the facilities at their home to winterize and store a boat that size. On Sunday, he took the cruiser to the marina for winter storage. Irene drove there and they stayed for lunch.

"I can't believe we're already well into the fall," Tom remarked. "It kind of snuck up on me."

"You've been preoccupied, honey. Now you can go back to enjoying the world around you."

"You're right. From the lake, I noticed the fall colors ... They're stunning."

Tom and Irene both usually had mixed feelings about this time of year. It was sad to pull everything out of the water after an active season with the kids and grandkids, but it signaled the approach of another enjoyable winter in Florida. After everything that had happened, Tom looked forward to the winter even more than usual.

The weather turned cool and wet on Monday. It was October 19th.

"It's a good thing we put the boats away when we did," Tom commented as he and Irene sat down for their usual light breakfast.

"Yes, and I think this pretty well spells the end of the tennis season, at least until we get to Florida."

After breakfast, Tom called Detective Carter.

"I have some new information and a question for you," Tom announced.

"Very good … Let's have it."

"First, I just wanted you to know that I have completed the list of relatives as you requested. I'll send it to you in an e-mail this morning. It's rather simple and I don't see anything there that will help you. On the other hand, as I was going through a bunch of family pictures, I discovered that my aunt Mary, Ronnie's biological mother, wasn't just my mother's sister, she was Mom's identical twin. So, my question is: does that change how much of a match we would expect between my DNA and Ronnie's?"

"Good question. I don't know. Let me call the lab. I'll call you right back."

After an hour, Tom hadn't yet received a call from the detective. He was about to call him again when his cell phone rang.

"Sorry it took so long to get back to you," said the detective. "I had to get a briefing on some other matters."

"I understand, no problem ... So what did you find out on the DNA front?"

"Your instincts were right on, sir. Cousins born from identical twins are expected to have a 25 percent DNA match, so the sample from the crime scene could possibly belong to your cousin Ronnie."

"Yes! I knew it had to be him!" Tom exclaimed.

"Well, we can't jump to that conclusion yet, but we can reinstate him as a prime suspect. We still have a lot of work to do before we can eliminate all doubt."

"Yes, I suppose you're right, but I feel very good about the direction the investigation is heading in. By the way, I have another bit of new information. You won't find any of Ronnie's DNA on the saxophone I shipped to you. I'm sorry, it was a red herring, a waste of time. The initials on the case are for Robert Goodman, Ronnie's father, not Ronnie. I found a picture of my uncle Robert playing a soprano sax in a small orchestra. You will likely receive the package this week. You can send it back when you get a chance."

"I will, and thank you for the information about your aunt Mary. It may very well help us crack the case. Have a good day."

Tom sat down with Irene and explained the significance of his discovery.

"It means that the 25 percent DNA match with mine makes Ronnie a prime suspect, once again. It all makes so much sense. It probably explains why my parents were the ones that adopted him, and why my mother tried so hard to love him like a son."

With six weeks to go before their departure for Florida, Tom and Irene began their annual packing ritual, beginning with their golf and tennis equipment.

"We had trouble getting a room at our favorite hotel in Atlanta last year," Irene reminded Tom. "Maybe we should book it now."

Part of their travel ritual was to stay at the Four Seasons Hotel in Atlanta and dine at the Bar Margot when they were travelling south to Naples. In the spring, they liked to stay at the St. Regis and dine at the Atlas when they were travelling north to their home in Westfield, New York.

"You're right, I'll get online and book it today. I'm looking forward to it."

Two weeks later, on November 3rd, 2015, Detective Carter called. It was ten o'clock in the morning. Tom was in the garage when his cell phone rang.

"I just wanted to keep you up-to-date," the detective declared. "I received the saxophone and decided to go ahead and send it to the lab even though we don't expect to find any of Ronnie's DNA on it."

"Okay, but how can that be of any help?" Tom asked.

"Well, we found a box of reeds in the case. Most were new, but there were three used reeds which may have retained some of Robert Goodman's saliva. This could allow the lab to establish a DNA profile for him. If there's a 50 percent match to the DNA from the crime scene, then Ronnie is undoubtedly our man."

"Great! How long before we get those test results?"

"We'll have to be patient. It could be three weeks or more. In the meantime, we still have to look at all possibilities."

"What other possibilities are there?" Tom asked in frustration.

"I'm working on a new investigative path, based on some fingerprint evidence we have just uncovered."

"What is it?"

"The lab did an extensive examination of the frame of the rototiller. It's mostly just a hunk of rust now, so it's impossible to lift fingerprints from it. But, near the motor mount brackets, there is an oily area, probably where the motor had leaked some oil which protected that particular spot from rusting. There are two clearly defined sets of prints in that area. One set is yours, the other is as yet unidentified, except that it matches a partial print on the small blade of your knife, the blade that was used in the stabbing. The partial print is not in an area of the blade where we recovered blood traces, so it's impossible to tell if the print was made before, during or after the stabbing."

"Those have to be David's prints, I would guess. I don't actually remember him handling my knife, but I suppose he might have held it at some time or other."

"Or, if he's the perpetrator, he could have found the knife in the dugout and used it to stab the victim, thinking he could pin the crime on you."

"That doesn't sound like the David I knew; and what about the DNA? We're not even related. How could the semen samples show a 25 percent DNA match with me?"

"That's right, but in my experience, when you have conflicting pieces of evidence, you have to chase each one down. Ultimately, a logical explanation usually emerges. In any case, it's time we have an interview with your friend David. What can you tell me about him?"

"His last name is Strohman. I haven't had any contact with him since 1965. I don't even know if he's still alive. I got on the Internet and searched for him, but I couldn't find a trace of him. I tried LinkedIn to no avail. I don't know what else we can do …"

"We have resources that you don't have access to. Dead or alive, we'll find him."

"Good luck, and let me know if there is anything else I can do to help. My wife and I are here until the end of the month, and then we're off to Florida. You can use the same cell phone number and e-mail address to reach me in Florida."

Tom was convinced that David wasn't the culprit. In his opinion, his old friend just didn't have the temperament to commit such a heinous crime. But, on the other hand, there were no obvious answers, and he felt he could wear a hole through his scalp scratching his head over this mystery. We're obviously missing something, he thought.

The next day, after breakfast, Tom took a mug of coffee into the den and sat down at his desk. He opened the bottom right-hand drawer, pulled out the box, and began reading the letters his mother had so carefully preserved.

Tom didn't know how his mother would have felt about her son reading her most private and personal correspondence, but he admittedly had shunned his past and this was one way to get reacquainted with it. The letters spanned a time period from the early 1940s to her death in 1994. She was a beautiful and refined woman who attracted many admirers. Some, as evidenced by their letters, became her lovers, if only for a short time. It seemed she was always the one who broke off the relationships, much to the chagrin of her idolizers. There were two men, however, with whom she had lasting relationships at the same time. One of them was a man called Ian Chapman, and the other was Tom's father, Fredrick. Both men competed for Elizabeth's heart and both proposed marriage. They didn't seem to be aware of each other. From the content of the letters, it appeared to Tom as though Ian Chapman would ultimately prevail. Tom was curious as to why it didn't turn out that way. There were no obvious answers in the letters. He wasn't quite through all the letters when Irene summoned him for dinner.

"What have you been up to in there?" she asked.

"You wouldn't believe it, Irene. I'm still trying to get my head around it …"

"What? What? Tell me …"

Tom swallowed a sip of wine and took a deep breath.

"From these letters, I have learned things about my family that were kept secret my entire life. My mother had several relationships, before and after she married my father. It's all so puzzling, I don't know what to think."

"Does any of what you're learning provide any insight into the case?"

"Well, not directly. If anything, it may make things murkier …"

"In what way?"

"I don't know … I may be overreacting, but, how do we know for sure who fathered who … And how sure can we be about any related DNA evidence?"

There was a pause. Irene frowned and looked up at the ceiling as if she was mulling some thoughts.

"I'm curious, Tom. I keep wondering why you're so determined to prove Ronnie guilty. Is it possible that you have gone through all this trouble because you're harboring some ill feelings toward him, after all these years? Could it be that you never got over the way he treated you, and this is some form of retribution?"

Tom thought about it for a few moments.

"It certainly didn't start out that way. I genuinely wanted to find the truth. Then, I wanted to make sure I wasn't the perpetrator. After that, I figured it would be a fair and just outcome if Ronnie turned out to be the culprit. I don't think I've been carrying a grudge, and I don't think I'm looking for revenge. I just think it would be a tidy and logical end."

14

On November 10th, Tom got another call from Detective Carter.

"We're pretty sure we've found your friend David. His mother was a writer. Was her name Nicole?"

"Yes, Nicole Strohman. His father's name was Patrick."

"Okay, that's got to be him, we've found him. He is still among the living. He is an ordained minister of the United Church of Canada."

"Canada?"

"That's right. He leads a small rural congregation in a small town, less than an hour's drive north of the border, a little bit north of the city of Kingston, Ontario. As far as we can tell, he is not married and has no children."

"I'm impressed. How did you find him so quickly?"

"I can't give you specifics about our investigative tools, but let me just say that anyone licensed to drive a motor vehicle in North America can be found in shared police databases."

"And you say he's an ordained minister ... Wow, that really does sound like David. Can't you get his fingerprint record from his driver's license application?"

"Not all jurisdictions take fingerprints for driver permits, and none of Canada's provincial authorities take fingerprints for driver permits."

"Shame ... So, when are you going to interview him?"

"Well, there's the rub. We found him easily, but we have no authority in Canada. We can't bring him in or question him. He's under no obligation to say anything to us. And, we don't have a shred of evidence to justify a request for extradition."

"So, does that mean we're just left with Ronnie?"

There was a pause.

"Not necessarily," the detective responded with some hesitation in his voice. "We still want to check out David, but we would need your help and I don't know if we should impose on you. You have already done so much ..."

"Listen, Detective, I've marched up to the edge of the precipice over this whole thing. For a couple of weeks, I thought I was going to be wrongly convicted of a crime and spend the rest of my days in jail. After all that, I'm willing to do just about anything to bring this whole story to a conclusion. I want to find the truth, as long as you really believe the effort is worthwhile. So, what can I do to help?"

"I'm going to give you David's contact information. I'd like you to call him and get reacquainted with him. Your goal is to try to get him to agree to meet with you. Then, if you succeed, I'd like you to meet with him and reminisce about your childhood days together. Eventually, steer the discussion toward the theft of the rototiller and your underground fort. I'd like you to gauge his reaction. See if he gets nervous or uncomfortable. Try to draw out something we don't already know. And, if possible ... If at all possible ... Try to get a sample of his fingerprints somehow, without being obvious. We don't want to tip him off that he's a person of interest in a murder case."

"I ... I don't know if I feel right about this. I'm not a deceitful kind of person."

"I know you're not, and I sense that you desperately want Ronnie to be the culprit. But I'd like you to look at it this way: by meeting with David and collecting whatever information you can, you may be helping us prove that he's not the one. And, if it's not him, and it's not you, it gets us closer to concluding that Ronnie is the one."

"Okay. I guess I can do it …" Tom said with hesitation.

Detective Carter provided Tom with a full civic address and a phone number for David.

"And," the detective continued, "I want you to know that, if you're successful in getting a fingerprint, it won't be admissible in court. It will just help us steer our investigation in one direction or another. And one more thing … I almost forgot the most important thing. He will surely be curious about how you found him. You can't tell him you got his coordinates from the police. So, our staff searched on Google for hours. And finally, after going through page after page of false leads, they found him in a small article in the *Tweed News* where he was named as the minister who presided over the wedding of a Marilyn Dawes and Gordon Thomas on June 20th of this year. So there's your answer."

"Got it. Thanks."

Tom told Irene what was going on. She was only mildly supportive.

"You be careful, Mister," she said in a stern voice. "He's not the nice little buddy you thought you once knew. And, if he's the one who committed that awful crime, he could be capable of God knows what …"

"He's a minister of the United Church, for heaven's sake," he responded with a bit of a chuckle.

Tom spent the rest of the day writing a script for his phone call. Then, just before dinnertime, he called the number the detective had given him.

"Hello," said a man's voice. It sounded a little raspy and Tom didn't recognize it.

"Yes, hello, is this David, David Strohman?"

"Yes, and whom am I speaking with?"

"Hi, David. It's Tom, your old friend, Tom Gibson. We were neighbors on Riverdale Circle back in the sixties."

"My heavens! Tom?"

"Yes!"

"What a surprise, after all these years. How on earth did you ever find me? And what drove you to look for me?"

"Well, it's a bit of a long story, but I'll give you the short of it. I've been retired for a few years, and to keep busy and to make a few bucks, I've been dabbling with real estate investments. Three months ago, I bought my former childhood home at 5 Riverdale Circle and turned it into a rooming house. I've got it filled with postgraduate students from the university."

"That's amazing!" David exclaimed. "And perhaps a little unusual."

"It was a good deal and I couldn't pass it up. Anyway, each time I step onto the property, it brings me back to the old days and all the good times we had together. That's what drove me to try to look you up. It wasn't easy to find you. But, the Internet is so amazing. After a lengthy Google search, your name popped up in a brief article in the *Tweed News*. It was about a wedding you performed last June. After that, it was a matter of looking you up in the Canada411.ca register. I still wasn't sure it was you until a few moments ago when you answered the phone and recognized my name."

"Well. I'm delighted to hear from you and I'm glad you're doing well. We should get together sometime and catch up on lost time."

"That would be wonderful. I'd love to get together. How about I come up there and I can treat you to lunch?"

David giggled.

"Did I say something funny?" Tom asked.

"Yes, sort of ... There are no restaurants anywhere near here, at least none that you would want to patronize. We can have lunch right here in the manse. My part-time housekeeper makes a wonderful Irish stew and leaves me a number of servings which I freeze and use at my discretion."

"Sounds great to me!"

"What kind of time frame were you thinking of?"

"I was thinking about sometime in the next two weeks, before the snow flies."

"We could have lunch on Thursday or Friday. After that, and for the next two weeks, I'll be working a few shifts serving lunches at the seniors' residence, and my availability will be more difficult to predict."

"Okay, how about Thursday?"

"Sure, let's go for Thursday."

"I'll bring a French baguette. I look forward to seeing you, David."

"Likewise, Tom. Have a safe drive."

After dinner, Tom went out to the loft and gathered a few childhood pictures he had seen during his previous searches and picked up one of the family albums in his office so he could show David his kids and grandkids. Then he went out to his vehicle to load David's address into the GPS. The shortest route, from his home near Westfield, was to cross the border into Canada at Buffalo, drive to Toronto and then east on the MacDonald-Cartier freeway for a couple of hours. David's church was located in a small village near the town of Tweed, Ontario, a short drive north of the freeway. The estimated trip duration was five and a half hours.

The next day, Tom wrote down a plan for his conversation with David. He rehearsed it several times and then drove out to the bakery to pick up a French baguette.

On Thursday, Tom had to get up at five o'clock in the morning so he could be on the road by six. He brought a toasted bagel and a thermos of coffee with him. It was still dark as he headed east on I-90. The temperature was barely above freezing, and Tom felt winter was around the corner. Fortunately, the road was clear and dry and traffic was light. He plugged his MP3 player into the sound system and listened to classical music. He tried to concentrate on his planned conversation with David but was often distracted by feelings of guilt. As much as he wanted to get at the truth, he felt uneasy about misrepresenting himself to his old friend.

The border crossing into Canada wasn't congested and flowed smoothly. But the density of commuter traffic into Hamilton and then into Toronto caught Tom by surprise. His GPS indicated he was going to arrive at his destination thirty-five minutes late. He called David to inform him. He got David's voicemail and left him a message. He made a brief stop at a rest area to stretch his legs and go to the washroom. Finally, Tom pulled into the small church parking lot at ten minutes before one o'clock.

Tom didn't spend a lot of time looking around. The small stone church was a charming example of early twentieth-century architecture. The wood-sided manse was obviously added at a later date. He saw only one other car in the parking lot; it was a Japanese compact car that seemed to be in need of serious bodywork. There was a bitterly cold wind out of the north. Tom closed up his trench coat and held his small photo album with one hand while he knocked on the door with the other. As the solid oak door opened, he recognized David right away. He had the same tall slim build and full head of hair, although most of it was white. His wire-rim glasses and tweed jacket with leather patches on the elbows gave him an intellectual appearance.

"Welcome, Tom!" he exclaimed as he extended his hand.

Tom shook his hand and then pulled David toward him and hugged him. Both men patted each other on the back.

"Thank you, David, it's so great to reconnect with you after all these years."

"Come on in!"

David took Tom's coat, and the two of them sat in a room that looked like a combination of living room and office. There was a couch and two stuffed chairs around a rectangular coffee table, two bookcases stuffed with books in one corner, and a desk with three wooden chairs in another corner. A fieldstone fireplace flanked by two tall windows dominated the wall opposite the church. An opening in the wall opposite the entrance led into the kitchen. A savory aroma wafted in from the kitchen.

"Can I offer you something to drink?" David asked.

"If you have any coffee ready, I'll have some of that, but don't go to any fuss."

"No fuss, I've got a pot brewing as we speak."

Tom walked around as David went into the kitchen. The decor was austere. A narrow hallway led to the church. There were no personal items, not even photographs. It was hard to imagine anyone could live there. Tom peered at the kitchen. It was small and primitive. A doorway on the opposite side seemed to lead to a bedroom.

"I'll just have it black, thanks."

David carried two mugs back into the living room. Tom gave a brief overview of his career and family history while they sipped their coffee. He opened up the album and grabbed a couple of loose pictures from their childhood. One of them depicted the two of them sitting on the front steps of David's house. The other showed them side by side in their gravity derby karts, at the starting line, smiling ear to ear. Tom turned the pages of the album and stopped at a picture of him and Irene with their kids and grandkids. He handed the album to David. Some of Tom's calling cards fell out. David picked them off the floor and placed them back in the sleeve inside the front cover.

"I'm sorry. Is this where they belong?" David asked.

"Sure, that's fine. You can keep one if you like. It has all my contact information."

David took one of the cards and dropped it in his shirt pocket.

"You're so fortunate," David commented. "You have a lovely family and you live a charmed life. By contrast, I live very modestly."

Tom watched his friend as he held the album and likely left a number of clear fingerprints on the cover. Tom had mixed feelings; he was satisfied about accomplishing one of his key goals, but he felt remorse for being deceitful. For all he knew, his old friend had committed no crime. Tom rationalized his actions by concluding that he was perhaps giving his friend an opportunity to exclude himself as a suspect, and, if it didn't exclude him, it was because he was guilty and deserved to be caught by any means, overt or covert.

"How did you end up in Canada, and in the church?" Tom asked.

"It's a long and not-so-happy story. I'm not sure it would interest you."

"Of course I'm interested."

"I came out of college with a commerce degree and was hired by a stock brokerage. It was a bit of a miracle because I had been suffering from … I'm not sure … I called them memory lapses. I found it difficult to concentrate under stress. In any case, my job was often stressful and I hated it. Instead of helping our customers build portfolios that were well suited for them, we were highly pressured to sell IPO stocks from bought deals. I was extremely unhappy. I started to drink heavily and got into a downward spiral. I had made plenty of money but had no real friends and no family. I eventually screwed up on the job and got fired. I reached the bottom of the barrel and blew whatever savings I had. I was on the street. I woke up from a drunken stupor one morning in the arms of a pastor. I had snuck into the church for shelter and warmth. He talked me into entering rehab and the church covered the cost. He said it was God who delivered me to his church. I believed him. It wasn't easy but I got through the program. During my last week there, I met a young lady who was also nearing the end of her rehabilitation. We hit it off. She was planning to move in with her mother who lived in a small town in Canada. She invited me to visit."

He paused to sip his coffee and then continued.

"I took her up on her offer. Her mother was a hardworking woman who ran a small dairy farm. She said I could stay two weeks, but only if I helped with the chores. I did my part and also found a part-time job as caretaker at the cemetery. I got other odd jobs and earned enough to pay room and board at a widow's house in the nearby village. I joined the church and one thing led to another. I was ordained eighteen years ago and have been leading this congregation for the past seven years. It's not high living, but I find it peaceful and satisfying and stress free."

"What about the young lady. Did you marry her?"

"Sadly, no ... I thought things were looking pretty good for us, then she had a relapse. She started to combine heavy drugs with alcohol. Her mother found her unresponsive one evening and called an ambulance. She slipped into a coma shortly after arriving at the hospital. She never recovered and died a few weeks later."

"Oh my God, how tragic!"

There was an awkward silence. Tom didn't know what else to say. He felt even guiltier about plotting to collect evidence from this man who had experienced nothing but hardships, yet didn't seem to carry any bitterness. He thought about simply asking David for a sample of his fingerprints to help prove his innocence. But he realized that if he asked, and David refused, the whole visit would be a waste of time.

"Well, I think you deserve congratulations for climbing back as you did," Tom finally commented. "But it sounds like a lonely existence."

"It's not as bad as it sounds … I do my rounds and visit the elderly and the sick. On Wednesday evenings, a group of us gets together for a few hands of euchre. We hold fund-raising events for the church, and on Sundays of course, we have Sunday school for the kids and our Sunday service for the whole congregation."

There was another quiet moment.

"What about family … Whatever happened to your sister?" Tom asked.

"My parents are long gone, but they were around long enough to see me at my worst. Dad died in 1989 and Mom lasted into 1992, although she suffered from severe dementia for the last two years of her life. As for my sister, Karen married a lawyer and moved to California. They have two grown boys. They dropped by for a visit six years ago, when the boys were still in high school. They were on vacation, driving an RV around the lower Great Lakes. I haven't seen them since. We exchange Christmas cards and that's about it."

The men fell silent again for a few moments.

"Now, how about digging into some stew?" David suggested.

"Sounds great … Smells wonderful. Let me go to my car and get the baguette."

Tom ran out and came back in with the French baguette.

"I should go to the washroom and wash my hands before I slice this bread," Tom suggested.

"The bathroom is on the left in the hallway," David informed him.

Tom ran water in the sink and washed his hands. As he did so, he looked around. The whole room was about eight by six, with a shower stall in the corner, a toilet, a vanity and sink, and a linen closet. There was a small wooden cabinet on the wall above the toilet tank. He left the water running in the sink and dried his hands. He opened the two small doors of the cabinet and checked out the contents. There were some medication vials and vitamin bottles. There was an electric razor, a hairbrush, and a can of talcum powder along with two extra rolls of toilet paper, a toothbrush, and a tube of toothpaste. Tom concluded this was the only bathroom in the manse. He turned off the tap and joined David in the kitchen. Tom cut a number of thick oblique slices of bread, and the two men sat down at the kitchen table to eat.

"This is probably the best Irish stew I've ever had!" Tom commented enthusiastically after a couple of mouthfuls.

"Yes, Mrs. McTavish uses lamb as the main ingredient and fresh vegetables from her garden. Then she makes these portions of stew and freezes them. She also makes a wonderful meat loaf."

They didn't say much as they gobbled their respective servings. Afterward, and following a couple of stifled burps, the men got up to clear the table.

"I don't have a dishwasher," David admitted. "Well, not a machine anyway. We can just rinse the dishes and place them in the sink. Mrs. McTavish will wash them tomorrow."

David wiped down the table with a damp cloth. He walked into the living room and returned with the two coffee mugs and Tom's album. He placed the mugs in the sink and began to wipe down the album.

"Better get my greasy prints off your lovely album," he said as he placed the album on the kitchen table, carefully using the cloth like an oven mitt.

A phone rang somewhere as the two men finished rinsing the dishes.

"Oh, I'm sorry, that's my phone. I'd better get it," David said as he walked into the bedroom.

Tom was dismayed by what had just happened. He couldn't tell if David was on to him, or just being considerate. In any event, he felt it was unlikely he could get David's prints on the album again. He could hear David conversing on the phone but couldn't make out any of the words. He walked back into the living room and looked around. He pulled out a couple of books from the bookcase and read the titles. He looked at a couple more. He leaned forward and checked out a few more titles without pulling the books off the shelf. It occurred to him that most of the books were biographies. How peculiar, he thought. A modem sat on top of one of the bookcases, indicating that David had Internet access.

He could hear that the conversation was still going on in the bedroom. He walked over to the desk. There was a laptop computer sitting in the middle of the embedded leather work surface of the desk, and a small lamp at one end, near the wall. Tom quietly opened the middle drawer of the desk. There were scissors, pens and pencils and paper clips, a stapler, and a small plastic Scotch tape dispenser. Tom was suddenly struck by an idea. He had seen this done in an old TV episode of MacGyver. He grabbed the tape dispenser and shoved it into the side pocket of his cargo pants. He went into the bathroom and closed the door. He opened the cabinet, grabbed the hairbrush by the bristles and placed it in the sink. He took the can of talcum powder and sprinkled powder all over the plastic handle of the brush. He pulled the tape dispenser from his pocket and ripped off a five-inch length of tape. He applied the sticky side of the tape along one side of the brush handle and pressed firmly along the whole length of the tape. He ripped the tape off the handle and dangled it in the air with one hand while he pulled his passport out of his shirt pocket with the other. Using his thumb, he opened his passport somewhere in the back pages, where customs officers normally apply their stamps. He carefully slipped the tape between the pages, then turned one more page, dropped in a few hairs he pinched off the brush bristles, closed his passport and slipped it back into his shirt pocket. He wiped down the brush handle and returned it to the cabinet, along with the can of powder. He rinsed out the sink and washed his hands. David was sitting in the living room when Tom emerged from the bathroom. Tom sat in one of the stuffed chairs.

"Hope everything is okay ... I mean with the phone call?" Tom asked.

"Oh yes, better than okay. It was Mrs. Campbell asking to book the church and me for a wedding next spring. We like weddings. We do quite well with weddings ..."

"Good, I'm glad it wasn't for a funeral or something like that."

"Actually, as much as we hate to lose any members of our congregation, we do quite well with funerals too," David admitted with a smirk.

Tom felt he needed to steer the conversation toward that period in their lives when they were neighbors.

"Do you ever reminisce about those days when we ran our Sunday derbies in our gravity karts down Riverdale Circle?" Tom asked. "Do you ever think back at that amazing motorized kart we built from that metallic tubing your Dad gave us?"

David looked straight into Tom's eyes.

"Tom, I know why you're here," David said in a calm and deliberate voice.

"What?"

Tom was in shock. He realized that David had been on to him from the start. He didn't know what to say.

"I know why you've come here," David continued. "After you called me, I searched your name on Google. I just wanted to catch up on what you've been up to. One of the first items that emerged was a recent article in the *Daily Record* in which you were named as the owner of the house where the police found the remains of a young girl who disappeared in 1964. I knew right away that your call was no coincidence."

Tom reflected for a few moments. He realized he needed to change tactics.

"You're right, David. This visit is related to that cold case, but not in the way you might think. I told the police that you were not the kind of person who could commit such a crime. I told them how I remembered you as a kind and gentle soul. I decided to come up here to reaffirm my convictions about you."

"Or, are you here to deflect the blame away from yourself? What I don't understand is why they haven't arrested you. After all, it was your house, it was your secret fort, it was …"

David suddenly stopped talking, as if he wanted to avoid saying something that could betray some knowledge of the details of the crime.

"Frankly, when I was confronted with the reality of this crime, I was convinced the culprit was Ronnie. And I'm still hopeful the evidence will point to him, although there is significant doubt about that. You see, they have fingerprints and DNA evidence from the scene, but none of it shows that Ronnie was ever in our fort … Nothing. That leaves a very short list of possible suspects. I'm afraid it comes down to you and me. And, David, I know with certainty I didn't do it."

Tom knew that Ronnie was still a viable suspect, but given David's suspicions and the way their conversation had suddenly turned, he decided at that very moment that he needed to apply pressure and get a reaction from his friend. He expected an emphatic denial. He was stunned by what ensued.

He observed some sudden changes in David's posture. His facial muscles seemed to sag. He looked up at the ceiling as if he was looking for guidance from God. His eyes started to well up. He slid off the chair and onto his knees. He cradled his face in the palms of his hands and started to cry. Neither of the two men uttered another word for quite some time as David cried quietly. He looked up at the ceiling once again.

"It's okay, David. I'm not the police. You can confide in me … Nothing you tell me can be used as evidence. Take the weight off your shoulders."

David stopped crying. He squared his shoulders, got up, and sat upright in his chair. He stared straight ahead of him and said nothing.

"David, is there something you want to tell me?" Tom asked.

"I'm not David."

"What?"

"I'm not David."

"I don't know what you mean …"

"David is a weak-minded wimp. He gets himself into trouble and then he can't stand the heat. He screws up and I have to step in and clean up the mess."

Tom tried to hide his astonishment. His mind was racing. He wondered if David was simply trying to play mind games, but concluded that it would have been inconsistent with what he knew of David's character. He also observed a sudden and very noticeable difference in David's voice and tone. He seemed more assertive, if not aggressive. Tom had heard about alleged cases of dual—or multiple-personality disorder, but he wasn't sure if they were regarded as real medical diagnoses or merely theories. He decided to pursue the conversation under the assumption that David was in fact suffering from a mental disorder.

"So, if you're not David, who are you?" Tom asked.

"I'm Chuck."

"Hi, Chuck, I'm Tom Gibson."

"I know who you are."

"So, where is David?"

"As usual, when he can't stand the heat, he checks out."

"I had a feeling he was about to tell me something about what happened to that young girl who disappeared in 1964. Can you tell me anything about it?"

"Sure, it was stupid. The dumb jerk was in his garage. He was about to close the door and sit in his usual spot so he could look at his *Playboy* magazine and masturbate. A young girl rode her bike up to him and asked for his younger sister, Karen. I don't know what got into him. He tried to hide his erection. He lied to her. He said his sister was playing in the fort next door and offered to take her there. He grabbed a flashlight and he lured her into that dugout. He pinned her down and started to masturbate while pressing his cock against her. She screamed. It was piercing. He covered her face while he finished his business. He was in some kind of dumb frenzy. When he was done, she wasn't breathing anymore. He shook her, yelled at her, and slapped her face but there was no reaction. He pointed the flashlight into her eyes and realized she was dead. He panicked and that's when I stepped in."

"What did you do?"

"He screwed up. He killed her … And for what? It was dumb. But, she was already dead. I had to deal with it. I saw your knife in the dirt. I decided to use it to stab her. I figured it would confuse the evidence and maybe point the finger at you. Then I wrapped her up in that stinky blanket and propped her up in the corner. I had to go to the garage and get a shovel to collapse the entrance tunnel. That's when I saw her bike. I dragged it to the dugout, tossed it in the hole, and shoveled a bunch of dirt on top of it. End of story."

Tom took a few moments to digest what he had just heard.

"You're probably wondering why I'm telling you all this," Chuck continued.

"Yes, I find you've been surprisingly frank."

"I know my stuff. David didn't admit what he did. I told you. That's considered hearsay. And you're not the police. If you tell them, that's more hearsay."

"But I knew David as a gentle soul. I would have expected him to turn himself in to the police …"

"You're bang on … At first, the poor sap tried to give himself up. Each time he felt that pressure, I took over and snapped him out of it. Lately, things have been calm and he has settled nicely. That is … Until you showed up and stirred the pot. Now he's ready to explode again. Let me tell you this," Chuck said as he gave Tom a steely-eyed look.

"After all this time, there's nothing to gain by going to the police."

Tom didn't know how to respond. He didn't want to rile Chuck in any way.

"When do you think David will be back?"

"I don't know. Things will have to calm down. It won't be while you're here, that's for sure. It may not be until tomorrow … Maybe you should leave."

Tom suddenly felt very uncomfortable. He had felt reasonably at ease in David's company, but with Chuck, it was a different matter. He didn't feel safe and convinced himself it wouldn't be prudent to stay or to turn his back on Chuck. He already had everything he had come for, and even more, so it was time to get out of there. He stood up.

"You're right, Chuck. I should get going. I have a long drive ahead of me."

Tom was startled when Chuck jumped energetically out of his chair and hurried to the door. He grabbed Tom's coat and handed it to him. Tom just folded it over his arm, not wanting his arms to be tied up in the sleeves with Chuck standing right there in his face. He felt around for his car keys and felt the tape dispenser in his pocket. He knew there was no way to return it to its rightful place and suddenly felt a cold sweat.

Chuck grabbed the door handle and turned toward Tom.

"I think you should leave David alone. Don't try to contact him again. He doesn't need those old memories roiled again," Chuck asserted firmly. "And don't get funny ideas about telling the police anything. You have a nice life and a nice family. We wouldn't want anything bad to happen …"

The cynicism in Chuck's voice sent a chill down Tom's spine. He left as Chuck opened the door, and not another word was spoken.

15

It was almost four o'clock when Tom drove out of the church parking lot. He felt a number of emotions. He felt relief in finally finding the truth, and some satisfaction in having done everything he possibly could to bring peace to that poor young girl's lost soul. He wasn't proud of using duplicitous means to trap his old friend, but he felt justified. He debated in his mind whether he should walk away from the case or stay involved until justice was served. It wasn't a decision he was going to make easily or quickly. And with Chuck in the picture, there was more at stake.

He called Detective Carter. He reached his voicemail and left a brief message. The detective called back a few minutes later.

"It was him! He did it! He's the murderer! He admitted it to me! Well, not directly. Chuck is the one who told me how it all happened! I was shocked!"

"Who the hell is Chuck?"

"That's his other personality! It's freaky, I know but …"

"Okay, okay … Let's slow down a bit. First, I can hear the road noise, so I know you're on your way back. This is emotional for you, so I don't think we should be going over the details right now. We can meet after you get home and I can get a full statement from you at that time."

"Sure, okay … But, I also have some physical evidence for you!"

"What do you have?"

"I lifted some fingerprints off his hairbrush!"

"I won't ask you how you did that, but you can tell me when we meet."

"I also picked up some hairs from his brush, so we can extract some DNA."

"Very good, very smart. We need to get that to the lab immediately."

There was a pause while Tom yawned out loud.

"I'm sorry, it's been a long day," Tom admitted. "Yes, I want to get it to you as quickly as possible, but I'm still almost five hours from the border crossing. If I drive on to your office, it will be ten hours before I get home. I think I'm just too tired to do that."

"Don't worry about that, Tom, just go straight home. I'm going to drive to your place. You just get home and get some rest. I'll bring a technician from our crime lab with me."

"Good, okay, that would be much better, thanks."

"Make sure you stop for coffee and walk around a bit."

"I'll do that. I have to stop to top up the gas tank anyway. The weather is turning nasty. We're getting some snow accompanied by strong winds. Visibility is becoming a problem."

"Drive carefully. See you tomorrow."

Tom's hands and ears were freezing as he filled his gas tank in the midst of a full blizzard. He warmed his palms and fingers around an extra-large cup of coffee, but his ears remained numb. Back on the road, it was a slow drive. The snow finally stopped as he reached the Queen Elizabeth Way between Toronto and Hamilton. He reached the border thirty minutes later.

The border guard asked Tom for his passport. As he handed it to the guard, he suddenly felt a hot flash. He panicked at the thought of losing the precious evidence in the back pages, either from the wind which was gusting between the customs booths, or from the border guard's handling of the passport as he scanned it through the reader.

"Where do you live?" asked the border guard.

"Westfield, New York."

"When did you leave the US?"

"This morning."

"Are you bringing back anything you acquired in Canada?"

"Just what's left in this cup of coffee."

"Good night, sir," said the guard as he handed the passport back to Tom.

Tom just glanced at his passport before returning it to his shirt pocket. He didn't want to draw attention to himself by searching through the pages. He pulled over just before merging onto I-90 and turned on his dome light. He wasn't wearing his glasses so he couldn't be sure, but it appeared the hair samples were gone. However, the strip of Scotch tape was still there. He was frustrated and disappointed that, after all his efforts, he may have lost a key piece of evidence, but he wasn't absolutely sure.

An hour later, Tom was safely home and in bed. Irene was sleeping soundly and he didn't want to wake her. He knew he would have ample opportunity to bring her up-to-date in the morning. Even though he had much on his mind, he was so exhausted he had no difficulty getting to sleep.

Tom was awakened from a deep sleep by Irene. It was just after eight o'clock in the morning.

"I'm so sorry to wake you, honey … Detective Carter is on the phone."

It took Tom a few moments to regain clarity of mind, and then he picked up the phone and greeted the detective.

"Good morning, Tom. I just wanted you to know that I'm on my way. I'm accompanied by Officer Anthony Pritchard from the police lab. I'm guessing we'll be there around ten o'clock."

"Very good, I'll be here."

"Just one quick question … I can't seem to find your street on my GPS."

"From the intersection of Main Street and Highway 5, proceed west on 5 and turn right on Shore Drive."

"Got it, thanks. See you in a little while."

Tom didn't have the heart to tell the detective he may have lost the DNA evidence he worked so hard to get. He immediately jumped to his feet and retrieved his passport from his shirt on the floor. He took it into his office and put on his reading glasses. He closely examined his passport, starting with the back page. He confirmed, as he had the previous evening, that the strip of Scotch tape was intact, but there was no trace of any hair anywhere in the document. He was crushed and felt he had been careless.

During breakfast, Tom described everything that happened during his visit with his old friend David, and Chuck.

"It seems amazing to me that, during that time when you were best friends and neighbors, you never witnessed that other side of him," Irene commented. "You were convinced he could never do something so horrific. This might explain it."

"You're right, I'm completely baffled. But is this dual-personality stuff for real?"

"Yes, there is increasing evidence that it is very real. I've read quite a lot about this in my work. I've even referred some kids to psychiatrists because I suspected they suffered from such a condition.

They now call it dissociative identity disorder. There are about two hundred new cases diagnosed in this country every year."

"But, Irene, I still have some nagging doubts. How do we explain the 25 percent match between the crime scene DNA and mine? David and I aren't related!"

"I don't know. Perhaps an answer will emerge in time. Or maybe we'll never know. I realize your disappointment that it wasn't Ronnie, but at least you know the truth, and that was the entire purpose of everything you have done. It's over."

Tom didn't have the heart to tell her about Chuck's not-so-veiled threat.

After breakfast, Irene and Tom agreed it was time to complete their preparations for their departure for Florida. They had it down to a routine, and each of them had their respective itemized list for packing and for preparing the house for a full shutdown. Tom was doing some routine maintenance on the hot tub in the sunroom when Detective Carter and his fellow officer arrived. Tom greeted them and introduced them to Irene.

"Gentlemen, did you want some fresh coffee? Irene asked.

"That would be lovely," Detective Carter replied.

Irene stepped away while the officers followed Tom into his office.

"Before I take your statement on your visit with David Strohman, I'd like Officer Pritchard to take custody of any physical evidence you have brought back," the detective suggested.

Tom pulled his passport from the middle drawer of his desk and handed it to officer Pritchard.

"Here, you'll find a strip of Scotch tape stuck on the second-last page. I used talcum powder to dust the handle of his hairbrush, blew off the excess powder, and then pressed that piece of tape along one side of the handle. I hope it picked up one or more fingerprints."

The officer slipped on some latex gloves and examined the passport. He pulled a headgear loupe and light from his kit and strapped it onto his head.

"Well, it's a little crude," he said, "but I see some latent prints. We'll have to see, after we transfer and digitize them, if your technique picked up enough detail for a definitive matching process."

"Okay, good, now how about the hair samples?" Detective Carter asked.

Tom hung his head, his shoulders sagged.

"I'm so sorry, officers, I'm afraid I've let you down. When I pinched the bristles on the hairbrush and pulled off some hairs, I placed them carefully between some of the pages in my passport and shoved the passport in my pocket. It seemed like the safest place for them. But when I got to the border, I had to present my passport to the border guard. The wind was horrendous. I don't know if the wind blew the hairs out. I only thought of it as I handed the passport to him. Or, maybe they fell out when he opened it to scan the bar code … I don't know. All I know is that the hair samples are gone … I'm so sorry."

Officer Pritchard examined each page very carefully.

"Sadly, I don't see any hair in here at all," the officer observed.

Irene walked in with a pot of coffee and three mugs. All three men chose to have their coffee black.

"I can't add anything helpful here, so I'll leave you three to yourselves."

"Before you go, Mrs. Gibson, let me ask Tom something."

The officer turned to Tom.

"What garment did you keep your passport in on your way home last night?"

"It was a shirt. I kept my passport in my shirt pocket for easy access."

"Where is that shirt now?" the officer continued.

"I tossed it in the laundry basket this morning," Tom answered.

"I need to see it," the officer asserted.

"I was just about to throw it into the washer," Irene declared. "I'll go get it for you."

Irene left and returned a few moments later with the shirt. She handed it to the officer. He slowly inverted the pocket while examining it through his loupe, poking away with a pair of tweezers. He smiled.

"I see one lowly hair in here. I don't know, at this time, whose it is, but it certainly could have slipped out of the passport while it was in your pocket. The hair is whitish gray, which, in of itself, is inconclusive because both you, Tom, and Mrs. Gibson have some gray hair."

The officer pulled a measuring tape from his kit. He held the hair with the tweezers while holding the tape alongside the hair.

"However, this hair is just under two inches long. That would suggest it doesn't belong to Mr. Gibson. If I'm not mistaken, you probably don't have any hair that length."

"No, I've favored a crew cut for many years. I don't think I have a hair longer than three quarters of an inch."

"So, there is a good chance it might belong to our suspect. However, I have to tell you there's only a 10 percent chance we will be able to extract DNA from this hair."

"What?" Tom exclaimed with surprise and incredulity. "I always thought hair samples or fingernails and such were a slam dunk for DNA evidence!"

Officer Pritchard placed the hair into a small plastic evidence bag.

"It's not that simple," the officer explained. "When the root is still attached to the hair, we can usually extract enough nuclear material to produce a complete DNA profile. However, what we have here is the shaft of a hair. This is the part which extrudes outside the scalp. We do not have the root."

Officer Pritchard paused to sip his coffee while Tom looked puzzled and dismayed.

"The shaft of the hair does contain some cells," the officer continued, "and these cells do contain some DNA. However, over a period of time, these cells degenerate and die through a naturally occurring process called cornification. Once these cells die, there is no way to extract nuclear DNA. It all depends on how long the hair has been out of the scalp."

"So, it sounds like time is of the essence. Let's get this hair into the lab ASAP!" Tom urged the officers.

"Yes, you're absolutely right ... Time is key. But again, it's not that simple."

"What do you mean! You could get in your car right now and take it to the lab. We can look after my statement later!"

The officer sighed and leaned toward Tom.

"The reality is that, our lab could and does handle DNA evidence extracted from the roots of human hairs. But, to analyze cells from the shafts of human hairs, a lab requires an electron microscope and other very expensive equipment. Because the success rate of extracting such evidence is only 10 percent, it doesn't justify the investment in that kind of equipment for regular police forensic labs. Only the FBI labs have that kind of equipment. So, we have to send our evidence to the FBI and it goes into a queue which is prioritized based on urgency. I'm not sure this fifty-one-year-old case will rank very highly in that queue."

Once again, Tom's shoulders sagged. Detective Carter could feel his frustration.

"Tom, let me tell you," the detective vowed, "I will pull any marker I have and use all my contacts in the FBI to get them to give this piece of evidence the urgency it deserves. I'll call them on our way back and try to get the process started right away."

The detective turned to his colleague.

"Come on, Anthony, let's go," he ordered. "I'll meet with Tom at a later date to get his statement."

He then turned to Tom.

"Tom, I'd like you to write down everything that happened and every word that was said during your visit with Mr. Strohman. I just don't want you to forget any of the details before we can get together to take your statement."

"No problem, I'll do that."

"When are you and Mrs. Gibson leaving for Florida?"

"We leave on the thirtieth."

"Okay, today's the thirteenth, so that leaves us two weeks. That should be fine."

Tom committed to dropping by the police station the following week.

"I have to visit the house and inspect the new sunroom anyway," Tom explained.

The officers left quickly and unceremoniously. Tom called Mike Larson and arranged to meet him at the house the following Tuesday, November 17th. He also left a message on Detective Carter's office voicemail to confirm he would drop by that same afternoon to make his statement.

THE HOUSE ON RIVERDALE CIRCLE

Irene and Tom spent the weekend finalizing their packing for Florida. Although their locker on the ground floor of their condo building was a generous one hundred square feet and climate controlled, they nevertheless hauled a number of items back and forth. These included golf clubs, tennis gear, computers, and various garments and footwear. They had booked a table for four for dinner and a live jazz night at the marina. They had invited their neighbors, Julie and Don Morrow, to join them. The four of them enjoyed a wonderfully entertaining evening. Tom selected sea scallops and giant shrimp on pesto linguini as a main course while Irene picked bison rib eye. The two of them got up to dance on several occasions. Tom managed a smile now and then.

Tom got on the road on November 17th and drove straight to the house where he met the Larson brothers. It was a bright sunny day, albeit a little on the cool side. The project was nearly complete. All Tom needed to do was to confirm his choice of flooring.

"With all the windows in here, it's a very bright room," Mike Larson explained. "We wanted you to see it in person so you could determine if you wanted to stay with your original choice."

Marcia, the real estate agent, showed up as the three men were looking at various flooring samples. The four of them agreed on a dark oak floor. Marcia introduced Tom to three of the tenants who happened to be at the house; Tom would have liked to have met the others, but they were out. Afterward, Marcia and Tom went to the riverfront complex for lunch.

"You've been discreet and sensitive enough not to ask about what's going on with the police investigation," Tom whispered, "and I thank you for that."

She nodded.

"I've only read a few short pieces in the *Daily Record*. I'm glad the site has been released and the sunroom project is nearing an end. The tenants will be pleased and it will make my job easier."

"Have they been asking questions?"

"Yes, but mostly about when things might get back to normal. I think they understand that the investigation is about something that happened more than fifty years ago."

Tom wasn't sure how much he should tell Marcia. She was his frontline representative in terms of his investment in the Riverdale Circle property, but it was strictly a business arrangement and he didn't feel inclined to share any of his history in that house, although he recognized that it was entirely possible that all of it would eventually become public knowledge.

"The police tell me they have pretty well wrapped up their investigation and they won't be coming back to the house," Tom assured Marcia. "And, you heard Mike Larson tell me he'll be done with the sunroom project by the end of the week. So, as far as our tenants are concerned, things get back to normal by Friday."

"I read about their discovery of the remains of a young girl who disappeared and was murdered more than fifty years ago. Do the police have a suspect?" Marcia asked.

"Yes, I believe they have identified the perpetrator. He hasn't lived in the United States for a number of years and I suppose they're working on an extradition. It's a very sad story, but it's also a very old story. I'm ready to move on."

Tom surprised Marcia by informing her that he planned to get the housed reappraised as an income property and, depending on the appraised value, might sell it.

"Now that all the rooms are fully rented and the property generates substantial income, I think the appraisal might exceed the normal residential value," Tom suggested.

"You may be right. I'm just taken aback by this sudden turn. Are you concerned that the history of the house and the fact that a murder was committed on the property may affect the value?"

"Not at all. If the renters aren't spooked and they continue to enjoy living there and pay their rent, then there's no issue. It just boils down to business and the return on investment."

"Okay, that's great! And I'll be happy to be your listing agent on the property, if that's what you want."

"Of course, the listing will be yours. I'll call you when the appraisal is done and we can get going. We'll have to execute the listing agreement, and the eventual transaction, by fax because my wife and I will be in Florida."

"Sure, that won't be a problem."

They finished their lunch and left without much further conversation.

Tom drove to the police station where Detective Carter was anxiously waiting for him. They sat in the same interview room where, not much earlier, Tom had been grilled by the detective. It gave Tom an uneasy feeling, but he was determined to deliver his statement, and Detective Carter seemed much more pleasant and relaxed.

"You remember Barbara, our stenographer," the detective said.

She shook hands with Tom.

"She will prepare a complete transcript for you to review and sign. Also, this interview is being video recorded, as per our normal protocol," Detective Carter added.

They got down to business and Tom recounted, in minute detail, his visit with his old friend David, quoting every word his friend had spoken, and describing the emergence of Chuck. It took almost two hours to get through it all. The two men broke for coffee while the stenographer retrieved the transcript. All three went back to the interview room to review the document. Detective Carter received a call on his cell phone just as Tom signed the document.

"That's great news, Hank. I don't know how to thank you. Please call me as soon as you get the results. Bye."

The detective ended the call and placed his phone on the table.

"That was my contact at the FBI. They have agreed to analyze our hair sample for DNA evidence and they're proceeding right away," the detective announced.

"That's great news," Tom responded enthusiastically. "If they find a DNA match to the crime scene, do you think you'll be able to use it in your extradition efforts?"

"Well, let's not get ahead of ourselves. Remember what Anthony said; there's only a 10 percent chance we'll find something. If we get lucky and find some useable DNA, I'm sure we'll get a match and of course we'll use it in our extradition case. His counsel will dispute its admissibility, as we expect, but your deposition should help tie everything together."

"And when do you think all this could happen? My wife and I are heading to Florida in a few days."

"Yes, I know. Don't worry. If we are clear to proceed, there are a lot of steps and it's a painfully slow process, although, as jurisdictions go, Canada is one of the better ones, as long as we provide written confirmation that we won't be seeking the death penalty. That will be easy in our case because the state of New York has had an effective moratorium on the death penalty for many years. But, it's possible this case may not go forward until you get back. But, if it does go forward, we may ask you to fly back for a few days to testify at a hearing."

"Very well … In the end, we'll do what we have to do. I'll let Irene know. Please let me know as soon as you hear from the FBI. That will be the key."

"Of course, I will, and thank you for coming in today … And thank you, once again, for everything you have done to help bring justice for young Jennifer. Not many people would have taken the risks and made the sacrifices. You have my admiration. And, by the way, I have announced that I'm retiring from the police force. This will be my last case. The police chief and I have agreed that I'll be turning in my badge on December 31st, and then will continue to provide consultation as needed to bring this case to its conclusion."

"Wow! Congratulations … I'm glad I was able to help and be part of this case."

"Thank you. I've been at this for forty-two years, starting as a beat cop. And now, it all seems like a blur …"

"So, what are your plans? What are you going to do with your time?"

"My wife and I have decided to travel abroad for a couple of years. We've never been anywhere, so we plan to catch up. After that, we both have our little hobbies and, of course, our six grandchildren."

"Sounds wonderful. You've earned it. I wish you all the best in retirement. And on that note, I'll bid you farewell."

Both men stood up and Tom hugged the detective. Tom felt a great sense of relief and accomplishment as he made his way down to the parking level. It was after four o'clock, and he knew he would run into some outbound traffic as he drove out of the city. He called Irene from his SUV, gave her a brief update on his day, and told her he was on his way home.

"Drive safely," she said. "I'll expect you around seven or so … It doesn't matter how long it takes you. I'll have a lasagna in the oven."

Tom listened to classical music and reflected on the events of the prior few months. He realized his decisions and actions had brought stress and anxiety for himself and for Irene. But, in the end, he believed he had been right to follow his instincts and abide by the moral code that had guided him his entire adult life. He also realized that, surprisingly, he wasn't all that interested in whether or not his old friend David would ever face justice. Throughout the ordeal, he had been driven by his relentless desire to find the truth. His actions, he felt, ultimately helped to arrive at the truth. That's what mattered most.

16

Tom had had an exhausting day, and the lasagna was exactly the kind of comfort food he needed. The Tuscan Chianti helped too. Irene brought him up-to-date on the family preparations for Thanksgiving.

"The kids and grandkids will all be here by midday on Wednesday. Trevor says they understand you and I are trying to consume whatever food we have left and they don't want us buying any groceries for the holiday weekend. So the kids are bringing all the food for every meal except for Friday's dinner."

"What's happening on Friday?"

"I've booked a table for ten people at Brazill's. We have a reservation for seven o'clock."

"That will cost an arm and a leg …"

"It will be my treat. It will be our last family gathering for a while, and we won't see any of them until they come down for their visits in Naples. Besides, I feel like celebrating."

"Celebrating?"

"Yes, the kids won't know, but you and I will be marking the end of a tumultuous few months and we'll be looking forward to relaxing in Florida."

"You're right. We're turning a new leaf."

"The only thing the kids have asked is that you keep the hot tub up and running for the little ones. They know you normally like to shut it down a week before we leave, but they'd like to use it. Trevor said he's willing to stay a little longer on Sunday to help you close it down."

Tom decided to go along, although the reason he liked to shut down the hot tub earlier was to reduce the humidity level in the house before closing down the house for the winter. He had learned that, as the air in the house turned cold, it could not hold as much humidity, causing condensation and possible staining on the walls. However, at this particular time, he felt it was more important to enjoy a perfect Thanksgiving with the family; everything else seemed secondary.

"Okay, sure. While he's shutting down the tub, I can look after the plumbing and all the other items on my shutdown list. All I know is that I'd like to be on the road by seven o'clock on Monday morning. That will get us into Atlanta by seven thirty in the evening."

The following few days seemed to fly by as Tom and Irene completed their long list of outdoor chores. As they sat down for breakfast on Wednesday, the anticipation of the arrival of the kids and grandkids filled the air.

"We have so much to be thankful for," Irene reflected. "And most of all, we're so fortunate to have our grandchildren. Thanksgiving wouldn't be the same without them."

Tom nodded. Just then, the phone rang.

"It's for you. It's Detective Carter."

"Good morning, Detective," Tom said enthusiastically.

Tom listened as the detective went on at some length. Irene watched inquisitively.

"I see … That's great news. Thanks for keeping us informed … Yes, you know how to reach us if necessary … Okay … Goodbye."

"What was that all about?" Irene asked.

"He said the FBI lab was successful in extracting nuclear DNA from that single hair sample and the DNA profile is an exact match with the DNA from the crime scene. So, they have their man. But we already knew that … But now, they have the hard proof they needed."

"So, what happens now?"

"They have already notified Canadian authorities that they are formally proceeding with an extradition request. They say that David and his counsel, if he has one, will be advised today."

"What about the admissibility of the evidence?"

"Well, that will be an issue. But, this is an extradition hearing, not a trial. The standards are not necessarily the same. They feel that the physical evidence, combined with my statement, might be enough to bring him to trial in the United States. Then, of course, the normal rules of evidence would apply and they would have to get a court order to obtain a DNA sample from David. Alternatively, if they aren't granted the extradition, they hope to convince Canadian authorities to order that David submit to a DNA test."

"But, will you have to personally appear to testify at this hearing?"

"Well, there's the problem. It seems a deposition by a witness doesn't carry much weight."

"Why is that?"

"Apparently, it's because the lawyer for the accused doesn't get a chance to cross-examine the witness. In a live testimony, the lawyer gets that chance and this makes the process fairer. So, without me in attendance at the hearing, the case is much weaker, so they say."

"Well, either way, you deserve congratulations. Without you, they would never have got this far. You're my hero, even though I have to admit, I had my doubts at some point."

"Thanks. I don't see myself as a hero, but I feel good about doing the right thing. It's like a huge weight has been lifted from my shoulders. Thanks again for hanging tough with me."

The two of them hugged and sighed. It was as if each hug helped them release a little bit more of the tension that had invaded their lives.

The kids arrived on schedule and immediately got to work on lunch. It was a bright and beautiful day, but a little on the cool side. Everyone wanted to eat lunch on the terrace, so Tom fired up two propane patio heaters while Trevor and Alan cooked the burgers on the grill. It was a great way to kick off the holiday weekend.

In the afternoon, the men lit a fire in the fire pit and another in a steel drum near the garage while the grandkids scooped up the leaves Tom had blown into piles, and tossed them into the fires. Meanwhile, the ladies baked a couple of pumpkin pies and prepared a good old-fashioned Irish stew for dinner.

A cold snap moved in on November 26th, Thanksgiving Day. Delicious aromas wafted from the kitchen all day. The little ones played games and spent hours in the hot tub while the men watched football. It was a typical family holiday. At dinner, everyone got a chance to express what they were thankful for before Trevor started to carve the turkey. After dinner, Tom ran a slide show of family photos on the big flat-screen TV in the great room.

Friday started out under dense fog but turned into a bright and sunny day. Temperatures turned milder. The young ones played on their tablets while the adults slept in. Eventually, Irene got up and started panfrying some bacon which, of course, lured the rest of them out of bed. After a huge brunch, Tom led the family on a two-hour trek along the beach. It was just what everyone needed to work off those extra calories.

Tom jumped into the shower just after five o'clock and then changed into khakis and a sport jacket, setting the tone for the dress code for the evening. He began serving cocktails around six but didn't have any himself. He and Trevor's wife, Anne, had agreed to be the designated drivers for their restaurant outing. They drove to Brazill's in two vehicles. It was less than a five-minute drive, but it would have been a difficult walk with the kids on roads that didn't have sidewalks or lighting.

The staff at Brazill's was outstanding, as was the food. It was a gastronomical adventure that lasted through multiple courses. Fortunately, the parents brought the kids' tablets to keep them busy. Irene settled the check just after ten o'clock, and the family was on its way back to the house. As they pulled into the driveway, Irene screamed out: "Tom! Look, the front door is wide open! You didn't leave it open, did you?"

"No, of course not! I clearly remember closing and locking it!"

The kids got scared and began to cry.

"Stay in the car. I'll tell the others to do the same and then I'll call the police."

Tom grabbed his cell phone, got out of the car, and walked over to Trevor's car.

"Looks like we've had a break-in. Stay in the car. We don't know if they're still in there. I'm calling the police."

Tom dialed 911 and reported what was happening.

"We have our kids and grandkids with us. We don't know if they're still in there. This could be a live situation."

Tom walked back to his SUV, got into the driver's seat, and locked the doors.

"They have a patrol car less than two minutes away. Another one will be here shortly after. They want us to stay put."

The first police car arrived, and Tom got out of the vehicle to meet the officer.

"Please stay right here until we check inside," the officer instructed as the second police car arrived. Two officers got out of the second car. One of them went into the house with the officer in charge. The other was told to check the perimeter of the house.

It took ten minutes for the officers to emerge from the house and link up with the third officer. One of them walked up to Tom.

"The house is secure, sir. Whoever it was is gone. You can go in, but we ask you not to touch anything. A crime lab technician is on his way. They want to dust for prints and determine if this break-in is linked to a home invasion and assault that took place across town last month. In the meantime, we need you to draw up a list of anything that's missing."

"Okay, Officer, but our first priority is to get the little ones to bed."

"Of course, go ahead, sir."

Tom gave instructions to the rest of the family, and they all went about their business. The officers and Tom examined the front door. The lock bolt socket and the wooden doorjamb had been blown out, either by a massive kick or some kind of ramming device. The damage on the door, near the handle, suggested it was some kind of ram.

"Was the alarm system armed?" the officer asked Tom.

"No, we only arm the system when we're away for an extended period of time."

A state police van showed up about twenty minutes later. An officer got out carrying what looked like a suitcase. Tom and Irene started to scope the house to see what might have been stolen. They started on the main floor. Surprisingly, it appeared nothing had been touched.

"Maybe they were targeting something specific," Tom suggested. Let's go check the master bedroom. Maybe they wanted jewelry."

Irene had a large jewelry box which sat on top of her dresser. While most of her jewelry was relatively inexpensive, she did have an antique broach, a diamond necklace, and a diamond ring that were each worth in excess of $10,000.

"I don't think anything is missing," she declared as Tom walked to his bedside table to check his watch collection.

"Oh my God, look!" Tom exclaimed as he pointed at the bed. Irene screamed.

One of her black nightgowns was neatly stretched out across the bed. They both knew it wasn't there when they left for the restaurant. They were stunned and scared.

"Who would do this? And why?" she whispered is dismay. "It's so creepy! I feel so helpless and, I don't know … violated in a way …"

Tom walked up to her and hugged her.

"It's probably just teenagers out on a crime spree. Maybe they're on drugs," Tom whispered as he tried to reassure her. "Let's go downstairs."

Tom explained to the lead officer what they had just found in their bedroom and confirmed that nothing seemed to be missing.

"All right, sir. I'll need you to show us where the nightgown is normally kept so we can dust the area for prints."

Tom led them upstairs and pointed to the door of Irene's walk-in closet.

"Is this closet door normally kept closed?" the officer asked Tom.

"Yes, and I know both closet doors were closed when we left for the restaurant."

THE HOUSE ON RIVERDALE CIRCLE

The lab technician dusted the door frame and the handle. He flipped down his magnifying glasses, pointed his flashlight, and examined the area closely. He shook his head.

"This whole area of the door has been wiped clean," he said. "There are no prints at all, not even from the occupants. We found the same thing with the front door."

"Very strange," the lead officer responded. "We have a break-in, a front-door entry using a ramming device, prints wiped clean … It has all the markings of a professional MO and yet, nothing is missing."

"The only room I haven't checked yet is my office," Tom stated. "But there really isn't anything of value in there, other than my laptop and tablet. But, I'll go check anyway."

"Please check your files for any important papers, sir. It's possible they weren't looking for valuables at all."

Tom went downstairs into his office. He cringed as soon as he looked at his desk. His heart rate jumped, and he had to rest one hand on his filing cabinet to steady himself. Everything in his office looked perfectly normal, everything except one item in the middle of the inset leather working surface. It was a Scotch tape dispenser. Not any dispenser; it was the one he had picked up at David's home and used to lift latent fingerprints from the brush handle. Tom recalled very vividly he had placed it in the middle drawer of the desk, beside his passport. And yet, there it was. Someone had opened the drawer, removed the tape dispenser, and placed it on the desk in plain sight.

"Oh my God," he whispered. "It was David, or more likely Chuck."

He understood right away why nothing was missing. He realized that the break-in was intended as a very forceful message of intimidation. He chose not to say anything to the officers. Instead, after the investigating team left, he called Detective Carter's cell phone and left him a message. It was after midnight, and he didn't expect to hear back until morning.

Tom asked Trevor and Christine how the grandkids were doing.

"They're fine," Trevor replied. "They're all asleep."

"Okay, good. Now let's secure the front door. For now, I just want to hold the door closed by using a two-by-four with four-inch crews into the upper part of the door frame."

After securing the front door, Tom suggested everyone go to bed. Once they were alone in the master bedroom, Tom and Irene sat on the edge of the bed. Tom explained what he thought was going on.

"Placing that tape dispenser on my desk was a very clear message. A written threatening note couldn't have been clearer."

"My God! Did you tell the police?"

"No, but I left a message with Detective Carter."

"This is hitting way too close to home. I don't want to expose our family to any danger. We need to get the hell out of here. I mean it! And you have already made your deposition. You can't take it back. What does he want?"

"I'm the only one he has admitted his crime to, and he probably understood why his Scotch tape dispenser was missing. He seemed to be quite familiar with extradition requirements. Maybe he knows that, eventually, they will need my live testimony in order to make their case for extradition. He's telling me to stay out of it."

"What are you going to do?"

"I don't know. All I know is that I don't want to put my family in danger. I'll need to speak with Detective Carter. Dealing with David is one thing … But Chuck, he's downright scary. I don't know what he's capable of."

"We'll have to get that door fixed. But I want to leave for Florida right now!"

"I know. I want to get out of here too. I can get a carpenter in here to fix the door and reinforce the frame. It might not happen for a few days but … looks like the lock is still fine. I can disarm and rearm the alarm system remotely from my cell phone. So, I think we should go as we planned."

"Good."

Tom and Irene hugged and kissed and then got into bed. Neither of them got any sleep. They got up just after seven o'clock and started preparing breakfast. Everyone was up by eight. At the breakfast table, Tom tried to reassure everyone that the break-in was likely an isolated incident but also suggested that, in an abundance of caution, they should consider packing up and going home after lunch. The grandkids were disappointed but the parents agreed.

"I'll get working on shutting down the hot tub right away," Trevor stated.

"Thanks, son. I'll get the compressor out so we can blow out the jets."

The house was quiet by two o'clock. Tom called the handyman who had helped him on previous occasions. He explained the situation, and Gerald agreed to drop by after running a couple of errands. Tom was pleased to see him pull up in the driveway just before four o'clock. Tom went outside to greet him.

"Hi, Gerald. Thanks so much for responding so quickly."

"No problem, Mr. Gibson. I was sorry to hear you and your wife were the victims of a break-in. It's usually so safe around here. But now, I don't know … First, there was that home invasion last month at Dr. McFadden's … He got stabbed, you know … And now this! I don't know what's happening but I don't like it … Did they get away with a lot?"

"No, not really, it's just the idea of strangers coming into our home …"

Tom didn't want to get into any details about what happened. Gerald was a very nice man and an excellent carpenter, but he was a bit of a gossip machine, and the last thing Tom wanted was a flurry of stories and speculation running around the neighborhood.

The men entered the house through one of the patio doors, and Tom showed Gerald the damage that had been done to the front door and frame.

"That must have been a mighty blow," Gerald commented as Irene came into the foyer to greet him. "Hi, Mrs. Gibson, I'm sorry for all this. But don't worry, I'll have it fixed in no time."

"I'm sure you will, and I'm not worried. We're leaving on Monday anyway and it will be nice to get away."

"That's right, Gerald. I forgot to mention we'll be leaving for Florida early Monday morning. I'll leave you a key for the side door and you can go in and out that way. I won't arm the alarm system until you're done."

Gerald pointed at the door frame.

"In order to prevent anything like this in the future, I think I'd like to install a new frame and brace it to a metal stud with two feet of steel plating where the lock bolt socket is, right here. All of it will be hidden behind a new and wider molding around the door frame."

"Sounds good to me. What about the door itself?"

"Well, this is a metal-coated door and you can see where it got slightly bent below the handle. That means it won't fit tightly against the weather strip on the frame. I'll bet there's a big dent on the outside."

"Yes, that's right."

"So, the bad news is that it can't be fixed. We need to replace the door. And, this is not a standard door. It's wider and taller. You must have ordered it from a custom door manufacturer."

"Yes, our builder recommended it. I still have the paperwork."

"So, I can't get the materials to rebuild the frame until Monday. Then, it will take me two days to get the work done. The door is another matter altogether. We can keep using this door until the new one comes in; it just won't have a perfect seal."

"Sounds good."

"In terms of cost, we're probably looking at a couple of hundred for the materials, plus five hundred for two days of labor. I have no idea what the door will cost."

"Don't worry about it. I think it was about three thousand originally. I'll get the paperwork out for you right now."

Tom went into his office, pulled a file from his filing cabinet, and pulled out a flyer and order slip. He made a photocopy and highlighted the model number of their door and the specifications.

"Here you go. That's the door supplier and door specs. And here's a card with all our contact information, including our place in Naples. Oh, and here are spare keys for the front and side doors."

The men shook hands, and Tom accompanied Gerald out to his truck. As the handyman pulled away, something frightful flashed through Tom's mind. He remembered that David had kept one of his cards with all his contact information.

"How stupid I was," he whispered to himself, realizing he and Irene would be no safer in their condo in Naples.

They had no alarm system in the condo. It was in a secure building with a gated parking lot, but anyone walking up the beach could gain access. Worse yet, he and Irene normally slept with the sliding door open, allowing the breeze off the gulf to come into the master bedroom, leaving the screened door as their only defense. Tom understood that some things were going to have to change, at least until David was apprehended. The tricky part was going to be to pay more attention to security without scaring the hell out of Irene.

Irene warmed up some leftovers for dinner.

"Are you going to file an insurance claim?" she asked as they sipped their wine.

"Yes, we're probably looking at a repair cost of at least $4,000, and our deductible is $1,000, so yes, I think I should file a claim. I'll call them while we're on the road on Monday and I'll give them Gerald's cell number so he can give their adjuster access."

They spent the evening reading in the great room and were both yawning by ten o'clock. They went to bed and enjoyed a better sleep than they had the previous night.

On Sunday, Tom loaded up the SUV with everything they were bringing to Naples. The rest of the day was spent winterizing the house. The task was somewhat simplified by the fact that, at Tom's insistence, the builder had installed hot and cold water manifolds in the basement, with individual water lines with drain-back valves for each sink, shower, toilet, and other water appliances throughout the house. Tom shut off and drained all pipes except for the kitchen and master en suite. After dinner, which consisted of more leftovers from their Thanksgiving dinner, Irene ran the dishwasher one last time. Afterward, Tom drained the lines that served the kitchen and poured RV antifreeze into all the drains and toilet bowls and tanks throughout the house.

On Monday morning, they were both up and going by five o'clock. After their showers, Tom winterized the master en suite plumbing and they were on the road by six. They stopped for breakfast about an hour into their trip. Tom called his insurance agent just after nine o'clock and got the claims process started. A few minutes later, his phone rang. It was Detective Carter. Tom described the whole break-in event and explained why he was sure it was David.

"I don't think he wants to harm us," Tom stated, "but he has gone through a lot of trouble to give us a blunt message."

"Yes," the detective agreed, "and we're not sure if we're dealing with David or Chuck. And, at this point, Chuck is an unknown. We really don't know what he's capable of. Where are you now?"

"Irene and I are on our way to Naples."

"Okay, good. That will make it easier for us to keep you two out of harm's way."

With Irene sitting beside him, Tom didn't want to admit to the detective that he had given David his card which contained all of his contact information, including their location in Florida. He knew he would have to make that fact clear to Detective Carter at the earliest opportunity; perhaps at their next stop.

"Did you say anything about this to the local police?" the detective asked.

"No, I didn't want to get into it with them. As far as they're concerned, it was just a break-in with no obvious explanation as to why nothing was apparently taken. Their theory is that we got back to the house before the robbers had a chance to round up any valuables."

"Did you mention to the officers about the tape dispenser?"

"No, again, for the same reason."

"Okay, I'm bringing the FBI into it. They'll find out pretty quickly if our guy crossed the border. I'll let you know as soon as I find out."

The call ended with Tom and Irene feeling apprehensive about the situation. A couple of hours later, Irene wanted to take a bio break so Tom pulled into a rest area. As soon as she got out of the vehicle, Tom called Detective Carter. He got his voicemail. He explained how David was fully aware of their location in Florida. He also explained that David likely didn't have any way of knowing when he and Irene were headed that way. After the call, he felt relieved that everyone was working from the same information, except of course the local police. Tom felt it was now Detective Carter's responsibility, or the FBI's, to decide what information to share with local authorities.

It seemed Tom was on the phone for much of the rest of the trip. He spoke to Gerald twice, the insurance agent, the insurance adjuster, and the Four Seasons Hotel in Atlanta, where they eventually pulled in a little after seven thirty in the evening. They checked in, freshened up, and went down to one of their favorite dining spots, Bar Margot. They loved it because it offered fine cuisine in smaller portions where they could sample a number of dishes, all in a relaxed bar atmosphere. They were back in their suite just after eleven o'clock and were fast asleep.

17

Tuesday morning, Tom slipped out of bed around seven o'clock and went out for a walk while Irene showered. He was back thirty minutes later and had his own shower. They had a light breakfast and started the final leg of their trip. It usually took them about ten hours to get from Atlanta to Naples. It was December 1st, and it was a bright and warm morning. The weather forecast for their journey was clear and warm all the way.

Tom's phone rang a little after nine o'clock. It was Detective Carter. He introduced FBI agent Mark Hanson who was at his side. The agent informed Tom that David Strohman's passport had indeed been scanned by a border officer at the Buffalo border station at 1:17 p.m. on Friday. They were waiting for a response from the Canadian border authorities to determine if and when he had crossed back into Canada. Their voices were loud and clear over the stereo speakers of the SUV, so Irene heard every word.

"So, it looks like you were absolutely right, Tom," the detective stated. "It had to be David who broke into your house."

"I never had a doubt," Tom responded. "As soon as I saw that tape dispenser on my desk, I knew it was him. He was sending me a message. The only thing I'm still scratching my head about is the nightgown. What was that all about?"

"It looks like it was meant to amplify the intimidation effect. He was letting you know that you need to worry about your family's well-being, in addition to your own. It doesn't mean he is necessarily capable of bringing any harm to you or your family, but it's possible he has concluded he has nothing to lose. And we have to be mindful of the psychotic element. David may not be capable of violence, but it certainly appears that Chuck could be a whole other story. So we need to assume he poses an immediate threat."

"So, what should Irene and I do?" Tom asked.

Tom heard the two officers chatting in the background.

"I can't hear what you're saying," Tom commented.

"Sorry, Tom," answered the detective. "We were just confirming what we want to do. I'll let Agent Hanson tell you where we go from here because he's the one who will be in charge."

"Right, so you and your wife don't have to do anything right now," suggested the agent. "As soon as I hear back from the Canadian authorities, I will be in touch with you. If he has gone back into Canada, we will alert our border agents to nab him if his passport is scanned at any border crossing into the United States. However, if he hasn't gone back to Canada, we will immediately implement a protection plan. We'll provide you with the details of that plan if and when we get to that point."

Tom looked briefly at Irene and whispered, "Are you okay with all of this, dear?"

She nodded.

"Very well, gentlemen. We're fine with everything. We'll just wait for your call and go from there."

The call ended on that note. Tom and Irene both felt some anxiety about the situation.

"I don't think I'll be able to relax until we hear that he's gone back to Canada," Irene admitted.

"I feel the same way."

The rest of the trip was quiet and uneventful. Tom was hoping to get a call from Agent Hanson before they got to Naples. It didn't happen. They got into their condo by dinnertime. After unloading the SUV, they decided they were too tired to shop for groceries, so they walked to one of their favorite nearby restaurants for dinner. Along the half-mile walk, they noticed a number of vehicles bearing Ontario license plates. There was nothing unusual about that, but given the circumstances in which they found themselves, every one they spotted made them wonder if it belonged to David.

They both chose grilled red grouper in a beurre blanc sauce for their main course and washed it down with a Napa Valley pinot noir.

"This is delicious," Irene whispered, "but I have to admit … All this tension has spoiled my appetite. But I'm glad we're down here. I hope we'll be safe …"

Tom's cell phone rang before he could comment. It was Agent Hanson.

"We have heard back from the Canadian authorities. David Strohman has not returned to Canada. So, he is still in the United States and poses an immediate danger. We are implementing our protection plan."

Irene couldn't hear what the agent was saying. She didn't need to. She could see Tom's concern in his facial expression.

"We also know that he's not driving his own car," the agent continued. "We know that he picked up a rental car at the Hertz location at the airport in Kingston, Ontario. That's the nearest municipality to his home. The vehicle is a silver-colored 2015 Ford Fusion bearing an Ontario tag number DFLN 864. We have an APB out for this car along the entire eastern seaboard."

There was a pause while Tom digested this new information.

"Where are you right now?" the agent asked. "Are you and your wife in your condo?"

"No, we're at a restaurant."

"Which restaurant?" the agent continued.

"We're at the Turtle Club restaurant on Gulf Shore Drive."

"Okay, stay there. I'm sending Agent Fielding to meet you. He'll send you a text when he arrives at the restaurant. He will escort you back to your condo. I would like you to pack a few things, enough for two or three days. Agent Fielding will take you to a hotel. You two will need to lay low for a little while and let us take this situation to its conclusion. Do you have any questions?"

"No, we'll sit tight and finish our wine."

Tom relayed to Irene what he had just learned from Agent Hanson and explained the next steps in the protection plan.

"Where did they book us a room?" she asked. "I hope they didn't pick some seedy motel."

"I don't care what they booked; we're not going there. I'm going to call the Ritz right now and book a suite," Tom whispered in an attempt to be discreet.

Tom tapped the Google icon on his phone. He keyed in the Ritz Carlton on Gulf Shore Drive and then called the number on the listing. He had no problem making a reservation.

"It's not going to be cheap," he whispered. "But I'm sure you'll like it. We can think of it as a second honeymoon."

"Well, after all, our fortieth anniversary is coming up in June."

They sipped the last of their wine, and a few minutes later, Tom received a text message from Agent Fielding.

"Okay, he's waiting for us at the front door."

Tom settled their bill, and they walked out to meet the agent. He was wearing his FBI badge but didn't need to. His appearance made it obvious. They shook hands.

"Follow me, please," he asked.

They climbed aboard his black Yukon SUV with dark tinted windows. It was a two-minute drive to the condo. Tom gave the agent the gate code, and they proceeded into the covered parking area and up to the main entrance of the building.

"We're in 104," Tom stated.

"Yes, sir. I know," the agent responded.

Tom unlocked the condo door and gestured to Irene to enter.

"Just a moment, please," the agent intervened. "Please wait here while I make sure the place is secure."

The agent walked in with his flashlight in hand. He returned a couple of minutes later.

"All clear, come on in," he said.

"I don't know if your agency has already booked a room somewhere," Tom stated, "but I've taken the liberty of reserving a suite at the Ritz Carlton. It's almost next door to the restaurant we just came from."

"I don't think that hotel is on our FBI-approved list," the agent responded. "The protocol in these situations calls for me to stay in the room beside yours in a hotel or motel where we have preapproved rates. The agency would never agree to pay for two expensive rooms in a luxury hotel."

"That's okay. This suite has a guest room. You can stay there. You'll have your own bathroom and this arrangement will be even more secure than adjoining rooms, and, I'm paying for it. It won't cost the FBI a nickel."

"Very well, sir, as you wish. Please round up what you need. I'd like to be out of here in five minutes."

After packing a few items, Tom and Irene followed the agent back out to the Yukon, and the three of them pulled up to the reception area of the Ritz Carlton where they were warmly received by the doorman and bell captain. Check-in was fast and easy. The assistant manager of the hotel escorted them to the suite.

"This elevator is dedicated to the royal suites on the penthouse floor," the assistant manager explained as they walked into the oak-paneled elevator. "Yours is the Club Two-Bedroom Royal Suite. You simply insert your key card here and press either Penthouse Level to go up to your suite, or Lobby Level to go back down."

The elevator door opened into a large foyer. They walked to their suite entrance where the assistant manager opened the door and invited his guests to step inside. As suites go, it was quite impressive, even for Tom and Irene who had seen their share of luxury suites. Tom felt justified in paying the price as a way to alleviate the stress for Irene. The assistant manager walked through the living room and opened a set of French doors.

"This is your own private terrace where you'll find your own hot tub and outdoor dining area."

There was a teak table surrounded by eight chairs under a thatched roof along with a tiki bar. Another thatched roof covered the hot tub. The views were spectacular.

"Here are your key cards and my business card. Please call me if you need anything at all," said the assistant manager as he bowed and left.

The Gibsons settled into their master bedroom while Agent Fielding went into the guest room to place some calls. It was late. Tom and Irene were exhausted. They went straight to bed and slept soundly in spite of the emotional highs and lows.

Tom woke up just before eight o'clock in the morning. Irene was starting to stir. Normally, in such glamorous surroundings, the two of them would engage in an amorous interlude. But the fact that an FBI agent was watching over them from the guest room dampened the mood. Tom got up and went out to the terrace where he slid into the hot tub. He came back into the suite and showered and shaved.

"Oh shit!" he shouted.

"What's wrong?" Irene shouted back from the bedroom.

"I forgot to pack my blood pressure medicine. It's still in the condo."

"Oh, no, what are you going to do?"

"Let's order up some breakfast and then I'll have to go back to the condo."

Tom walked to the guest room and knocked on the door. There was no answer. Tom opened the door. The agent wasn't there. The bed was made and the agent's knapsack was there. At that moment, the agent walked into the suite holding a large thermos. The aroma of strong coffee wafted into the suite.

"Good morning, sir!" the agent said cheerfully. "Did you have a good sleep?"

"Yes, yes, we had a great sleep … But we have a small problem.

Tom explained about the need to go pick up his medication at the condo.

"No problem, sir. I'll take you back there as soon as you're ready. Your wife will have to stay here behind locked doors while she's on her own."

"Okay, that's great. We'll just order up a bit of breakfast and I'll be ready to go."

Irene ordered a full breakfast that featured eggs Benedict. Tom had a bagel and coffee. Agent Fielding inspected the room service attendant before allowing him into the suite. They ate on the terrace.

It was a bright sunny day with a steady offshore breeze. It wasn't nine o'clock yet, and the temperature was already past eighty degrees.

The agent and Tom went back to the condo. As Tom unlocked the door and pushed it open, he felt some resistance and then a gush of air blew past them and into the hallway.

"Something's wrong! That's a cross draft!" Tom exclaimed. "One of the sliding doors on the gulf side must be open!"

"Stay here," the agent ordered as he walked past Tom into the condo.

He came back a few moments later.

"All clear, you can come in!"

The two men walked into the master bedroom where the curtains were fluttering in the wind. Agent Fielding examined the wide-open sliding door while Tom cringed at the sight of one of Irene's nightgowns stretched across the bed.

"It's him! That's his MO!" Tom shouted as he pointed at the gown. "That's what he did when he broke into our home."

"Look here," said the agent as he pointed at the door frame. "He used a pry bar to force open the door and snap the door latch apart."

"Didn't your guys keep a watch on this place? How could this happen right under their nose?"

"Yes, of course. We have a car out on the street. They were watching for any incoming or outgoing traffic. This guy must have walked up from the beach. I'll get the lab guys over here to dust for prints."

"It will probably be a waste of time. He wipes down everything."

"We still have to follow protocol. And we'll have to check the building security cameras."

The agent called his office and reported the new developments while Tom retrieved his medicine from the master bathroom. They were back in the hotel suite ten minutes later. Tom reluctantly wanted to bring Irene up-to-date.

"Irene! I hate to tell you this, but we had a break-in at the condo!"

There was no answer. Tom looked in the master bedroom and in the en suite.

"She's not here!" he exclaimed.

"I'll check the terrace," Agent Fielding said as he pulled open one of the French doors.

He came back into the condo and shrugged his shoulders.

"Goddamn it!" Tom shouted in frustration. "He's playing us like a fiddle!"

"We don't know if he's got anything to do with this, at least not yet."

"I'll call her on her cell phone," Tom suggested.

He called up the directory on his cell phone and called Irene. They immediately heard the ring in the master bedroom. They ran in and found Irene's purse on her night table.

"I don't like this," Tom admitted with a sense of panic. "She rarely goes anywhere without her purse."

The agent called his partner who was on watch in the lobby of the hotel. Tom listened attentively as the men spoke. A few moments later, the room phone rang.

"Is this Tom Gibson?" the voice asked.

Tom held the phone slightly away from his ear and signaled to the agent to come and listen.

"David, you son of a bitch, where's my wife? What have you done with her?"

"It's not David. And you need to calm down and listen, Tom," the voice continued. "Your wife is fine. Irene is on her way back up to your room."

Hearing Chuck refer to her by her name was chilling for Tom. He had never mentioned her name in any conversation with David.

"So, yes, she'll be safely back in your arms in a few moments. But, it could have turned out very differently. Thanks to my little visit at your house last Friday, I know a lot about you and your family. You have a very nice family, but you're all very vulnerable. So you need to take this as a warning. Listen very carefully. There's going to be a hearing before a federal judge on February 11th. You need to stay away. You have nothing to gain by going there and testifying. And they can't make you do it. So be smart and stay away."

Tom and Agent Fielding heard a click, and that was it. He had hung up. Before they had a chance to react to what they had just heard, the door opened and Irene walked in, holding a key card in her hand.

"Irene! Where were you?" Tom exclaimed in a tone that betrayed his frustration. "Why did you leave the suite? We were so worried about you!"

"I got a call from Agent McInnis. He asked me to join a meeting with you and the security team. He said you were meeting just outside the entrance to the spa. So I went down there and waited. I didn't recognize anybody. Then a bellhop came to me and handed me a message saying the meeting would have to be rescheduled. So I came back up."

"Mrs. Gibson, I hate to tell you this, but there is no Agent McInnis. You were tricked. You were in danger."

"He was here ..." Tom added calmly. "David was here. He's the one who impersonated an FBI agent and asked you to come down to the spa. And, our condo has been broken into. Just like the break-in at our house, he took nothing but he laid out one of your nightgowns across the bed."

"This whole thing is turning into a nightmare! Can't you guys do something?" she asked as she turned to Agent Fielding. "Why haven't you nabbed this guy? He's been right under your nose, for heaven's sake!"

Her fear and frustration were evident. Tom hugged her.

"They're going to tighten the security detail," Tom whispered. "We'll be okay. These are just scare tactics. He wants to intimidate us so I won't testify."

Tom chose not to mention that David had just called, at least not yet. He felt Irene was too fragile to hear how brazen he, or rather Chuck, had become.

"I'm going to go to the hardware store and pick up a new lock for the sliding door in the condo," Tom announced. "I have to get that door fixed today."

"I'm going with you," Irene quickly replied. "I need to get out of here for a while."

"You should also pick up some pieces of wood to insert in the door tracks so, even if someone breaks the lock, they won't be able to slide the door open," Agent Fielding suggested.

"Yes, you're right. I should have done that long ago," Tom agreed. "I'll have to drop by the condo first and measure the lengths I'll need for both sliding doors."

"Maybe you should also get some pieces that are just a bit shorter so we can leave the doors slightly open at night and still be safe," Irene suggested.

"Good idea. That way, we can still enjoy that offshore breeze at night."

"You two go ahead. I'll have an agent stay fairly close to you without getting in your way. Meanwhile, we're going to recalibrate our team."

"You know, Agent Fielding," Tom commented, "it might be a lot easier for you and your team to do your job if we just go back and stay in the condo. You won't be as spread out because it's a much smaller area to cover, and Irene and I will be happier."

"I'd like that," Irene added.

"It's entirely up to you," replied the agent. "We can't force you to do anything you don't want to do. We'll reset our protection plan with the assumption you're moving back into your condo today. Do you want us to drive you there?"

"No thanks. It's a short walk. We'll be fine."

By late afternoon, Tom and Irene had restocked the condo, Tom had fixed the lock on the sliding door, and sawed a one-inch diameter doweling to the appropriate lengths to secure the sliding doors. The FBI had installed two webcams, one on a flagpole on the beach side and one in the main corridor of the building. Two agents were posted in a vehicle outside the condo building at all times.

18

On December 4th, Tom installed a new tap in the kitchen sink. He was turning the water pressure back on to test it when the phone rang. It was Agent Fielding.

"Good afternoon, sir!" He sounded quite cheerful. "This is Agent Fielding."

"Yes, I recognize your voice, Agent."

"I have very good news for you, sir. We have confirmation that our suspect has crossed back into Canada. And, because we have flagged his passport, if he tries to come back into the United States, border agents will arrest him immediately."

"I thought you were going to say that you got him. That would have been really good news. But, I guess this is good enough. It will give us some peace of mind. Thanks."

"So, it also means we will be lifting our protective detail. You and your wife will be on your own, but, I am still on the case and will remain your contact point with the FBI here in Naples. Agent Hanson will remain in charge overall. Are you okay with all of that?"

"Yes, that's fine. I'll let Irene know. She'll be relieved."

Irene was out on the patio, reading the *Naples Daily News*, when Tom broke the news to her.

"Oh, thank God. Does that mean we can resume our normal life? Can I call the tennis club and ask them to set up some matches for us?"

"Yes, absolutely!"

While Tom appreciated the prospect of this welcome tranquility, he realized he had an important and difficult decision ahead of him. For the next few weeks, life would seem normal on the surface while a battle of sorts would be raging in his mind.

The Gibsons spent the following two weeks getting reacquainted with their winter friends, playing tennis, walking the beach, and dining out at their favorite eateries, some of which featured live entertainment. They flew back north and stayed with their daughter, Christine, her husband, and the three boys over Christmas. Trevor and his family joined them for dinner on Christmas Day. Tom and Irene were back in Naples by January 4th.

The call which Tom had dreaded came on January 6th. It was a beautiful and warm morning. He and Irene had just returned from the tennis club. Irene answered after a couple of rings. Seeing the expression on her face, Tom knew who was calling.

"It's for you, Tom. It's Detective Carter."

"Hello, Tom here!"

The detective engaged in some small talk for a few minutes, asking about the family, Christmas, and the weather. He wished Tom and his family a happy new year.

"Happy new year to you too, Detective," Tom responded.

Carter then turned to the business at hand. "Tom, I'm sitting here with the prosecuting attorney on the case. His name is Robert Stearns. We're on the speakerphone in his office, given that I don't have an office anymore."

"Good day, sir," exclaimed the attorney.

"Hi to both of you! And yes, you're retired now, aren't you, Detective?"

"Yes but, other than the fact I don't have an office, a badge, or a gun, my work schedule hasn't changed a bit."

He sighed.

"Tom," the detective continued, "I've been in constant contact with Agent Fielding of the FBI and we're well aware of what went on there. We're very sorry we failed to prevent that sordid business. Hopefully we can bring all this to its rightful conclusion very soon."

"That would be very much appreciated," Tom conceded.

"On that note, I wanted to share our plans with you and tell you where we are in the process."

"When he made that threatening call," Tom intervened, "David said something about a hearing on February 11th."

"That's right, Tom," the attorney confirmed. "There is an extradition hearing before a federal judge in Ottawa, Canada's capital, at eleven o'clock in the morning on February 11th. This is the second step in a three-step process, and the only step that involves live testimony."

"And, I'm assuming you want me there to testify in person," Tom stated.

"Yes, of course, that would be ideal," the attorney admitted. "But you don't have to make that decision right now. What we would like to do is this: we would like to meet with you here on February 9th and outline our case and our options to you and examine the likely outcomes. Then, and only then, you can mull it over and decide if you want to accompany us to Ottawa for the hearing."

"Would you be willing to do that, Tom?" asked Detective Carter.

"I don't know. I'll have to discuss it with Irene and get back to you. How about I call you by end of day tomorrow?"

"Sure, Tom," the detective agreed. "That will be fine. By the way, I still have the same cell phone and that's how you can reach me from now on."

The call ended, and Tom invited Irene to join him for a walk along the beach. He conveyed the pressure he was getting from Detective Carter and the prosecuting attorney.

"They want me to attend a briefing at the prosecutor's office on February 9th and then decide if I want to accompany them to the extradition hearing in Canada on the 11th."

"I'm sure you realize they're going to use that briefing to browbeat you until you give in. As far as I'm concerned, I think you've already gone way beyond your civic duty ... And, after what we went through, I'm not confident our law enforcement people can do a good job of keeping us safe from this person who seems to have become some kind of madman."

"Yeah, I can't say I blame you for feeling that way."

"And what if he decided to go after our kids or grandkids?"

"I know. We can't let that happen. I think I'll sleep on it tonight and call them tomorrow to let them know I've done as much as I can. They have my detailed deposition. It will have to do ..."

"Didn't you tell me that live testimony is considered much more powerful because it gives the defending attorney an opportunity to cross-examine?"

"Yes, that's my understanding. But I don't know what other evidence they have, or how heavily their case relies on my testimony. I guess that's what they propose to discuss at the February 9th meeting they want me to attend."

They stopped for a drink at the patio bar at the Turtle Club. It was a popular spot where people gathered to watch the sunset. They recognized some of their friends from the condo building and from the tennis club. They waved at them, but Tom was not inclined to join them because he didn't feel up to socializing. The sun disappeared into the gulf waters at exactly 5:51 p.m. Tom and Irene walked home in the dark and got to work on dinner. They shared a thick cut of New York strip loin and two Alaska king crab legs, all prepared on the grill. They enjoyed their candlelight dinner in the lanai.

Tom slept sporadically that night, torn between his sense of duty and his desire to keep his family safe. He finally concluded his family took precedence, but it didn't do anything to appease his conscience. He dozed off occasionally, only to wake up a few minutes later. Just after sunrise, he decided to get up and take a walk on the beach. Irene was still sleeping soundly. As he walked by the pool, he saw a shadow in the water. He walked up to the edge of the pool, and his heart began pounding.

"Oh, my God!" he shouted as he jumped into the pool to retrieve a young girl floating facedown in the shallow end of the pool.

He was panting. As soon as he got to her, he flipped her over so as to get her face out of the water. He screamed, "Oh, Geena, No! It can't be! Geena!"

He grabbed her in his arms and rushed to the stairs at the corner of the pool. He climbed out of the pool and set her body down on the pool deck. He didn't know if he should get his phone to call 911 or start CPR. He decided that every second counted so he should administer CPR.

"Irene!" he shouted as loud as he could. "Irene, get out here!"

He saw a few lights come on in the building.

He was kneeling beside Geena. He leaned over her with his hands crossed over her chest and began pumping rhythmically while he counted, just as he had been trained to do in the CPR class he had taken at the tennis club at home.

"One, two, three, four …"

He looked up and prayed to God to let her come to and breathe again. His eyes had welled up so much he could hardly see. He shouted for Irene again. More lights came on. As he looked down, Geena's face turned gray and gaunt. Her chest suddenly became soft and brittle and collapsed under the pressure of his hands. He screamed.

"Wake up! Wake up! Honey, wake up!" Irene yelled at him. "You're having a nightmare! Wake up, Tom!"

He opened his eyes. He was crying. The relief he felt as he realized it was a nightmare was not quite enough to overcome the emotions he had felt as he thought they were losing their granddaughter. His heart was still pounding. It took several minutes for him to settle down.

The doorbell rang. Irene threw on a bathrobe and walked to the door, opening it up just a crack while leaving the safety chain on. She was even more cautious than usual. It was their next-door neighbor wanting to know if they needed help.

"Is everything okay in there? Are you all right? Do you need help?" he asked.

"No, no, Lorne. Thanks. Tom had a nightmare. He's fine now. Thank you."

She went back to the bedroom. Tom was in the washroom, splashing water in his face.

"I'm so sorry," he said.

He described what had happened in his nightmare.

"It was Geena, our granddaughter!" he exclaimed. "It was so horrible. She drowned in the pool and I was trying to resuscitate her while I called for you! But then … After a while, it wasn't Geena. It was that young girl, the one David murdered! My hands went right through her chest!"

"Thank God it was only a dream …"

There was a pause while the two of them mulled over the same thought; was Tom's nightmare triggered by a sense of guilt for deciding not to testify at the hearing, or was it driven by fear for the safety of his family?

"I haven't had a nightmare or vision for a long time. I thought I was done with them. I thought that finding the truth was enough for me to have a clear conscience. Why this nightmare, and why now?"

"I remember you saying that a pattern seemed to have emerged where, whenever you stepped away from the case, the nightmares came back. Perhaps, subconsciously, you feel you haven't quite done everything you can to bring this case to a just conclusion."

"You may be right. But, how could I justify putting my family in danger just to avoid future nightmares?"

"Listen, I don't want to imperil our kids and grandkids either, but if I were you, I would look at it differently. The justification for seeing the case through this final step, the only justification that makes sense, is to help bring justice for that helpless young girl, and, to put this murderer away for good so we never again have to feel threatened. I think I've changed my opinion on what you should do. I think you should go, but it's ultimately up to you."

"You're so right ... And you're so smart. I'm going to call Detective Carter and tell him I'll go up there and meet with them on February 9th."

Tom had a tennis match scheduled for eleven o'clock in the morning. He dropped Irene off at the hair salon on the way. He played well and stayed focused throughout the match. He got a call on his cell phone as he sat at the juice bar with his fellow players. It was Irene.

"Hi, honey, I just wanted to let you know that I walked home and you don't have to hurry back to pick me up."

"Okay, great. So, I think I'll stay here and have lunch with the guys."

"That's fine. Just remember you have to call Detective Carter before the end of the day."

"I will. Thanks."

It was four in the afternoon when Tom called Detective Carter on his cell phone.

"Carter here," he answered.

Tom was a bit taken aback, firstly by the fact he wasn't greeted by voicemail, and secondly because there was no mention of the title "detective" when he answered.

"Can I still call you Detective Carter?" Tom asked.

"Oh, hi, Tom. No, I'm no longer officially Detective Carter; I am now just a consultant, a private citizen called Carter. But after everything we've gone through Tom, you can just call me Phil from now on."

"Phil, okay. It's going to seem strange at first, but sure. The reason for my call, Phil, is to confirm that I will be going up there to meet with you and Prosecutor Stearns on February 9th."

"That's great news. We're close to the finish line. I'll let Stearns know right away. He's going to want to reimburse you for your airline ticket."

"Tell him I said thanks, but it won't be necessary. I'll fly in on the eighth and stay at the Del Monte. If you could send me an e-mail with the address where we're meeting, I would appreciate it."

"I'll do that right away. It won't be from my department e-mail, it will be from my new personal Gmail account."

As soon as the call ended, Tom called his travel agent and booked a first-class flight with an open return date, as well as a room at the Del Monte Lodge Renaissance. An hour later, he got a call from Marcia, the real estate agent.

"Hello, Tom. It's Marcia. Nice to speak with you again. Happy new year to you."

"Happy new year to you as well."

"I don't want to be presumptuous but, the last time we spoke, you indicated you wanted to sell the house on Riverdale Circle and you said you would assign the listing to me. I'm calling because, even though you and I haven't signed a listing agreement yet, I have a serious buyer willing to make an offer. He owns several other rooming houses in the area and is very familiar with that market. I took the liberty of showing him the house and he is ready to proceed."

"Okay, Marcia … Good work. Why don't you draw up a listing agreement and send it to me as a pdf attachment to an e-mail. I'll sign it, scan the signature page, and send it right back to you. And since you have a buyer, there's no need for an MLS listing, you can make it exclusive."

"Perfect. You'll have it within the hour."

"The other thing is that I have to be up there on February 8th for a few days, so if we could close the deal around that time, I could be there to sign everything in person."

"I'll do my best to make that happen. There is no move involved, so as long as he has his financing in place, there shouldn't be a problem."

Tom felt good about his decision to meet with the prosecutor and, in all likelihood, testify at the extradition hearing, and he was buoyed by the fact Irene remained supportive. He still had a nagging feeling that he was subjecting his family to some risk, but he justified it by the belief his contribution to the case would bring a final end to the threat.

A week later, Tom's sister arrived for a ten-day visit. She had recently recovered from a bout of pancreatitis and appreciated the opportunity to get away. Tom and Irene found her less jovial than usual and understood that her condition was known to bring on episodes of depression. They did their best to buoy her spirits. Sarah had been a high school teacher and retired in 2011. She married relatively late in life to the owner of a successful car dealership. She was thirty-nine at the time and he was forty-eight. It was her first marriage and his second. They had no kids together, but he had two boys from his first marriage. The boys lived with their mother. In 2010, after a brief battle with acute leukemia, her husband succumbed to the disease. It was a tragic loss followed by a protracted battle over his estate. Tom had helped Sarah with the legal fees, and she ended up with the bulk of the estate. It was, in Tom's opinion, a fair outcome, given that the first wife had remarried and the boys had been left with a generous trust fund. The ordeal strengthened the bond between Tom and his sister.

The three of them dined at the Turtle Club on Sarah's last night in Naples. Tom drove her to the airport the next day. When he got back to the condo, he found Irene sitting on the couch, crying softly.

"What's wrong? What happened?" Tom asked.

She took a moment to wipe her tears.

"I just got a call from Christine ... They ... they had a break-in ... at their house. They took the boys to their swimming lessons last night ... When they came back, the front door was wide open ... Just like at our place," she explained.

"That doesn't mean it was related to our situation. It's probably just a coincidence," Tom interrupted.

"No," she continued with a calm and deliberate demeanor. "Nothing was taken and one of her nightgowns was laid across the bed in the master bedroom."

"Holy shit! It's him. That bastard is at it again. But, I thought the FBI said they flagged his passport ... How did he get back in the country?"

"I don't know. He always seems to be one step ahead of them."

"I can't believe their incompetence! This should be pretty straightforward for them. I'm calling Carter right now. Do you want me to tell him I've changed my mind about testifying at the hearing?"

"No, I don't think so. I don't think I could endure years of uncertainty. Let's get this damn thing over with," she stated in a soft but authoritative tone.

Tom stooped over her and kissed her on the forehead. He got on his cell phone and called Carter.

"Phil, we have bad news," Tom announced.

"Why, what's wrong?"

"He's back. David is back in the United States and broke into our daughter's house."

"How do you know it's him?"

"Same MO. He left the front door wide open, didn't take anything …"

"Don't tell me he left a nightgown on the bed …"

"Yep, he sure did! It's him! There's no doubt about it. Our kids have no idea what this is all about. We haven't shared anything about the case. So, I thought he was going to be nabbed at the border if he ever tried to get in again. I want to know what happened. How did they screw up?"

"Let me get Agent Hanson on the phone. I've got his cell phone number. I'll call you right back."

It was more than an hour later when Carter called Tom back.

"Hi, Tom, Carter here. Sorry it took me awhile to get back to you. Agent Hanson just got back to me and has been able to confirm that David Strohman crossed the border at Hill Island Bridge to Interstate 81 two days ago. He was driving a 1999 Subaru Forester with Ontario plates. We have an APB out on that vehicle."

"How could they let that happen? They were supposed to arrest him at the border! What went wrong?"

"He crossed the border using a Canadian passport. We had no idea he had dual passports. The good news is that they have now flagged this passport as well. But, we don't yet know if he has crossed back into Canada."

"Well, that's just great!" Tom stated in the most sarcastic tone. "Here I am, doing everything in my power to help you, subjecting my family to risks … And your guys aren't holding to your end of the bargain. How complicated can it be?"

"I understand your frustration, Tom, and I agree we have screwed up. But, Agent Hanson told me they now have surveillance units in place to protect your family."

"I just don't know what this guy is going to do next, or what he's capable of …"

There was a long and awkward pause.

"Are you still planning to meet with us on February 9th?" Carter asked.

There was a pause.

"I think so, but you guys aren't making it easy. I think it will depend on how the situation stabilizes, and whether or not I feel confident that the FBI is doing its job."

"I understand. By the way, I've sent you a note with the address where we're meeting. You'll need to register at the security desk. They'll have your name on a scheduled guest list."

Tom recognized Carter's convincing technique; it was called "the presumptive close" approach, often used in corporate sales. He was surprised that a retiring detective was familiar with it. He didn't know if it was the result of Carter's experience and intuition, or if it came from formal training.

"I'll let you know if I have a change of heart. Meanwhile, why can't you extradite him on these break-ins?"

"Well, it wouldn't be that simple. First of all, other than confirmation that he crossed the border at times that gave him the opportunity to perpetrate those break-ins, there is nothing else that ties him to those events; no fingerprints, no eye witnesses, nothing. In addition to that, only offences that are punishable by five years or more in prison are eligible for extradition. So, these break-ins wouldn't qualify because there was no violence involved."

"I see ..."

"So, the best way to put this guy away for good is to follow through on our plans. We're close, Tom. Today is the 29th. The hearing is in two weeks!"

"You're probably right. I just don't need any more stress. Please use whatever means you have to convince Agent Hanson to apply the resources he needs to do his job and protect our family."

"I promise I will."

The call ended on that note. Tom sat beside Irene and explained what was going on.

"Do you want me to tell them I've changed my mind?" Tom asked her.

"No, but let's hope we can get this ordeal over soon. I've had it!"

Tom called Christine and talked with her for almost an hour. He wanted to make sure she was okay. He paced over every square inch of the condo while he was talking. She seemed freaked out by the event and worried about the boys' safety. Tom was torn. He wanted to let her in on the whole situation, but he felt it wouldn't do much good until he had something more definitive to tell her about the conclusion.

"Alan has arranged for an alarm system to be installed tomorrow," she explained. "I guess we were naive about this sort of thing because we live in such a nice crime-free neighborhood. In any case, we'll be happy to get away for a while and come down to Naples. We plan to be on the road next Friday. We're going to take it easy and spend two nights on the road. We'll be at your place by midday on Sunday."

"Sounds great! We can't wait to see you."

Tom concluded Christine was a little shaken but seemed determined not to live in fear.

"Do you think it may be time to tell them what's going on," Irene asked.

"I don't think so. I want to take this to its conclusion first, and then tell them the whole story. I don't want them to live in fear. I don't think they're in any real danger."

"I hope you're right …"

The two of them went out for a walk along the beach. They always found their beach walks soothing and relaxing. They didn't say much, but Irene clearly felt Tom's growing impatience.

"The Conleys have invited us to join them and two other couples for a murder mystery dinner night at their golf club on Sunday," Irene announced. "Would you like to go? I'll understand if you don't feel up to it, given the circumstances."

"Actually, that kind of diversion may be exactly what we need. Sure, let's go."

The couples met for cocktails in the club bar at five o'clock on Sunday. Tom and Irene had known Pat and Bob Conley for many years and also knew Sue and Mike Reynolds. All of them had been members at the tennis club. Bob introduced the fourth couple to everyone. The McRaes had just purchased the condo next door to the Conleys.

The discussions got more animated with each cocktail. Bob was telling a golf joke when he was interrupted by a loud disturbance at the bar. Two men and a woman were engaged in a heated argument. The room hushed. Finally, the woman stomped down the hallway toward the dining room with one of the men in tow.

"Well, good riddance," Bob commented.

Conversations resumed following a bit of a buzz around the room. Suddenly, a gunshot rang out from the hallway.

"What the hell!" Tom shouted as he jumped to his feet.

Everyone else at the table, except Irene, started to chuckle.

"Oh, I get it," Tom mumbled as he sat back in his chair, slightly embarrassed. "This is part of the setup for the murder mystery, isn't it?"

The rest of them nodded and giggled. The call to dinner came a few minutes later. There were eight dinner guests and one cast member at each table. The theme of the evening was the classic love triangle. The victim was one of the two men who were arguing in the bar. The cast member sitting with Tom and Irene and their friends played the role of the murder victim's wife. After many false leads, she turned out to be the culprit. Irene was the only one at their table who correctly identified her as the murderer. The mystery was well acted and the food was outstanding. Everyone enjoyed the evening and made plans to play tennis the next day. Tom and Irene were home just after eleven and went straight to bed.

19

On the morning of February 8th, Irene drove Tom to the airport. He found it difficult to leave. The idea of leaving her on her own didn't sit well with him, particularly given the fact they had not yet received confirmation that David had reentered Canada. He was sufficiently worried that he called Detective Carter to find out if there was any news on David's whereabouts.

"No, Tom, I'm sorry. I have not heard from Agent Hanson yet. I'll check with him again. But, as you know, we're dealing with Canadian border authorities and there is some delay in relaying that information back to the FBI. He could be back there by now."

"Yes, I understand. So, tell me, is he going to be at the hearing on Thursday?"

"According to our prosecutor, he is required to be represented but he doesn't have to be there himself."

"So, you're telling me he could be down here threatening or harming my family while the hearing is going on in Canada."

"That's right, but Hanson has a pretty extensive security detail around your family."

"Yeah, right … So far, I'm not impressed. In any case, if you hear from Hanson, please let me know. I would feel a lot better knowing he was back in Canada."

"I promise I will."

Tom's flight landed on schedule and he took a cab to the Del Monte. It was around four o'clock. Marcia and one of her coworkers were waiting for him in the lobby. After checking in, he led the two of them into a small conference room.

"The reception desk people suggested we use this meeting room," Tom told them.

Marcia laid out a series of documents which the three of them signed, one by one. It took twenty minutes to go through them all.

"Looks like all the tenants will be staying. The buyer is very pleased about that," Marcia informed Tom. "And you'll be netting, after the sales commission, about thirty thousand dollars, before taxes and before your lawyer's fees. I don't know how much he's charging you. I hope you're happy with that."

"Of course, Marcia, I'm fine with it. You did a great job with the renters and with the sale and, as you probably suspected, it was never about the money ... I want you to know how much I appreciate everything you did."

"You're very welcome, Tom. It turned out well for me also. I'll get all this paperwork to your lawyer tomorrow morning."

They said their goodbyes and Tom went up to his suite. He was checking his e-mail on his tablet when his cell phone rang.

"Mr. Gibson, this is Agent Hanson."

"Oh, good. Just call me Tom. Are you calling to confirm David is back in Canada?"

"No, actually, I have some bad news. I have Agent Fielding on the line with me from Naples."

"What? Why? Did something happen to Irene?"

"Your wife was involved in a motor vehicle accident this afternoon," Hanson said.

"Oh, shit! Is she okay?"

"She sustained some non-life-threatening injuries … She's going to be okay."

"Can I speak with her?"

"Hi, Tom, this is Agent Fielding. I'm at the NCH Baker Hospital where the ambulance took her. She is conscious and in stable condition. She can't speak with you right now because they are prepping her for surgery."

"Surgery? What surgery?"

"She has a ruptured spleen and that's what they're going to take care of immediately."

"So, what happened?"

"We were with her all the way. Our agent followed her to the airport and then tailed her as she ran a few errands. She was on Tamiami Trail when a car suddenly changed lanes and forced her over the median and into oncoming traffic. She collided with a delivery van. It was a violent collision but your SUV protected her very well. The driver of the delivery van didn't fare as well. The EMS attendants pronounced him dead at the scene."

"Oh, my God," Tom gasped.

"The vehicle that caused the accident didn't remain on the scene. Our agent had to make a choice to either pursue the vehicle, or stay with your wife. He chose to stay with your wife, as he was required to do, but got a pretty good description of the car and a partial identification on the tag. We have an APB out on that car right now."

"Was it an accident? It all seems too coincidental to me. What does your agent think?" Tom asked.

"Tom, we haven't fully debriefed him yet," Agent Hanson interjected. "He's preparing his full report as we speak."

"Okay, officers, I'm going back to Naples. I'm going to catch the next flight out of here. I'll call Detective Carter on the way and tell him I won't be attending the meeting tomorrow. I'm not sure about the hearing in Ottawa … We'll see how things go."

"We understand, Tom," Agent Hanson agreed.

"Let us know what your itinerary is and I'll have an agent pick you up at the airport," Agent Fielding added. "And, by the way, you're going to be on the market for a new vehicle. I'm afraid your Audi Q7 is a write-off."

"I don't care about that. I just want to make sure Irene is okay. I'll text you with my flight information as soon I get confirmation. It'll be a late arrival because there are no direct flights. I'll likely have a stopover in Atlanta. We're usually looking at five hours or more."

"No problem, we'll be there," Agent Fielding responded.

Tom grabbed his bag and hustled down to the front desk. He quickly explained why he had to leave. They were very sympathetic and did not charge him for his room. During his cab ride to the airport, he called Delta Airlines and was able to book a flight to Atlanta and a connecting flight to Naples. It was a tight connection in Atlanta, and his was the last flight of the day to Naples, so there was considerable risk in his itinerary. He texted it to Agent Fielding and let him know about the risk, promising to alert him if he missed his connection for any reason.

As it turned out, the first flight landed twenty minutes early and Tom made his connecting flight. He landed in Naples at eleven forty. Agent Fielding was there and drove him straight to the hospital. Irene was sleeping soundly when he arrived. He slept on the sofa bed in her room.

The next morning, Tom was awakened by the activity in the room. Irene was being tended to by the hospital staff. Tom jumped up and held her hand while they were checking her blood pressure. As soon as they were done, he leaned over and hugged her.

"How are you doing, dear?"

"Oh, I'm fine. In fact, I'm starving. Are we going to have breakfast soon?" she asked as she looked at one of the nurses.

"Yes, Mrs. Gibson," the nurse answered. "But, because it's your first meal after being under general anesthetic, it's going to be very light."

"Tom, you didn't have to come back ..." Irene whispered.

"Oh yes, I did. I didn't feel right about leaving you alone in the first place. So, tell me what happened."

"Sir, I just want to warn you that she is still recovering from surgery," the head nurse said. "So please keep that in mind and go easy for the next day or so."

"Of course. Sorry, dear, we don't have to get into it now."

"No, No, it's okay. I want to tell you how it happened. I made a couple of stops on my way back from the airport. It was actually a little eerie. I don't know if it's because my suspicions have been driven so high with everything that's happened, but a car pulled up beside me, on my right, and I felt the driver was looking at me. Then he pulled up ahead of me and veered right into my lane. I think his car bumped into me. I just instinctively turned away from him to avoid a collision. After that, I saw a flash and everything went dark. I woke up in the hospital with a pain in my stomach."

"Okay, that's enough for now. Just take it easy."

Tom was convinced it was no accident, but he didn't want to say anything that would upset Irene. A small breakfast arrived, consisting of bouillon and a poached egg. Tom went down to the cafeteria to get something to eat. Agent Fielding accompanied him.

"I want to let you know, Tom," the agent said, "we have located the vehicle that caused the accident. We found it in one of the parking lots at the airport. It had been stolen from the valet parking compound at one of the local hotels. Our forensic team is going over it as we speak. The first bit of visible evidence they noticed was a large dent and scrape on the rear quarter panel on the driver's side."

"So, I was right. It was no accident."

"It's a little early to draw a definitive conclusion, but all indicators point to a willful act of aggression."

After breakfast, Tom called his son and daughter to let them know what had transpired.

"Mom is okay and she'll call you later today after they finish their latest series of tests," he said to both of them.

Christine reacted by wanting to change her travel plans.

"The five of us were going to drive down on Friday and arrive on Sunday anyway," she said. "So, instead of driving, we'll fly. We're coming down today if I can get a flight. I'll text our flight plans to you as soon as I get a confirmation."

"Okay, sweetheart. I would pick you up at the airport, but I don't have a vehicle right now."

"No worries, Dad. We're going to pick up a rental car. Trevor says he wants to get a van. When is Mom going to be discharged from the hospital?"

"If all goes well, probably this afternoon."

"Great! See you soon, Dad. I love you."

"I love you too, sweetheart."

Tom went back up to the room and spent the rest of the morning with Irene. They allowed her to go down to the cafeteria for lunch with Tom, but they went over the menu with her and showed her which choices she was limited to. She was delighted to hear that Christine and Alan and the three boys were coming early.

"Well, it's not a sure thing yet. It depends on the availability of flights," he said.

Just as he was speaking, his cell phone buzzed with a text message from Christine. She confirmed their itinerary.

"Okay, there it is," he said. "She got the flights. They'll be landing just after eight o'clock tonight."

"That's wonderful. Now, you and I have to talk," she said as her tone sounded more somber. "You have a job to do, and you can't do it here with me in Naples. You need to go back up there and attend that hearing. We need to put an end to this."

"What worries me though, the thing that grinds at me, is that there's been no confirmation that he has reentered Canada. He could very well still be right here, watching, stalking, waiting for his chance to hurt you. Maybe he just wants vengeance at this point. He's probably not thinking logically. Who knows what he can do ... Especially if Chuck is in charge ..."

"Listen ... I'm in good company here. The hospital staff are all over the place. Then, Agent Fielding and his team will be here to look after me and Christine and her family. We're going to be fine. Go. Please go. I mean it."

"Okay, I'll go. I've already missed the prep meeting, so I'll have to go directly to Ottawa and meet Carter and the prosecuting attorney there. I need to call them. I'll take you back up to the room and then I'll get on the phone."

The doctor popped into the room just as Irene was settling into her bed. He confirmed that all the tests were good and she could be released by late afternoon. Tom called Detective Carter to bring him up-to-date and to confirm his intention to go directly to Ottawa for the hearing.

"I'm delighted your wife is doing well. We can all breathe a sigh of relief. Let's hope we can get this over soon. Stearns is going to want us to meet for at least an hour before the hearing. What are your travel plans?"

"I'll book a flight for tomorrow. I'm sure there are no direct flights. If you can text me the address where the hearing is taking place, I'll book a room at the nearest hotel."

"That's good. Stearns will probably want to meet at the hotel tomorrow night."

Tom called his travel agent. She searched for flights while they were on the phone. He was surprised when she found a direct flight to Ottawa on Westjet, a Canadian regional carrier.

"But, there's no first class or business on this flight, Tom. On the other hand, the flight is only three hours, so you're saving a bunch of time."

"Great! Go ahead and book it with a return late on Thursday."

"What about a hotel room?"

"I'll need a room near the federal court, wherever that is."

"Okay, let me see … I'm searching it on Google now … Here it is … Looks like 90 Sparks Street and … looks like the nearest decent hotel is the Sheraton Ottawa Hotel. It's just a short walk to the federal court building."

"Good work!"

"I'll send you the confirmations by e-mail."

Irene was discharged from the hospital at four o'clock. Agent Fielding drove them back to the condo, and the protection detail hunkered down.

"I had some groceries when the accident happened," she said as they sat on the patio, "but I have no idea what happened to them."

"Don't worry about it. The agents salvaged your purse from the scene, the rest doesn't matter. I'll order out. What would you like?"

"I feel like Thai, but I'm not sure my stomach can take it yet."

"Okay, I'll just order something simple, like mango salad, spring rolls, and dumplings."

"Sounds wonderful."

After dinner, Irene was tired but didn't want to go to bed until after the kids had arrived. It was after nine o'clock when one of the FBI agents called Tom to say that Christine and her family had just arrived. Tom and Irene went out to the parking lot to greet them. Everyone was excited but tired. The grandkids were in bed by ten. Afterward, Tom and Irene explained what was going on and why there were FBI agents on duty around them. Christine and Alan were stunned by the revelations, and by the realization that they too had been under a protective blanket for some time.

"I hope you're not angry with us for taking this long to fill you in … We just didn't think it would come to this."

"I don't know what to say," Christine admitted. "You two have been living a horror story … I feel so bad for you … Don't worry about us, we'll be fine, but what happens now?"

Tom explained the steps to extradition and the role he was about to play.

"So, I'm glad you kids are here with Mom," he said. "I feel a lot better about leaving her and doing what I have to do. Thank you for being here."

Everyone was tired and went to bed relatively early.

Tom was already awake and just lying in bed when he heard the grandkids milling about. He got up and made some breakfast for them. Irene was still sleeping soundly. Alan was the next one up, followed by Christine.

"What are you going to do about getting a new vehicle?" Alan asked Tom.

"I'm going to call my insurance company right away and start the claim process. And, if you don't mind, I'd like you to drive me to the Audi dealership. It's just beside the municipal airport on Airport Pulling Road."

"Sure, just let me know when you want to go."

It only took about ten minutes on the phone to get the claim process started. The claims agent told Tom it would likely take a week to ten days to settle. Tom didn't want to wait that long to get a new vehicle, so he and Alan drove out to the dealership. On the way out, Tom explained to the FBI agent on duty where they were going. He called in to report.

It turned out the Audi dealership missed out on an easy sale. They didn't have a Q7 in stock. The sales agent tried to convince Tom to wait.

"Let's see, today is Wednesday, I get can get a fully loaded one from another Florida dealership and have it here by Monday," the salesman assured Tom.

"Let me check around first and I'll call you if I want you to place the order."

As they got back into Alan's rental van, Tom asked him to drive to a Nissan dealership.

"If you just go north on Airport Pulling and turn right on Pine Ridge Road, it will be right there, about ten minutes from here," Tom indicated.

"No problem."

"Before I bought the Q7 I did a fair bit of research, and for me, it was a toss-up between the Q7 and the Nissan Armada. So, if the Nissan dealership has one in stock, they'll have my business."

As they pulled into the dealership, Tom was pleased to see several Armadas on the lot and another one in the showroom. Tom introduced himself and his son-in-law to one of the sales representatives. They quickly found one that was equipped to Tom's liking, and the deal was done. Tom called his bank and initiated an electronic fund transfer.

"Can I drive it home now?" Tom asked.

"Not quite, Mr. Gibson," the salesman replied. "First, we have to apply for a tag with the Department of Motor Vehicles and place a temporary tag in your window. We also have to do some dealer prep on your Armada. But we can have it ready for you right after lunch."

"I guess that will have to do. I'll be catching a flight at that time, but you can deliver it to our condo and drop off the keys. You have our address. My wife will be there with our kids and grandkids."

"Sure, Mr. Gibson, we can do that. Do you want us to give your wife a tutorial and an introductory drive on the Armada when we drop it off?"

Tom didn't want to get into any discussion about how complicated that might be, with FBI agents in tow, but decided to defer to Irene.

"You can offer it to her and see what she decides. Otherwise, I'll go over the key items with her when I get back."

The men were back at the condo for a couple of hours and then on the road again, this time on their way to the international airport. On their way out, Tom informed the FBI agents about the impending vehicle delivery from the Nissan dealership. Tom's flight took off on time at twenty minutes after three o'clock. The flight on a Boeing 737 was bare bones in terms of services, but the young flight crew was exceptionally pleasant and helpful. They also displayed a refreshing sense of humor and kept the passengers in stitches. Tom, in all his travels, had never experienced anything quite like it. Their service seemed to be well suited for the many families on board who were likely returning home from vacations in Florida.

20

There was a collective expression of disgust from the passengers when the captain announced they would be landing in the midst of a heavy snowfall.

"We're about to start our descent, so please buckle up," the captain said over the PA system. "We should be at the gate in about twenty minutes. The temperature right now in Ottawa is minus eighteen Celsius. We have twenty centimeters of fresh snow on the ground with another fifteen to twenty on the way."

Tom figured that meant the temperature was about zero Fahrenheit with eight inches of snow already on the ground and six to eight inches to go. He quickly realized his deck shoes and flimsy trench coat were clearly insufficient.

A taxi ride that would normally have taken twenty minutes took over an hour. Tom had only been in this city once before, on a business trip, many years before he retired. He checked into the Ottawa Sheraton Hotel. There was a message waiting for him, asking him to call Phil Carter on his cell phone. He called as soon as he had settled in his room.

"Hello, Phil, Tom here ... I just checked in."

"Great! I'm in the lounge with Robert Stearns. Have you had dinner yet?"

"No, I'm not really hungry but I'll join you anyway."

"Okay, let's meet at the main restaurant right here in the hotel. It's called the Carleton Grill. We're going to walk over right now."

"Very well. I'm just going to call Irene and I'll head down."

Tom spoke with Irene and was delighted to hear everything was going well and she was regaining her energy.

"Alan took us all for a ride in the new SUV," she said. "Great choice! I didn't realize it was so huge. It's very roomy inside, but I'm sure I'm going to find it a challenge to park."

"Don't worry, it's got a very effective park assist feature. You'll do fine."

After the call, Tom freshened up a bit and headed down to the Carleton Grill. He found the two men at a table near the window. They stood up to shake Tom's hand, and the three of them sat down and examined the menu. Tom ordered a single malt whiskey as they chatted about the weather and then got down to business.

"I'll be doing most of the talking," Stearns explained. "I'll describe the content of your testimony and explain your willingness to give firsthand account. It may not be necessary for you to actually testify; your presence may in of itself be sufficient for the judge because it will have satisfied the opportunity for cross-examination by Strohman's lawyer. So, it's possible his attorney could ask you some questions."

"I'm fine with that," Tom commented.

"Now, the key part of your testimony," the prosecutor continued, "is the face-to-face conversation you had with Strohman at his home, where he, or his alter, openly confessed to killing the girl."

"Isn't that just my word against his?" Tom asked.

"Yes, but it has value nonetheless, particularly in the context of the surprises we plan to spring on them."

"I don't suppose you want to tell me what those surprises are, do you?"

"No, because that could be considered prejudicial before your testimony."

"Okay, and what about the fingerprint and DNA evidence?"

"Again, it will have some limited value. His counsel will argue vehemently that it is inadmissible because it was obtained in a clandestine fashion and without a warrant executable in a Canadian jurisdiction."

"So, what are the chances we'll get the extradition order, and when do we find out?"

"Good questions. Our chances are at least 50 percent."

"That's all! What the hell?" Tom exclaimed. He was in shock. "I thought we had him cold."

"A lot of it depends on the presiding judge. We'll be able to better estimate our chances once we see what kind of questions are asked. Now, you also asked when we will find out the judge's decision. The answer is simple. The judge will make a determination right there, at the end of the hearing. The decision can only go two ways: they can either refuse the request for extradition in which case Strohman is a free man, or they can recommend extradition and refer it to the minister of justice who has the final say. In that case, Strohman is ordered to be taken into custody. From what I've been told, the minister rarely overrules a judge's recommendation."

The men enjoyed their meals and agreed to meet in the lobby of the hotel at nine thirty in the morning for breakfast.

"It's just a short walk to the court building," Phil Carter explained. "We should plan to be there thirty minutes before the scheduled start time of the hearing."

"I'm not walking out there in that snow with these shoes," Tom interjected, pointing at his feet. "I plan to take a cab."

The men retired to their rooms. Tom had picked up a local newspaper in the lobby. He quickly found the crossword puzzle and took it to bed. He started to yawn halfway through the puzzle. He put it down and got up to grab a water bottle out of the small refrigerator. He placed it on the night table, set his cell phone to wake him up at seven o'clock, and turned off the lamp before cuddling into bed.

Tom had been tossing and turning for a least an hour. He was lying on his right side. He felt thirsty. He reached over to the night table and felt around for the water bottle. He grabbed it and rolled over on his back. Holding the bottle over his stomach, he twisted off the plastic cap, or tried to. It was on so tight his fingers were just slipping around the cap. He pulled away his blanket and sat up on the edge of the bed. With the bottle wedged between his knees, he once again tried to twist off the cap.

That was when he felt a presence in the room. He wasn't sure if he had heard stealthy steps, or the slight ruffle of clothing, but he was sure there was someone in the room, somewhere behind him. There was no point in turning around because it was so dark he couldn't even see the bottle he was holding. Then, he heard some breathing, slow and deliberate, inhaling through the nose and exhaling out of the mouth. Tom felt a cold sweat across his forehead and temples. His heart was pounding.

"David, is that you?" he asked. There was no response, just more breathing.

He suddenly heard the unmistakable snapping sound of a rifle cocking.

"David! There's no need to do this! It won't solve anything! It will only make matters worse!"

The breathing got louder and closer.

"It's not David ..."

Tom immediately recognized the cold and defiant tone of Chuck's voice.

"What's the fourth planet?" Chuck asked.

"What?"

"What's the fourth planet?"

"Mars, for God's sake, David! What is going on? What are you doing?"

"I told you ... It's not David ..."

"Okay, Chuck. Listen, there's no need for this. Let's talk this over!"

"How many zeros in a billion?"

Tom was quiet for an instant, trying to figure out if he should turn around and try to grab the riffle, or perhaps make a run for the bathroom.

"This is a test. How many zeros in a billion?"

"Nine ... There are nine zeros in a billion. What's that got to do with anything?"

"What year did World War I start?" Chuck continued.

"1914!"

"That's right. It started on July 28, 1914. What else happened on that day?"

Tom tried to think. He knew that date meant something, but his thoughts were blurred. He couldn't come up with anything.

"That was the day your father was born," said Chuck. "This year, we would be celebrating his 102nd birthday if he was still alive ... He was our father too, you know ... You, David, me ... We're all brothers. Too bad. So long, brother."

"David! Chuck, please! You don't ..."

There was a sudden and momentary flash accompanied by a loud bang. Tom felt numb in his upper back and could hear nothing but a loud ringing in his ears. He wasn't in pain but could feel liquid running down his lower back. His water bottle dropped to the floor. His arms slumped. He could faintly hear a voice but couldn't make out the words over the ringing. He began to feel faint. He couldn't utter a word, but one thought came to his mind: "Irene, oh, Irene, I'm so sorry!"

He rolled off the bed and onto the floor in a fetal position. The ringing began to fade, then nothing.

At some time later, perhaps after several hours had elapsed, Tom opened one eye. He was soaked and felt cold. He crawled toward the window and extended one leg to push open one of the thick drapes, just slightly. A bit of predawn light invaded the room. He opened both eyes and looked toward the bed, expecting to see a pool of blood. Instead, he saw a wet spot where his water bottle had emptied on the floor.

"Oh, thank God," he whispered to himself. "It was just another bloody nightmare."

He crawled into bed and cocooned under the blankets. He continued to shiver for a while, partly from exposure and partly from the emotional trauma he had just experienced.

He slept soundly for a couple of hours then got up and jumped in the shower. He was exhausted, physically and emotionally. He knew he had to see this process through to its conclusion, but never, in his entire life, had he ever yearned to be somewhere other than where he was.

Tom met Carter and Stearns in the lobby at 9:30 a.m. as planned. They had a light breakfast before heading to the federal court building. It was still snowing, but the snow removal crews had been working all night, and the roads and sidewalks were all in good shape.

"Let's walk," Stearns suggested. "The court building is less than two hundred yards from here, and I don't see any cabs anyway."

Tom shivered in his trench coat as the wind and snow swirled around him. He was happy to step through the revolving door of the court building. After going through a security check and registering in the visitor's log, they followed a security guard to courtroom 4 on the eighth floor. They removed their coats and sat in a waiting area outside the huge oak double doors of the courtroom. Tom felt tense. He wasn't looking forward to facing David.

At ten minutes before eleven, another man joined them in the sitting area. He was well dressed with long wavy white hair and a goatee.

"Are you here for the extradition hearing?" the man asked.

"Yes, my name is Robert Stearns. This is Phil Carter and Tom Gibson."

"Oh, yes, Mr. Gibson … David has told me a lot about you. My name is Gary Penfield. I am acting as counsel for Mr. Strohman."

"Is David going to be here today?" Tom asked anxiously.

"No, he will not."

Some idle chitchat followed. There was no discussion of the case, but there was considerable commentary about the stormy weather. Tom began to relax somewhat after learning David would not be present.

One of the big oak doors opened. A uniformed man stepped out. It was the bailiff. He invited the men into the courtroom and instructed each of them as to where they should sit. A woman was sitting at a small desk in front of the judge's large elevated desk. Just as the men settled into their seats and the two lawyers pulled documents from their briefcases, the judge walked into the courtroom from a side door and was introduced by the bailiff. He was carrying a leather binder.

"This hearing is now in session," announced the bailiff. "Honorable Pierre Demers presiding."

The judge sat down and quickly got down to business.

"Could I ask each of you to stand and take a moment to introduce yourselves," the judge asked.

The men complied and the judge introduced the stenographer.

"Let me start by going over the rules with you," the judge continued. "First and foremost, this is not a trial; it is a hearing. Witnesses, if there are any, will be sworn in, just as they would in a trial, but therein lies to only resemblance. Mr. Penfield, as you undoubtedly know, the extensive disclosure rights given to Canadian citizens facing a domestic criminal trial are not available to you and your client in extradition procedures."

"I understand, Your Honor," replied David's lawyer.

"We are here today to accomplish three things," the judge continued. "The first is to determine if a crime was committed. I have received the evidence from Mr. Stearns. So, let's see ... We have human remains. They have been positively identified as belonging to a Jennifer Dawbrowski, the same young girl who was reported missing in August 1964. We have a crime scene from which physical evidence was recovered. So, yes, we have sufficient evidence to confirm that a crime was committed. For the information of our American colleagues, according to the Criminal Code of Canada, there is no time limit for the prosecution of such crimes. There is no statute of limitation here for any serious crime."

The judge paused and shuffled some papers.

"Our second task is to establish whether or not we have dual criminality," the judge went on. "This should be relatively simple in this case. If the events of August 1964 had occurred in Canada, would they be considered a crime and would they be subject to the same prosecutorial charges as those applicable in the jurisdiction where the crime was actually committed? The answer, of course, is yes. So we have satisfied the dual criminality requirement."

The judge turned a few more pages in his binder, picked up his pen, and scribbled something.

"Now," the judge said, "let's get down to the meat of this hearing. This is where we examine the evidence and determine if there are sufficient grounds for me to recommend Mr. Strohman's extradition to the United States and specifically to the state of New York. Mr. Stearns, please present your case."

Robert Stearns stood up.

"Thank you, Your Honor," he began. "The evidence we have already submitted shows that Mr. Gibson and Mr. Strohman are the ones who dug out the space under the rear porch of the house located at 5 Riverdale Circle in the enclave of River Heights Estates in Rochester, New York. This has been corroborated by Mr. Strohman in the brief submitted by his counsel. The so-called fort was initially dug to conceal the frame of a rototiller which the two boys had stolen from a nearby property. As far as anyone can tell, the two boys were the only ones who were aware of the existence of this fort and no physical evidence from the crime scene has proven otherwise. So, as far as we know, only these two boys had access to the crime scene."

"May I ask you what physical evidence is in your possession, other than the proof of identity of the victim," the judge interjected.

"Yes, Your Honor, I was just getting to that. Thank you."

Robert Stearns flipped several pages from his file.

"We have two sets of fingerprints which were recovered from a portion of the frame of the rototiller. One set has been confirmed as belonging to Mr. Gibson and we presume the other set belongs to Mr. Strohman, since the two of them have admitted to stealing it."

"Excuse me, Your Honor," interjected David's lawyer.

"Yes, Mr. Penfield, what is it?"

"Isn't it entirely possible that this second set of prints could belong to a third person? As far as we know, my client has never provided a set of fingerprints."

"Your Honor, please allow me to elaborate," Stearns responded. "The frame of the rototiller had been underground for fifty-two years when it was recovered by our forensics team. It was completely covered in rust which obliterated all latent prints with the exception of those on a part of the frame which had been directly under the motor and which had been covered in oil. The oil prevented the oxidation of that portion of the frame and helped preserve the fingerprints. The boys were the last to handle the tiller as they removed the engine and buried the tiller. The spot where the prints were located would have been inaccessible as long as the engine was mounted on the frame. Therefore, it is logical to conclude that the prints could only have belonged to Mr. Gibson and Mr. Strohman."

"That would be a reasonable conclusion," the judge commented. "Please continue."

"Also recovered from the crime scene was a camping knife. A photo of it was included in the material we provided to you. The same two sets of prints were found on the knife. Well, actually, there were multiple prints belonging to Mr. Gibson as well as a partial print belonging to the same person as those found on the tiller frame, presumably Mr. Strohman, as deduced in my previous statement. The portion of the print that was recovered was sufficient to confirm an exact match. Furthermore, that partial print was located on the specific blade which was used in the commission of the crime."

"Excuse me, Your Honor," interjected David's lawyer, once again.

"Do you have a question, Mr. Penfield?" asked the judge.

"Yes, Your Honor. I would like to know if any of the fingerprints were smeared in blood. I would like to establish whether the fingerprints came to be on the knife before or during or after the crime was committed."

"That seems to be a vitally important question," the judge commented. "What is the answer, Mr. Stearns?"

"Thank you, Your Honor. There was no blood on any portion of the knife where the prints were located. So, we can only determine, from the fingerprints, that both boys handled the knife at some time. But this is only part of the physical evidence and other evidence we have. So, if I may ..."

"Go ahead," the judge instructed.

"We have recovered DNA from the semen found on the victim's clothing. With this evidence, we have been able to establish a full DNA profile of the perpetrator. We believe this profile is an exact match to Mr. Strohman."

"Excuse me, Your Honor!" exclaimed David's lawyer.

"Yes, Mr. Penfield."

"My client has never submitted a DNA sample and none was obtained by any legal means, although we suspect that Mr. Gibson may have illicitly obtained a sample from Mr. Strohman's residence during his visit in November of last year. I submit that any evidence obtained in that fashion is inadmissible."

"That's correct," the judge confirmed. "If there is to be a trial, no evidence obtained without a proper warrant would be admissible. Let's move along, Mr. Stearns. You mentioned nonphysical evidence. What do you have?"

The prosecutor turned a few more pages in his file and continued.

"On November 12, 2015, our witness, Tom Gibson, visited his childhood friend, David Strohman, at his home in Ontario. The two of them hadn't seen each other since 1965. This was an opportunity to get reacquainted. Mr. Gibson has described this conversation, word for word, in a sworn statement and is here today to testify, in person and under oath. In his testimony, he recounts how they had lunch together in the manse of the United Church and reminisced about their childhood days. During that conversation, Mr. Strohman described in detail how he lured the young girl, Jennifer Dawbrowski, into the fort, assaulted her, and ultimately killed her."

"Your Honor! Your Honor!" protested David's lawyer. "Objection, Your Honor!"

"This is not a trial, Mr. Penfield," the judge stated impatiently. "You may voice your position, but the objection process is not applicable here. What would you like to say?"

"Thank you, Your Honor. My client, David Strohman, acknowledges that he met at his home with Mr. Gibson in November of last year, but he emphatically denies ever admitting any involvement in any crime other than the theft of the rototiller. So it is simply a matter of Mr. Gibson's word versus my client's and has no validity in this hearing."

"I would tend to agree, Mr. Stearns," the judge admitted. "Why should this hearing consider this testimony which, some people might conclude, is self-serving hearsay?"

"Your Honor," Stearns replied, "we would all agree that such accounts would normally carry no weight. However, in this case, I plan to demonstrate how this testimony merits your full consideration. You see, during their conversation, Mr. Strohman exhibited clear symptoms of dissociative personality disorder."

"You're going to have to provide some explanation, Mr. Stearns," the judge instructed.

"Yes, of course, Your Honor. When Mr. Gibson confronted his old friend with the inevitable fact that one of them was the murderer, a sudden change came over Mr. Strohman and a completely different personality emerged. He called himself Chuck, and he went on to describe in detail several aspects of the crime which could only have been known to the murderer and to the investigative team. I'm referring to details which were never made public. Mr. Strohman could not have known about these specific details unless he was involved in the crime. That is a fact."

"Your Honor, this is all very absurd!" Mr. Penfield protested.

"Yes, Mr. Stearns, I have to admit that, when I went over the deposition by Mr. Gibson, it seemed quite strange," the judge commented. "The testimony describes an admission of guilt, but not by David Strohman. The words are attributed to this alter, and thereby provide some plausible deniability by Mr. Strohman."

David's lawyer nodded approvingly as the judge spoke.

"In any case," the judge continued, "you mentioned that you had some examples of details allegedly described by Mr. Strohman which were not made public and could only have been known to the perpetrator. Could you please provide us with some examples of these undisclosed details?"

"Yes, Your Honor. Firstly, in his alleged admission, Mr. Strohman told how, after he lured the victim into the dugout, he never tried to remove any of the girl's clothing but masturbated while he was in contact with her and covered her face with one hand when she started to scream. He then describes how she had stopped breathing and how he was unable to revive her. In a panic, he picked up his friend's knife, pulled out one of the blades, and stabbed her several times. He then describes how he wrapped her up in the blanket which the boys had laid out over the dirt floor of the dugout and moved her to one of the corners of the dugout."

The prosecutor paused for a moment, knowing that his next few words would be crucial to the outcome of the hearing.

"Now, Your Honor, I would like to compare that with the evidence and conclusions drawn by our forensics team, weeks before the November 12th meeting of the two men. First, there was no evidence that any attempt had been made to remove any of the girl's clothing. The semen recovered from the crime scene was entirely on the outside of the victim's clothing. There was no semen found inside the pelvic cavity, suggesting that there was no penetration. Next, the stab wounds were superficial and could not have been the cause of death. Furthermore, they caused minimal bleeding, confirming that they were inflicted postmortem. There was no evidence of physical trauma to the victim's body, or specifically, to the bones. Cause of death was determined to be, with a high degree of certainty, asphyxiation. And finally, there was the blanket. She was indeed wrapped in a blanket. All of these forensic findings mesh in uncanny precision with the details provided by Mr. Strohman in his alleged account of what happened, and, most importantly, none, I repeat, none of these details were ever disclosed to the public. There is only one possible explanation for this convergence of Mr. Strohman's alleged admission and the trail of forensic evidence. He had to be the murderer."

"Your Honor! Please, Your Honor," protested David's lawyer. "There is indeed another possible explanation."

"Go ahead, Mr. Penfield," the judge ordered.

"Thank you, Your Honor. I maintain that there is another simple explanation for all of this. If Mr. Gibson was the culprit, that would explain everything. It would also explain why he is so anxious to pin the crime on his old friend."

"I would tend to agree, Mr. Stearns," the judge opined. "Why isn't Mr. Gibson a prime suspect?"

"Your Honor," Stearns replied, "of course we considered Mr. Gibson our prime suspect from the outset of our investigation. But he has been categorically exonerated by virtue of irrefutable DNA evidence. The semen on the victim's clothing was NOT his."

There was a pause in the proceedings as all participants digested what had just been said. The prosecutor was the first to break the silence.

"Your Honor, we can ask Mr. Gibson to testify at this point, if you wish to hear directly from him, or if Mr. Penfield wishes to question him. Otherwise, this concludes our case. I would just like to add the following: we realize that, uppermost in your deliberation is the desire to avoid any miscarriage of justice. In that regard, I can assure you that, if this extradition is allowed to proceed, we will execute a warrant as soon as Mr. Strohman enters the United States, whereby we will legally obtain fingerprints and a DNA sample. If his DNA profile doesn't match the DNA from the semen recovered from the crime scene, he will immediately become a free man. Only if there is a conclusive match will he be remanded for trial."

The judge spent a few moments scribbling some notes in his binder, then turned to David's lawyer.

"Mr. Penfield, to your knowledge, has your client ever been diagnosed with this dual-personality disorder?" asked the judge.

"No, Your Honor, not to my knowledge. My client has been an ordained minister of the United Church for many years and an exemplary and respected member of the community in which he lives. Furthermore, if he was involved in this crime which occurred in 1964, he would have been thirteen years old. Offenders older than twelve years and younger than eighteen years are subject to the rules under Canada's Youth Criminal Justice Act, which is separate from the adult criminal justice system and has a different approach to incarceration and rehabilitation."

"Those are valid points, Mr. Penfield," the judge admitted. "However, as a point of law, the Youth Criminal Justice Act went into effect in 2003 and is not retroactive. The rules which were in effect in 1964 were under the Juvenile Delinquents Act, which did not apply to offenders over the age of twelve. In those days, offenders aged thirteen and over were tried in adult court."

Justice Demers took a few moments to go over his notes.

"I have seen and heard enough to render a judgment as to the request for extradition," he declared. "It is not the objective of this hearing to prove, beyond reasonable doubt, the guilt of the accused. My responsibility here today is to ascertain whether or not the evidence presented would be sufficient to commit the accused to trial if the crime had taken place in Canada. It is my ruling that the evidence presented constitutes a prima facie case. Therefore, I hereby order Mr. Strohman's committal to the minister of justice with a recommendation that he be extradited as requested."

Tom and his two allies in the room shared a sigh of relief but were discreet and careful not to make it look celebratory. Stearns turned to Tom and winked. That said it all and, for Tom, meant that his efforts and the emotional roller coaster he and his family had endured were worth it.

"What if he appeals this decision?" Tom whispered to the prosecutor.

"There is no appeal process in these hearings. This is final, subject to the approval of the minister of justice," he replied.

"Mr. Penfield," the judge continued. "Can you please tell us the current whereabouts of your client?"

"Actually, Your Honor, I have no idea where Mr. Strohman is at this time."

Tom gasped in disbelief.

"When was the last time you spoke with your client?" the judge asked.

"It was on January 26th, when I informed him that the district attorney's office from the state of New York had confirmed with Canadian authorities that it intended to send a prosecutor and witnesses to the hearing. I have left numerous messages and have been unable to contact him since that day."

"That was the day before he snuck back into the US," Tom whispered to the prosecutor.

"Hear me well, Counselor," the judge stated in a stern voice. "Your client has until five o'clock tomorrow afternoon, February 12th, 2016, to turn himself in to the nearest detachment of the Royal

Canadian Mounted Police. If he fails to comply, I will issue a warrant for his arrest. Is this clear?"

"Yes, Your Honor, very clear."

"Thank you. This hearing is adjourned," the judge declared.

21

Tom shared a cab with Stearns and Carter en route to the Ottawa airport. It was almost two o'clock, and they were starving. They agreed to grab a bite and perhaps a beer at the airport. Tom's flight to Naples was scheduled to depart at 5:30 p.m. while the other two were booked on a 4:00 p.m. hopper to Rochester. The snow had stopped, and the bright sun rays sparkled on the fresh coat of snow which covered everything but the roads. Upon check-in, the men learned that their flights were delayed slightly because all flights had to queue into the deicing station on their way to the active runway.

After going through the security checkpoint, the three men sat down in the D'arcy McGee Restaurant and Pub.

"Wasn't that the name of the federal court building?" Tom asked.

"That's right," Stearns answered.

"What a coincidence!" Carter commented.

"Well, not quite," Stearns continued. "I've been a history buff all my life. There are many places in this city which are dedicated to the memory of Thomas D'arcy McGee. He was an Irish-born politician who ultimately became one of the fathers of the Canadian Confederation in 1867. Ironically, he was assassinated a year later by an Irish splinter group opposed to any cooperation with the English."

The men raised their beer mugs and toasted the fact that justice had won the day and then toasted D'arcy McGee. Carter's phone rang at that very moment. He mumbled a few words but mostly listened.

"I see ... Yes ... How far up did it ... Yep ... Good work ... No, I agree, it doesn't really change anything ... Yep ... Yep ... Okay."

"What was all that about?" Stearns asked.

"That was Agent Hanson. He just received a report from Agent Fielding."

"Are the kids and Irene okay?" Tom asked anxiously.

"Yes, yes, they're fine. The report came as a real surprise to Hanson."

Tom and the prosecutor listened attentively. Their curiosity had been piqued.

"It's about your wife's car accident," Carter continued. "The security video from the hotel where the car was stolen captured an image of the thief. He's well-known to the police. Hotels were alerted and it paid off. He was spotted scouting another valet parking compound and was picked up as he tried to get away with another car. They grilled him and charged him with a number of offences, including of course, manslaughter, because of the death of the delivery van driver that was struck by your wife's SUV. It turns out that, in the hope of earning some leniency, he sang like a bird. He was one of three drivers hired by a towing company to cause accidents at predetermined spots in southwest Florida. The company was always the first to have a tow truck at the scene, of course, because they knew when and where the accidents were going to happen. What a racket. They have chased this thing all the way up and charged management personnel as well as the owners of the company."

"So, it wasn't David after all!" Tom exclaimed.

"No, he had nothing to do with your wife's accident," Carter answered.

"Well. I feel somewhat relieved because it means that, while he did certainly break into three of the family's homes and threatened us, he never crossed the line and actually caused us any harm, at least to this point. I was worried because we still don't know where he is."

"That's right," Stearns commented. "And he really has no place to go, which is why we have to assume he may be increasingly dangerous."

Tom accompanied the other two to their gate. They exchanged hardy handshakes and said their goodbyes.

"I'm sure I'll hear from you when it's all over," Tom said as he looked straight into Phil Carter's eyes, "but I'm guessing we won't get the opportunity to meet again. I wish you a wonderful retirement. You have certainly earned it."

"Thank you, Tom, and most of all, thank you for all you did to help us solve this case and bring justice for young Jennifer. Not many people would have hung in all the way, as you did. You must have been quite a formidable businessman in your day ..."

"I had my moments, but I have to confess ... I'm enjoying being a grandfather a lot more."

The two men hugged and didn't say another word as Carter and Stearns turned toward the Jetway and boarded the plane.

Tom called Irene and gave her a brief synopsis of the day's events, including the report regarding her accident. She was equally relieved.

"My flight should get in around nine tonight," he informed her. "Please tell Alan he doesn't need to come out to pick me up. I can take a cab."

"Okay, see you soon. I love you."

"I love you too. See you in a few hours."

The flight to Naples was full of young families on school break. Tom had hoped to enjoy a nap, but the cabin was noisy and the seats were cramped. Thankfully, he had packed his noise-cancelling headset. He plugged it in, chose a classical music channel, and slept like a log for almost two hours.

He was awakened by the captain's announcement that they were beginning their descent.

"We estimate arrival at the gate at two minutes past nine," said the captain.

There was a lot of excitement among the younger passengers when the plane landed. They were undoubtedly anxious to begin their winter vacation on the beaches. Tom was eager to spend some time with his grandchildren. Naturally, Alan ignored his father-in-law's advice and met Tom in the arrivals concourse. Tom was grateful.

"No problem at all, Dad! Besides, I'm really enjoying driving your new Armada."

On the way home, they spoke about various things they could do with the three boys over the next couple of weeks. One of the first things on the list was to take the family on a cruise through the Everglades.

Tom gave Irene a prolonged hug when he got home. He could feel the tension melting away and was ready for a new beginning. The boys had been asleep for some time. The four adults enjoyed a drink on the patio. The night sky offered a spectacular celestial display. Tom brought out his telescope and tripod and focused on the Orion nebula. It was straight south, over the gulf waters, at a declination of about five degrees. Everyone was awed.

"I'd like the boys to see this," Christine suggested.

"Sure," Tom replied. "We just need to keep them up until eight o'clock. Orion will be just a little east of where it is now. They'll love it."

The next two weeks were filled with wonderful outings, relaxing times on the beach, and memorable family moments. It was exactly what Irene and Tom needed. Christine, Alan, and the boys headed home on February 27th, three days before Trevor, Anne, and Geena arrived.

Tom couldn't help but recall how, two years earlier, his nightmares began after watching Geena play in the huge sand castle they had built together on the beach. He was hopeful it would be different this time. He was reasonably optimistic that all his efforts to find the truth and to help bring justice for Jennifer Dawbrowski would afford him a clear conscience and peace of mind. In that regard, Tom sat down with Trevor and Anne on their first night in Naples, after Geena had gone to bed, and described everything that had been going on. They were in disbelief but relieved the ordeal was at or near its conclusion and everyone was safe.

The five of them spent most mornings, over the next ten days, at the tennis club. Trevor and Anne had been strong players since their college days, and Geena had dedicated considerable time and effort to her tennis lessons at home and was showing signs of potentially becoming a very good player. It was generally too hot to play in the afternoons, so they spent time on the beach and visited some of the tourist spots. Out of the blue, Trevor suggested they go down to Key West. Tom was able to book two rooms at the Marquesa Hotel for two nights.

"Tom, don't forget to let Agent Fielding know what we're planning," Irene suggested.

Tom called the FBI agent and told him about their plans to take the Key West Express ferry and spend a couple of days and nights in Key West.

"Okay, Mr. Gibson," the agent said. "Thanks for letting me know. "We have a standing deal with the Fairfield Inn, so I'm sure we can get a room there for one of our agents. I'll send you a text and let you know which agent will be shadowing you and your family. Have a good trip."

Irene and Tom had never been there, so the jaunt to Key West was a new experience for all of them. They loved the trek on the ferry, during which they spotted a number of dolphins and other sea life. The weather was ideal, with temperatures slightly more moderate than those in Naples where the mercury had been climbing to ninety degrees by noon every day. One afternoon, Trevor and Tom went on a SCUBA diving expedition while the girls went shopping. They chose dining spots which featured live entertainment, the Pier House the first night and Chicago's the second night. By the time they got back to the condo in Naples, they all needed some rest.

It all seemed to go by so quickly. Before they knew it, it was time for Trevor and his family to go home. Tom took them to the airport on Sunday, March 13th. The next day, Agent Hanson called to say the FBI was cutting back on the security detail.

"At this point, we believe you and your family are under minimal risk," he told Tom. "You have my direct number and you can call it at any time of day or night. We have a fast response capability if you should find yourselves in any difficulty. This applies to your kids as well, so you should make sure they have my number. It's time for us to back away."

Tom understood and, in a way, felt this change could help lead them to a sense of normalcy. He and Irene had been sleeping well, with no signs of the type of anxiety that had haunted him over the past two years. The only angst he occasionally felt, as he reflected on the events that had transpired, was a feeling of self-doubt. He had second thoughts about his decision to follow his instincts and pursue the case to its conclusion. Perhaps David was right, he thought; perhaps there was nothing to be gained by anyone. He wondered if David had really deserved his fate. He confided in Irene, and she explained that these were part of a normal thought process after any consequential decision.

"I think I can give you some helpful tips that may help you move on," she said. "First, ask yourself: if you were presented with the same circumstances today, would your decision be any different?

Second, and perhaps more importantly, has your decision changed your core values? Think about it in those terms, over the next few days, and I think it will ease your mind."

"Thanks. That's a good place to start."

22

The tennis club hosted the Goodbye Snowbirds cocktail party on March 27th. Many of the senior tennis club members had been spending their winters in Naples for many years and had become a close-knit group of friends. Most were from northern states as far away as Minnesota, but there were also quite a few from Canada. Their friendships transcended the seasons, and many of the members made a point of travelling and visiting each other in the summer and fall.

After the party, Irene and Tom accompanied four other couples for dinner at the Turtle Club. Most of them were heading home the next day. Even though the dinner signaled the end of their winter sojourn, the atmosphere was light and cheerful. The toasts were warmly humorous. They all knew they would be back together in late fall, and most looked forward to resuming their lives with family and friends at home. Tom and Irene weren't planning to head back home for another two weeks. That last fortnight in Florida was always quiet and restful for them. This time, they felt they would appreciate it even more than usual.

On March 30th, Tom wondered why he hadn't yet heard anything from Agent Hanson regarding the apprehension of David Strohman. He called Phil Carter and left a message on his mobile voicemail. Carter called back within an hour.

"It's good to hear from you, Phil," Tom said. "I was calling you because I haven't heard anything from anyone. I've had no update. Did David turn himself in? Is he in custody? Has he been extradited? Is he going on trial?"

"I'm sorry, Tom," Carter replied. "I have been in touch with Agent Hanson on a regular basis, and even though there hasn't been much to report, we should have been keeping you in the loop. I apologize. I wrongly assumed Hanson kept in touch with you, given that he is still responsible for your security. He probably assumed I was looking after it because I have a more established relationship with you. Again, I'm sorry. The truth is that the last trace we have of Mr. Strohman is when he crossed the border into the US on January 27th. The APB has come up empty. Right now, I'm sorry to say, his whereabouts are a complete mystery. There are warrants pending for his arrest on both sides of the border. I don't know what else to say."

"Okay, Phil, I guess you're doing whatever you can. But I have to admit I find it frustrating, and even troubling, that all these law enforcement resources have been unable to collar him. It's not like he's a professional crook or anything, he's a minister of the church and he has very limited resources."

"I know, Tom, I'm as frustrated and baffled as anybody. But I promise to call you every week, no matter what happens, or as soon as anything breaks."

"That was Detective Carter," Tom explained to Irene as he went on to share the crux of his conversation with the detective. It was evident to Irene that Tom's frustration was turning to anxiety.

"Don't let it get to you, honey. It's just a matter of time."

On April 8th, at six o'clock in the morning, three days before he and Irene were scheduled to head home, Tom received a call from the alarm system monitoring company's control center, informing him that the alarm system at their home in Westfield had just been tripped. After confirming his access code, Tom asked what they knew about the possible intrusion.

"So far, only one motion sensor has been activated. It's the one in the basement," the security agent reported. "Do you want us to call in the local police, sir?"

"Normally, with only one sensor tripped, I would say no. But, given we had a break-in last fall, I'd say yes. Please go ahead and call in the police to check it out."

"Very well, sir, we're calling them right now."

It wasn't the previous break-in that motivated Tom to ask the control center agent to call in the police. It was the nagging thought that David had still not been located and could be lurking in the area. An hour later, Tom's cell phone rang.

"Is this Mr. Gibson?" the voice asked.

"Yes."

"Hello, Mr. Gibson, this is Officer Phillips, Westfield police. You may not remember me. I was the lead officer that responded after the break-in at your house in November."

"Yes, of course I remember."

"I've just finished inspecting the perimeter of your house. There is no sign of forced entry anywhere and all the doors are closed and locked. The ground is still soft from the recent thaw and there are no footprints other than mine. I spoke with the control center and they said that no other sensors have been activated and the system has reset itself. So, I think everything is okay here."

"That's a relief, Officer. I'm sorry we dragged you out there for nothing."

"No problem at all, sir. After experiencing one break-in, I would have done the same. Have yourself a good day, sir."

Irene and Tom spent most of the weekend cleaning the condo, moving some items into their storage locker and packing up the SUV. They never rented out the condo, but they occasionally loaned it to close friends. That's why they always liked to leave it sparkling clean and uncluttered.

They were on the road by eight in the morning on Monday. Tom had booked a room at the St. Regis in Atlanta, and they hoped to check in around seven o'clock that evening. They were three hours into their trip when Tom got a call from Agent Hanson.

"Hello, Agent Hanson. Have you got good news for us?"

"Well, sir, I have some news for you, but I wouldn't call it good news, at least not yet."

Tom and Irene were intrigued as they looked at each other and wondered what the agent was about to tell them.

"That sounds kind of ominous," Tom replied.

"I just wanted to let you know we've located David Strohman's car, the 1999 Subaru Forester. It was spotted in a wrecker's yard. The only reason the owners noticed it was because it was left in an area where they don't normally park Japanese cars. At first, they thought it might have been a stolen car, so they reported it to the police. There were no plates on it so it took awhile to identify the owner. The local police and the county sheriff asked for our assistance. It took us awhile but we finally matched the serial number with a license plate number from Ontario which was the subject of an active APB. We confirmed, without a doubt, that it is Strohman's car. There was nothing in the car, except a portable GPS device, and surprisingly, no fingerprints. It was wiped clean. It took about a week to get a positive ID. We have no way of knowing how long the car has been there. It could have been parked there anytime between January 27th, when he crossed the border, and about a week ago, when the car was spotted. We just don't know."

"Well, that's progress, I suppose," Tom commented, trying to remain positive. "That means he can't be too far away."

"That's probably a safe assumption, sir, but therein lies the problem."

"I'm afraid I don't understand …"

"The car was discovered at Harris Auto Wreckers, in Westfield, just minutes from your house."

Tom's jaw dropped, and Irene covered her face with both hands. There was a long silence.

"Mr. Gibson, are you still there?" the agent asked.

"Yes, Agent Hanson, we're still here, but I have to admit, we're in shock. Our house alarm went off on Friday, but the police didn't find anything."

"Yes, we're aware of that. We have been in contact with them. We advised them that we were posting two agents at the property as of today, without getting into a lot of details with them. He may have tried to get in and somehow tripped the alarm, or maybe it was totally unrelated. We don't know. In any case, don't worry, we have you covered."

Somehow, Tom didn't find Agent Hanson's words very reassuring. But, he didn't want to chastise the agent at this point, mostly because he knew it would only upset Irene even more.

"All right, please keep us posted," Tom asked as they ended the call.

A section of Interstate 75 was closed to traffic south of the Gainesville exit. Strong easterly winds had swept heavy smoke from a brush fire across the highway and had reduced visibility to nothing. Tom had received an alert on his GPS and had exited I-75 a few miles earlier and diverted to Highway 441. The detour added about half an hour to their trip, but they realized it would have been much worse if they had followed the traffic. They pulled into the St. Regis Hotel in Atlanta a little after seven thirty. They were both tired. They had a drink and a light dinner. They were in bed before ten.

23

Tom was totally exhausted when they drove into Westfield. The second leg of their trip seemed to have taken forever. Strangely, he couldn't recall pulling into or exiting the interstate, or seeing any of the landmarks along the way. He was angry that he let himself fall slightly unconscious or go into some kind of semiconscious trance like a commuter going to work. Fortunately, they had arrived safely nonetheless.

They were both puzzled as they pulled into their tree-lined driveway. There were three vehicles. There were two pick-up trucks and an old beater of a car that looked like it should have been in a wrecker's yard.

"Just stay in here, while I check what's going on," Tom told Irene.

He got out and stepped up to the front door. There was a "wet paint" sign stuck on the window of the door. Tom felt that was quite strange but concluded that Gerald had come back to put one more coat of paint on the door before he and Irene got home. He couldn't get his key into the lock. Perhaps Gerald had to change the lock, he thought. He faintly heard voices inside. He turned the doorknob, but the door wouldn't open. Maybe the kids decided to come up with some friends to welcome us home, he speculated. He rang the doorbell. After hearing some steps nearing the foyer, the door opened. Tom was shocked as a haggard-looking obese woman opened the door.

"What do you want?" she uttered aggressively. "Whatever it is, we're not interested."

"What are you doing in my house?" Tom exclaimed while gesturing with his arms.

She turned toward the inside of the house.

"Lou, you'd better get over here," she yelled.

A few moments later, a large, burly man with a full beard walked up to the doorway.

"What is it?" he roared as he was chewing on something.

"This man says we're in his house," she said with a sneer.

"Who the hell are you, and who put you up to this?" the big man asked defiantly.

"I'm Tom Gibson. My wife is in the car. We live here. This is our house, for God's sake! I'm calling the police!"

"Okay, that's enough, you fucking weirdo," the man yelled as he placed his hands on Tom's shoulders and violently shoved him away from the entrance.

Tom stumbled backward and fell on the walkway. He felt dizzy and his vision was blurred. He was hyperventilating. He suddenly felt a pair of warm hands on either side of his face.

"Are you okay, honey?"

"They're in our house! They've taken our house!" he yelled.

"No, honey. Nobody's taken our house … Everything is okay," she tried to say in a calming voice.

He looked at her, and then looked around him in a bit of a daze.

"Wake up. Everything is fine. You had a bad dream. We're fine. We're fine. See, we're in our hotel room."

Tom looked around again. His breathing eased.

"Oh shit! I'm sorry. I did it again. I'm so sorry."

"There's nothing to be sorry about. It's not your fault. You have no control over these nightmares. Obviously, you're still feeling anxiety about David's whereabouts, and the discovery of his car, and the house alarm ... But we're fine. Have a sip of water, and let's try to get some sleep. We have a long drive tomorrow and we still have a chance to get about four hours of sleep before we get on the road."

"Okay."

The couple managed to get some sleep and got up, a little weary, at six o'clock. They grabbed coffee and bagels to go and were on the road twenty minutes later. After refueling twice and picking up some lunch at a fast-food drive-through, they turned onto Shore Drive twelve hours later. Road conditions had been ideal all the way. Tom may have sped a little, but he was determined to get home before sunset, making it easier to get the plumbing up and going and getting the house warmed up to normal room temperature.

"The sun will set at seven fifty-seven today, so that should leave me about an hour and a half to get the house back to normal," he commented as they approached their driveway.

They waved at the two FBI officers in the black SUV parked on the road, opposite their driveway entrance. It gave them some sense of security. Tom unlocked the front door and disarmed the security system. Irene helped him unload the Armada.

"Something stinks around here," she commented. "Did you forget to take some of the garbage out to the roadside bin?" she asked.

"It's possible. We left in a bit of a rush. I just don't remember. I'll take a look in the garage after I get things going in the house."

After an hour, the water pressure was up throughout the house and all the drains were flushed of the RV antifreeze that had protected them from freezing. Hot water wasn't an issue because of the two instant water heaters. Tom just needed to flip the breakers on. The furnace came back on without any hiccups, and air was circulating nicely around the house. Meanwhile, Irene did most of the unpacking. The two of them had all this down to a routine.

They ordered pizza for dinner, making sure to add an extra one for the FBI agents. The order was delivered forty minutes later, and Tom walked out to the end of the driveway, introduced himself, and handed over one large all-dressed pizza to the agents. They were very grateful. It was a brisk evening with strong wind gusts out of the east.

"Thank you, sir," one of the agents said. "Our appetites perked up when we stopped the delivery van for inspection and got a whiff of the aroma."

"You are most welcome. My wife and I thank you for being here for us," Tom responded, standing there with his trousers flapping in the wind.

After dinner, Tom watched a bit of news while Irene wrote up a shopping list. They were comfortably in bed by ten o'clock, happy to be settled back in their home. They both enjoyed the best sleep they had had in a long time.

The bedside clock's red beam on the ceiling showed it was 6:40 a.m. when the sun's first rays reflected off the lake and into their bedroom. Tom and Irene stayed in bed for another hour and a half. They finally got up and showered.

"All I can offer you for breakfast is a granola bar and coffee," Irene admitted.

"That's fine."

After breakfast, Irene wanted to go out and do some shopping. It was a beautiful sunny day. There was hardly a ripple on the lake.

"Do you want me to use my car, or just take the Armada?" she asked.

"I have to hook your battery up and charge it. So just take the SUV. I'm not planning to go anywhere."

"Okay, I have a few stops to make. I should be back by lunchtime. I'll let the agents know where I'm going."

She drove to the end of the driveway, stepped out of the SUV to chat with the agents, and then drove away. Tom walked out to the garage. In the absence of any wind, the odor from the garbage in the garage was more noticeable. He unlocked the side door and opened it. He was jolted back by the stench and by a swarm of flies. He covered his mouth and nose with his arm and reached past the door frame to activate all three bay door openers. He also flipped on all the light switches. He walked around to the front of the garage to retrieve the garbage and take it to the bin at the end of the driveway. There were still hundreds of flies, maybe thousands, buzzing around inside the garage. Tom was stunned to find no garbage in the usual area alongside the recycling bins. He thought some raccoons might have gotten in and spread it around. He was still covering his mouth and nose. He felt overwhelmed and thought he might throw up. His eyes were watering. Irene's convertible seemed intact. Everything in the garage looked normal. He looked at the far left corner where the stairs led up to the loft. He thought some animals could have dragged some garbage up there. He walked up to his workbench at the back of the middle bay, opened one of the tool cabinets, and grabbed the breather mask he normally used for spray painting, along with a pair of work gloves. He walked out of the garage to get some fresh air before putting on his mask and gloves. He slowly walked toward the stairs and noticed a large shadow over the landing, halfway up the stairs.

"What the hell …?" he shouted into his mask.

There were so many flies, it took him a few moments to realize a body was hanging over the landing. There was a yellow extension cord around the neck, strung from the rafters in the loft. Tom desperately wanted to know who it was. The face was visible but unrecognizable because of the extensive decomposition. The eyeballs were dangling over the gaunt cheeks, and blackened flesh was dripping down like jowls past the chin. It was the most disgusting thing he had ever seen. There was a continuous drip from the body down into a puddle of body fluids on the landing. The corpse was covered in a full-length overcoat. There was a boot lying sideways in the puddle.

Tom ran out of the garage, threw off his mask, fell to his hands and knees, and threw up in the middle of the driveway. He heard voices in the background and then heard some steps running up to him.

"Mr. Gibson! Mr. Gibson! What's wrong?" one voice yelled.

Tom was unable to utter a single word. He pointed to the inside of the garage as he continued to cough up his meager breakfast.

"Stay with him!" one voice ordered. "I'll check it out."

Tom looked up briefly and saw one of the FBI agents draw his gun as he walked carefully into the garage. The other officer kneeled down beside Tom.

"Are you okay, sir?" he asked.

Tom nodded, and then wiped his face with his sleeve. The agent helped him up to his feet.

"There's a body ... hanging ..." Tom muttered while pointing into the garage. "I can't tell who it is ..."

The other agent came out of the garage with his cell phone in hand. Tom couldn't make out exactly what he was saying, partly because he was speaking softly and partly because he was using codes and police jargon. He stuck his phone back in his jacket pocket and turned to his partner.

"The cavalry will be here shortly," he said. "Why don't you take Mr. Gibson inside and make sure he's all right. I'm going to secure the perimeter."

Once inside, Tom started to feel better. He grabbed a couple of water bottles, offered one to the agent, and then opened the other. He downed half the bottle in one gulp, then just took a few deep breaths.

"I'm sorry, this is not the kind of thing you see every day …" Tom whispered. "I thought I was pretty tough, but I wasn't ready for anything like that. I don't think I could ever …"

"No need to apologize, sir," the agent interrupted. "You would have to be inhuman to be unaffected. Trust me, you never get used to it."

A number of emergency vehicles and other unmarked cars and trucks began to arrive.

"On her way out, Mrs. Gibson told us she didn't want any escort and wanted to spend a couple of hours shopping on her own," the agent stated. "You may want to call her on her cell phone and prepare her before she gets back. Otherwise, she may freak out when she gets here and she may think something happened to you."

"You're right. I'm going to call her right now."

Tom reached her as she was entering the Target store in Erie. That's where she usually liked to go for major shopping. He gave her a brief update, leaving out the gory details.

"I didn't want you to worry when you got home and saw all these emergency vehicles," he explained.

"I don't know if I'm horrified or relieved," she admitted. "Are you sure it's David?"

"I can't imagine who else it might be. He's been there for some time … I don't know how long … So, I imagine a positive identification is going to require some lab work."

"Yuck! So, is that what we were smelling when we got home last night?"

"I'm afraid so. And it's much worse today, with the bay doors open. Anyway, just take your time. Have lunch there, somewhere. You'll have to park on the road when you get back. I don't know how long it will take for them to clear the driveway."

"Okay. I'll probably be back by midafternoon."

The agent had gone out and joined the other law enforcement officers while Tom was on the phone. From his den window, Tom could see almost a dozen vehicles including a local police car, a county sheriff's truck, a fire truck, an ambulance, and several unmarked SUVs and vans. The agent came back to the house as Tom completed his call with Irene.

Tom was asked to sit down with the agent and give a detailed statement regarding the circumstances that led to the discovery of the body. It was relatively simple and only took a few minutes.

"I'm sure it's David Strohman ... What do you think?" Tom asked the agent.

"There hasn't been any official identification yet, but the team has already recovered a wallet. It belongs to Strohman, so you're probably right."

"How long do you think he's been there?" Tom asked the agent.

"It's hard to say, sir. The last trace we had of him was when he crossed the border on January 27th, and of course the ensuing break-in at your daughter's house in Syracuse, which we attribute to him. Since then, nothing ... The coroner will be able to pinpoint the exact TOD."

"TOD?"

"Sorry. Jargon which means time of death."

During his conversation with the agent, the smell of decaying flesh and the image of maggots crawling in and out of the eye sockets were permanently ingrained in Tom's mind.

"This looks like it will be the last chapter of this case for you and your family," the agent continued. "Agent Hanson will want to meet with you one more time to close up any loose ends. It probably won't happen until he gets the full report from the lab."

"That's fine. I'll be—"

Tom's response was interrupted by the ring of his cell phone. It was Phil Carter.

"Just heard from Agent Hanson," Carter informed Tom. "Looks like we have a conclusion."

"It would certainly appear that way."

"Are you okay, Tom? I know it had to be an awful experience."

"It was a horrific scene. I'm glad it was me that found him, not Irene. I'll get over it. How about you, Detective? Does this mean the end of the road? Are you really going to retire now?"

"Yes, absolutely. I promised my wife this would be my last case. By the way, I want to give you a heads-up you're going to get a letter from my boss. Watch for it."

Tom was intrigued but didn't want to pry. He sensed that Carter was being intentionally coy and wanted to keep it somewhat of a surprise.

"Okay, Phil, I'll watch for it."

The men ended the call with Tom scratching his head about the letter.

Tom called his kids and explained what was going on. He decided to accept Christine's invitation to spend a few days with her and her family until the dust settled. After Irene got home, Tom helped her unload and store all the groceries. The two of them packed a few things, informed the agents about their plans, and left for Syracuse. The boys were excited to see them and helped break the tension that had continued to fester in the minds of the adults while David was still at large.

Two days later, Tom received a call from Agent Hanson.

"Hi, Mr. Gibson. I just wanted to let you know that we're releasing the scene. You can come back and start getting your life back to normal. But I want to warn you … You're going to need to bring in some professionals to clean up."

"I understand and I have done a few searches on the Internet. I'll get that going."

"Good. The other thing is that I'd like to meet with you one more time, probably in a couple of weeks. I'll call you and we can pick a time that works for both of us."

"No problem at all. We can meet in town for lunch."

"Sounds great. Have a good day, sir."

Tom called a reputable company to take on the task of cleaning up the garage. He agreed to meet one of their representatives at the house at two o'clock the next business day, which was Monday, April 18th.

The Gibsons travelled home on Monday morning. Tom signed a contract that day, and the cleanup crew arrived early Tuesday morning. They were there for two days. They brought tons of equipment and worked nonstop. They were self-sufficient and even had their own portable toilets.

On Wednesday, there was a letter in the mail addressed to Tom from the Office of the Chief of Police in Rochester, New York. Tom was curious, thinking it could be an expression of gratitude for helping the department crack the case of Jennifer Dawbrowski. It was no such thing. It was an invitation to attend a retirement luncheon for Detective Carter. The event was scheduled for April 29th in the Carmel Room of the Del Monte Lodge.

"Do you think I should go?" Tom asked Irene.

"Of course you should. If Detective Carter asked his boss to invite you, it's because you made a significant impression on him and he wants you there."

"There's probably going to be some serious drinking going on. I'll have to book a room for Friday night and drive home on Saturday. Are you still okay with that?"

"Sure, go for it."

Tom called the RSVP number at the bottom of the letter and confirmed his intention to attend. Later that afternoon, he and Irene dropped by the tennis club and signed up for league play as well as a couple of upcoming tournaments including an interclub tournament scheduled for May 28th. It was the best indication yet that their lives were returning to normal.

On April 29th, Tom got on the road before ten o'clock. It seemed he had made this trip so often he could do it in his sleep. He wondered how many people would be at the luncheon. He deduced that it had to be no more than thirty. He was familiar with the Carmel Room and figured that, with its total floor space of about five hundred square feet, it couldn't possibly hold more than that for a sit-down meal.

As it turned out, he was absolutely right. He saw a chartered bus in the parking lot and assumed it was used to shuttle the majority of the luncheon guests so that they could avoid drinking and driving. When he entered the meeting room, Phil Carter gave him a big hug and introduced him to the twenty-six other guests. Except for Phil's brother from Arizona and a reporter from the *Daily Record*, all the other guests were law enforcement officers. Two were from the FBI, including Agent Hanson, and the rest were from the Rochester Police Department, the county sheriff's office, and the New York State Police.

A bar had been set up in one corner of the room. Two bartenders were busy serving drinks. Phil dragged Tom up to the bar and showed him the variety of whiskeys on the drink menu.

"Most of these are Irish," Phil said, "but there are a couple of others here, including some single malts that you're probably familiar with."

Tom settled on a shot of eighteen-year-old Macallan.

"Good choice!" Phil exclaimed. "Even though it's not Irish, that stuff is so smooth it will land on your tongue like a butterfly with sore feet!"

Tom concluded that Phil had already had a couple of shots of his own. Phil's brother turned out to be an interesting fellow. He had been a tennis club pro all his life and, although he had recently retired, still played in the ATP Champions' Tour.

The speeches started after the main course. Each guest stood up and said a few kind words about Phil. Most were work-related anecdotes and tributes. The chief, who was also the host of the luncheon, gave the longest speech, retracing the detective's career from beginning to end. It was interesting, if not very humorous. Tom improvised a few words around the wisdom he had witnessed when working with Phil on his last case. The last word went to Phil, of course. He had something nice or witty to say about each of his guests. For a man who did not habitually partake in public speaking, he was very eloquent. Tom was impressed, particularly considering the amount of whiskey that had been consumed.

There was some more heavy-duty drinking after lunch, and the event didn't wrap up until after five o'clock. The goodbyes took forever. Tom had been so right about booking a room. He wasn't hungry for dinner. He live-streamed some jazz music on his cell phone and worked on a crossword puzzle in his room, and when he couldn't stop yawning, he flopped into bed and slept soundly until about five o'clock in the morning. He got up, went to the bathroom, and crawled back into bed. His head felt a little heavy. The music was still playing softly, and he had a brief and innocuous dream that he was listening to a transistor radio with an earphone.

On the way home, his recollection of that little dream triggered a memory of the small transistor radio he listened to as a young boy, when he hid in his secret room to elude Ronnie's persecution.

"Whatever happened to that little old radio?" he whispered quietly to himself.

Suddenly, he felt a hot flash and started to hyperventilate. He had to pull over on the side of the road and stop. The answer to his question, he had just realized, was that his radio was still there, in that secret room. But that wasn't what got him worked up. The more troubling question was: why was the radio left there? For the first time in his life, he came to grips with a reality he had avoided all these years. As a young preteen, and after he had discovered that the walls of the tunnel leading to his underground fort had collapsed, his only refuge was his secret room. There was a span of about two weeks between the demise of the fort and Ronnie's departure to boarding school. During that period, Tom sought safety in his secret room as he had on many previous occasions. But, for some inexplicable reason, he didn't feel the serenity it had offered in the past. He felt anxious and jittery. He even contemplated suffering through Ronnie's beatings rather than hiding in that place. And after Ronnie was shipped off to school, Tom never went back into his secret room, not even to retrieve his transistor radio. Why? Why did he fear the very place that had been a safe haven for him? It had to be, Tom concluded, because something had changed. A beautiful young girl, Jennifer Dawbrowski, had been murdered and was right there, just inches below his feet, when he sat in his secret room.

After a few deep breaths and a couple of sips from his water bottle, Tom got back on the road. He conferred with Irene as soon as he walked into the house. He described what he had felt at the time, how he was so uneasy in that room, and why he never went back.

"Do you think it's possible that I felt something?" he asked her.

"I don't know. There is so much we don't yet understand about the transition to death. And I can't really find any other explanation for what you were feeling."

It took Tom a couple of days to come to terms with these new revelations. The fact that he had played a role in solving the case helped him find peace of mind.

The following Tuesday, instead of going out for lunch, Tom and Agent Hanson agreed to meet at the house and share a meal on the patio with Irene. Even though he was on duty, the agent accepted a cold beer while Tom and Irene sipped some Chablis. It was such a beautiful and warm day that Tom had to raise the umbrella over the patio table.

"At the risk of ruining a perfect day, I have to go over some business with you," the agent explained.

"We understand, and we're ready. Time heals and our perspective on this entire ordeal is improving by the day," Tom assured him.

Agent Hanson placed his briefcase on his lap, opened it, and pulled out a manila envelope.

"Let me start by stating what you already know," Hanson said. "The lab was able to confirm that it was indeed David Strohman who was found dead in your garage. This was proven beyond any doubt by matching the DNA profile of the body to that which, thanks to you, Mr. Gibson, we already had on record. It was also, as you know, a perfect match with the DNA profile of the semen extracted from the crime scene of the 1964 murder."

The agent looked at Irene.

"I'm sorry to use direct and graphic language in your presence, Mrs. Gibson, but there's no other way to get this done."

"Oh, don't worry. I'm an experienced psychologist and I've witnessed much worse," she assured him.

The agent pulled some items out of the envelope and placed his briefcase beside his chair.

"We found four items on the body," the agent continued. "There was a piece of paper on which several addresses were written, including yours and your children's. We assume he used these to enter into the GPS device which was recovered from his vehicle. The same addresses were found in the memory of the GPS device, under the Previous Destinations tab. We also found his wallet which contained several forms of identification. His were the only fingerprints found on the piece of paper, on his wallet, and on the items in the wallet. There was this garage door opener. This is your opener. We have tested it and it definitely belongs to you and I'm returning it to you."

"I'll be damned!" Tom exclaimed. "That has to be one of the spares from the drawer in the foyer table. We never noticed it was missing. He must have taken it during the break-in in November."

"That is our assumption as well," the agent commented. "And finally, there were two letters. One is a suicide note. This is a scanned copy, not the original which, for several reasons, remains locked in our evidence container. The letter is addressed to you, Mr. Gibson, so I am delivering it to you."

Agent Hanson handed the document to Tom. It was handwritten but very clearly legible.

"Do you mind if I read it now?" Tom asked the agent.

"Not at all, sir. We have gone over it extensively, but I'm sure your wife is curious about what he had to say."

Tom read it aloud:

> Dear Tom,
>
> I'm addressing this letter to you because you are the patriarch of the only semblance of a family I have left. I want you

to know I never intended to harm any of you. But, there was something in my inner self that simply and desperately wanted to cling to a meager and paltry existence.

I have to admit I never understood what on earth inspired you or led you back to the old house on Riverdale Circle and drove you to so doggedly seek the truth about that fateful day, many decades ago. On the other hand, I accept that there are inexplicable forces in this world, some evil, some beautiful, which are stronger than any of us.

Over the past twenty or so years, I have helped the elderly, the poor, and the lonely. Each act of kindness was done for its own intrinsic benefit to the needy, and not because I was in search of any redemption. I understood a long time ago that no amount of good deeds could ever atone for that instant of madness in 1964. I have always known, from that moment on, that I had written my fate to suffer through a living hell.

I nevertheless still feared death and all of its unknowns, but I have finally found the strength to overcome my demons and I'm now ready to welcome death as a final relief from everything I know.

David

The three of them sat in silence, profoundly moved by the words of a man about to die. In spite of all that had happened, and all the assurance Irene had given him about having any second thoughts, Tom couldn't help but feel some degree of guilt. Strangely, he felt no remorse for seeking the truth after all these years. No, the guilt stemmed from his conviction that, in the fall of 1963, if he hadn't stolen the rototiller and if he hadn't recruited David to help him, none of the ensuing events would have occurred and David would have had the opportunity to live a normal life.

"Why does he refer to me as family, just as Chuck did in my nightmare at the hotel in Ottawa?" Tom asked in bewilderment.

"I mentioned the fact that there were two letters," the agent responded. "The second letter answers that very question. This second letter was an old letter addressed simply to David. It was from his mother, Nicole Strohman. It was dated August 21, 1990, with instructions that it be handed to David upon her death. We believe she died in 1992. Normally, we wouldn't share something like this with you, but the contents of this letter will be of interest to you and provides some answers to that last nagging question in this case."

"What could possibly—" Tom murmured as he was interrupted by the agent.

"You know who Fredrick Gibson was …"

"Yes, of course, he was my father."

"Well, as you will see in this letter, David's mother tells him how she and her husband used to have dinner parties with your parents. On one of those evenings, they drank even more than usual and apparently swapped partners for a night. She became pregnant and realized that Fredrick was the father. She was even more convinced after David's birth. She had never confided in anyone before she wrote the letter."

"I'll be damned! David was my half brother! Just like Chuck said in my nightmare! That explains the 25 percent DNA match with me!"

"That's right."

Tom recalled Detective Carter's wise words when he was faced with conflicting evidence. It was something to the effect that we needed to follow each piece of evidence and the answers would eventually emerge.

Tom read the letter quietly, nodding occasionally in acknowledgement. His sense of guilt was amplified by the revelation that David was his half brother. He recalled that his father used to treat David better than he did any of Tom's other friends. He speculated that his father must have suspected that David was his son, even if Nicole Strohman had never told him.

"Well, that pretty well wraps up the case," said Hanson. "I should get going. And, by the way, as I walked by the garage today, and two of the bay doors were open, I couldn't help but be impressed with the great job they did cleaning up in there."

"Yes, we're very pleased. The only thing they couldn't salvage was Irene's car. They said it would have been fine if it was a hardtop. There was nothing they could do with the convertible top that would have restored it to its original condition. Other than that, they did an amazing job."

Tom fell silent for a moment. He recalled that the company which carried out the cleanup had a motto. Its motto was: AS IF IT NEVER EVEN HAPPENED.

Tom wished it could be that simple.

THE END

ABOUT THE AUTHOR

Al Aubry worked at the IBM Corporation for thirty years, starting at the bottom and working his way up to a senior executive position. During his career, he developed a reputation for turning around underperforming organizations and starting new businesses. His speech-writing skills were sought out by several of IBM's top executives, and he accepted numerous speaking engagements at the bequest of IBM customers.

Aubry was in his forties when he retired from IBM in 2000. He has kept busy serving on corporate boards and devoting considerable time as a volunteer in support of charities and community initiatives. He relishes the time he and his wife spend with their seven grandchildren, and remains an avid tennis player and golfer. Lately, in his spare time, he has found significant enjoyment in writing fiction.

Mr. Aubry holds a degree in liberal arts from Colgate University in Hamilton, New York, as well as a master's degree in business administration from McMaster University in Hamilton, Ontario.

CPSIA information can be obtained
at www.ICGtesting.com
Printed in the USA
LVOW08s1559250717
542590LV00002B/500/P